PRAISE F
JAMES R. K
Chasing Nigl

"**CHASING NIGHTMARES FOLLOWS** four college students trying to find the real quickness of life. It is a thrilling, grand adventure, terrifying at times, triumphant at others, rife with danger and with mystery as well. A master of intrigue, James Kincaid tells us just enough to make us participate in solving these mysteries, joining the four young people in their grand adventure."

— Peter Grudin, author of *Right Here, a Novel*

"**KINCAID SENDS FOUR KIDS** on a hayride to hell, driving us along right behind — and inside — them. You'll come out on the other side of this incredible read feeling smarter and more alive.

— Julian Wolfreys, author of *Silent Music, The Great European Bestiary*, and *Draping the Sky for a Snowfall*

"**NOT YOUR TRADITIONAL** horror story. Chasing Nightmares is redeemed by love but also by the broad sympathies it conveys through sophisticated, polished writing."

— N. John Hall, author of *Trollope: A Biography, Bibliophilia: A Novel, Max Beerbohm: A Kind of Life*, and *Correspondence: An Adventure in Letters*

Wendell & Tyler: We'reOff

"**IF YOU COULD MIX** David Sedaris with Maya Rudolph and add a pinch of J.D. Salinger, you'd get something like ***Wendell & Tyler***. Kincaid's novel has all the open-ended fun of a great vacation, but the travelers turn out to have brought serious baggage as well. Wendell and Tyler are great characters, fresh and unexpected, and it's a joy to spend time with them."

—Nancy Glazener, author of *Reading for Realism* and *Literature in the Making: a History of U.S. Literary Culture*

Wendell & Tyler: On the Road!

"A TALE OF STAR-CROSSED, ill-matched potential lovers as contemporary teenagers thrown together on the American road, this terrific read takes Kincaid to new places — in various senses of both national and emotional 'place.' The gradual if resistant disappearance of distance between two highly attractive denizens of what counts as the country of the young these days is managed with Kincaid's habitual wit and antic quirkiness — but also with a persuasive, attractive honesty about the difficulties of emerging self-knowledge."

—Gerhard Joseph, author of *Tennyson and the Text* and *Tennysonian Love: The Strange Diagonal*

Wendell & Tyler: End of the Road!

"ZOWIE! Tyler thinks Wendell is a pain in the ass; Wendell thinks Tyler is a thorn in everyone's side. Ironically, each dreads what the other seems likely to say in public. A gentle excitement builds as Wendell and Tyler haltingly open up to each other, often with unexpected consequences. And who knows? Maybe by the end of the trilogy, such bondings can redeem the flawed and failed America they are traveling through. Maybe. Maybe not. No matter, the trip is hilarious. This is the funniest American novel since Joseph Heller's *Catch-22.*"

—Philip L. Krauth, author of *Proper Mark Twain* and *Mark Twain & Company*

Annoying the Victorians

"VINDICATED. Finally, a book that explains why I didn't go to grad school to 'study' literature. This entertaining book pokes fun at the academic system's 'publish or perish' rule, whereby faculty are expected to write something, anything, no matter how ridiculous, to prove they are studious... My advice to anyone who feels tempted to pursue an academic career in literature is to read ***Annoying the Victorians*** instead."

— books4parents , *Amazon Reviews*

CHASING NIGHTMARES

by James R. Kincaid

Cambridge Books
an imprint of
WriteWords, Inc.
CAMBRIDGE, MD 21613

© 2017 James R. Kincaid. All Rights Reserved
First Print Edition, July 1, 2017

Publisher's Note: This is a work of fiction. All characters and events portrayed in this book are fictional, and any resemblance to real people or incidents is purely coincidental.
All rights reserved. No part of the book may be reproduced in any form or by any means without the prior written consent of the Author or Publisher, excepting brief quotes to be used in reviews.

𝕮𝖆𝖒𝖇𝖗𝖎𝖉𝖌𝖊 𝕭𝖔𝖔𝖐𝖘 is a subsidiary of:

Write Words, Inc.
2934 Old Route 50
Cambridge, MD 21613

ISBN 978-1-61386-400-5

Fax: 410-221-7510

Bowker Standard Address Number: 254-0304

DEDICATION

To my dearest friend Julian Markels
"Give me that man that is not passion's slave and
I will wear him in my heart's core, ay,
in my heart of heart, as I do thee."

CHAPTER 1

It all began comfortably and ended somewhere else. I want you to know that it's not my fault — that plunge, that disconnect.

There they were, settled in cozily, warm and cuddled, even if it was February, since it was also Los Angeles. They were in a well-appointed library, four college students. I was somewhere else, never mind where, but tuned in, hoping these four would sink happily and thoughtlessly into their privilege and let the stories set out for them carry them along. That's not asking too much. My guess is that these stories set out for them, that is, their present lives, were somehow clumsily revealed to them by somebody I work for, naming no names, and that the four kids were insulted by the banality of it all, the sense that they were nothing more than what they should be and would travel obediently to the destinations established with their best interests in mind.

However it came about, these four decided, as you will see, to pull against the traces, violently so. In the process, they made my job, which I used to enjoy, no fun at all. I know you are not interested in me, nobody is. I'm not whining, mind. It goes with the territory. I'm a teller of tales, and that's the way it should be. Still, I don't think I am being unreasonable, asking for some recognition. The wages are not high.

* * *

"Just why are we doing this? Tell me."

"Doing what, Katie? Sitting here, going to school, breathing?"

"Yeah."

There they were, the four of them, in the "Chat — But Quietly, Please" section the library had cordoned off for those still willing to go amongst the books but unwilling to shush. The other three friends stared at Katie as if they really did know what she meant, were waiting to demonstrate how fully they were locked into her view of things.

But they knew enough not to stage a competition to see who could out-intuit the others. They needed to find ways to join into a chorus.

Cobb went first: "Hell, we're not chained here, not just here, you know, in the library. That's not what I mean. It's not the library that's the issue. Like Katie says, the question is why we're here. Just *Why*. I mean, you know, *Here*."

"Sure, Cobb. That says it all." Joss slithered her eyes over Cobb with what she figured was a withering scowl. Then: "So, why don't we just not be here, or rather, *Here?* Why not throw ourselves out of the here, somewhere other, anywhere. We're not chained, like you say so memorably, Cobb, so why do we act as if we were?"

"Don't you sass me, girl!"

Brad, ignoring his roommate, said, "I agree, Joss, assuming I understand what it is I'm agreeing with. It's not going to be any different, out there, but we ourselves might be, different — or discover something different. In any case, we'd be leaving — sallying forth, as they say."

"Advancing on the enemy, or finding one," Katie took up. "An enemy would be nice. I'm for anything that'd be different, inside or out. Different might be alive, too. Cobb's maybe right about us manufacturing our own shackles, but he so seldom is."

She smiled as she said this, though, reached over and ruffled Cobb's very long hair.

What followed was circuitous and repetitive, though not self-congratulatory, not too much. They had wit and candor enough to recognize they were not the first 21-year-olds sensing that, inside and out, there was nothing they could locate that was not vaporous, dreamlike — and, worse than that, standard-issue. Mostly, they talked so as to give form to what they already agreed upon. Provide it with an approximate shape and then slap some glue on it so it would hold. They knew they had breached a barrier of some sort, just by getting the right words out there. Somehow, they had moved down country — and they did not intend to be driven back.

* * *

That's not how they put it. They talked instead about.... I'll let you in on the meaty part of it. Before I do that, maybe I should tell you just who I am, this voice you're welcoming into your living rooms, as we used to say in radio days. Once you have me located, you can pay full attention to the story: what these kids are saying, their clothing and mannerisms, the surroundings, my apt descriptions of the buildings and rooms (along with reflections on life in general), and not be distracted with nagging concerns about your sources. Then you won't have this irritating voice in your ear, hissing, "That's all very well, but who is telling me all this? What's the origin and how much can I trust it?" That sort of thing.

On the other hand, if I open up and drop this coy pretense that the words are appearing from nowhere, give you some personal details, you might be interested enough in me to keep reading, even if these kids strike you as foolish.

I was going to say, "Strike you as too much like what you once were, wish you were still, might yet be." That sounds pompous, though, and, for all my faults....

* * *

"Are we being spoiled brats? You know, wanting more excitement and figuring we deserve it? So, we're restless, dissatisfied, unfocused. Who isn't among privileged college kids? We have no real concerns, survival concerns. Plenty to eat — some of us, Brad, eating more than plenty."

"You saying I'm fat and self-indulgent, Cobb, which is no news to anyone and a palpably pathetic plea for prolonged peering at your own lithe form. Note that sweet alliteration? Artful."

Cobb smiled and winked, parodying himself and his undeniable litheness. To be fair, he really didn't care about it, hardly noticed.

"Entertaining as you male animals are and anxious as Katie and I have to be to watch you go at one another, maybe we could get back to the issue? Katie, talk some more. Get us closer. Just talk. We sort of know, but only sort-of."

"Thanks, Joss. I think it all came up to the surface so I noticed it just now, but it's been there inside me. In my inmost heart. That sounds silly, but it's so. You really want me blabbing on?"

"Yeah," said Joss, followed a beat later by the boys.

"Okay, I'll make this brief," said Katie.

"No, you won't," Brad said, then, "I'm sorry."

"Your apology is as fake as...," began Cobb.

"Katie's promised brevity," added Joss, with a smirk.

"That's what I mean," Katie continued, "just what I mean. Finishing one another's sentences or just leaving them dangling, since we know without a doubt where they're going. No surprises, not ever."

"That's because we know each other so well, are so perfectly fitted, an engine oiled with — er — tacit understandings developed over weeks, of harmonious gatherings. Don't you think — maybe?" Cobb offered it really and truly as a question.

"No!" Katie said, drawing mutters and stares from the scattered others lounging in the Chat Quietly. "No! It's just the opposite. It's because we don't know each other at all, each other or anything else. We have approximate notions, workable and routinized images and vague outlines that allow us to...."

"What?"

"Become more and more efficient, get through things quickly and smoothly, operate in the world with little friction and with less...."

"Awareness?"

"Yeah, but worse than that, less presence. We withdraw from others, even from objects, most of all from ourselves."

"Katie, this something you read for class?"

"I read it right now, Joss. Victor Shlovsky. Listen to this. Want to hear?"

"I know him. Shlovsky. Radical theorist. Denounced by Lenin."

"By Trotsky, Cobb, you idiot."

"Anyhow, Katie, tell us. Don't skip the boring parts."

"I'll just read it. And I will skip bits, thanks very much."

If we start to examine the general laws of perception, we see that as perception becomes habitual, it becomes automatic. Such habituation explains the principles by which, in ordinary speech, we leave phrases unfinished and words half expressed. We apprehend objects only as shapes with imprecise extensions, see the object as though it were enveloped in a sack. We know what it is by its configuration, but we see only its silhouette. The object, perceived thus, fades and does not leave even a first impression; ultimately even the essence of what it was is forgotten.

"Here's Tolstoy:"

I was cleaning and, meandering about, approached the divan and couldn't remember whether or not I had dusted it. I could not remember and felt that it was impossible to remember — so that if I had dusted it and forgot — that is, had acted unconsciously, then it was the same as if I had not. If some conscious person had been watching, then the fact could be established, but.... And if the whole complex lives of so many people go on unconsciously, then such lives are as if they had never been. And so, Shlovsky goes on, life is reckoned as nothing. Habitualization devours work, clothes, furniture, one's love, and the fear of war. 'If the whole complex lives of so many people go on unconsciously, then such lives are as if they had never been.' And art exists that one may recover the sensation of life; it exists to make one feel things, to make the stone stony.

"Holy shit, Katie! 'Such lives are as if they had never been.'"

"That's dreadful—lives made vacant."

"Dreadful and true."

"Make the stone stony. I love that. Recover the sensation of life."

"Think we can?"

"We'd damned well better."

"Try. At least we can try."

* * *

This, then, was the start to it all, the motor that drove them on the quest to try. They had come to feel that they had no life at all unless they turned their own faltering, formless beings into dangerous works of art. That they didn't realize exactly how to do it or even what they were doing is no mark against them: had they known, it would not have been worth trying.

And it was worth trying, despite everything. I will stake my life on it. Turning your life into a nightmare is far better than letting it drift, become nothing more than vapor dissolving into the indifferent sky.

Of course, that's easy to say, easy for me, since I'm not the one plummeting into nightmare.

So, true to their desperate vow to find the wildest and

most open adventure, they head off for class and then to eat dinner, study, brush their teeth the requisite number of times, and slink off to bed. There's wild adventure for you.

But I'm not in a position to ridicule. Truth is I don't understand too well what they're up to, these four. No use pretending. Being in the dark would make it easy to mock them—just covering my own ass—but, you see, I'm too honest to do that, though honesty is not my leading trait. I don't know how I stumbled into this mode of honest disclosure, a very bad place to be. While I'm here, though, I really must tell you that it doesn't matter much about me, as I'm not in charge. What I am is what you can best understand as a "sayer." Not like in soothsayer or nay-sayer, but different, more like a teller, but not quite that either. Got it?

Enough about me. I'm really anxious to see what will happen, what I will be allowed or required to tell you. As I mentioned, it's not up to me. I work for another, another who has never nominated me for employee of the month.

Chapter 2

The very next morning, they met for breakfast, ready to spring.

At the risk of trying your patience, let me interrupt myself here to respond to some of your e-mails. A few do not deserve a response, so I'll just display them for your contempt. I haven't changed a word.

* * *

"The only reason I'm reading this is that you're my uncle, and my mom, who is your sister and all, makes me, so could you get something happening, anything pretty much? My mom is sure to ask me and won't believe me when I say to her, 'What's happening, Mom? Not one shit thing.' If you had somebody punch somebody, I could tell her that. Maybe it could rain, even, or somebody could fall down. Just saying."

* * *

"I like the opening of your story very much, I guess, though I think you could cut some of this, just to make it more interesting — interesting being what it's not. I'm happy to pass on this advice. I've taken several creative writing classes. I'm no expert, but I've studied openings."

* * *

Those are not worth saying, and I'm sorry I did. No revising, though. That's a major rule by which I must abide.

Here's one e-mail I thought was worth attending to, as it didn't abuse me. I don't have a lot of self-confidence. Also, this one brings up a point that had occurred to me and then slipped my mind.

* * *

"I'm having trouble keeping these characters straight. Maybe that's just me. If you think I'm right, though, you could just tell us things like what they look like, how they dress, hobbies. Also, they could talk different, too. One could stutter, for instance, or say "like" and "you know." What are the buildings like, the weather? Where are they?

Do any of them have sex?"

* * *

I appreciate that one and can sympathize with his/her confusion, as I share it, and am now moving to correct the flaw. Cobb, Brad, Joss, Katie. I have a vivid image of each of them, inside and out. Thing is, I just need to convey all that. Have any tips? The stuttering idea I think wouldn't work, as it'd be a bit like making fun of a handicap.

Anyhow, I'm going to try something I've been advised (strongly) not to do, which is simply giving you a list of players — they're only the four, for now — and their leading characteristics, as I see them. I find that the most direct routes are always the best, even if they are a little predictable. Actually, I've not found that to be true, but I cannot find another way, so this will have to do.

I'm not confining myself to the physical, though right now I am not too clear on anything else. I'm not trying to include in this brief summary absolutely everything I do know, just enough so you have a handle on each one and don't keep thinking, "Now, *who* is this talking?" or "Is this the fat one?"

Katie. Katie is twenty-one, but they are all twenty-one, so that doesn't help. It was Katie, you remember, who first proposed that they abandon competence and court the unknown. She's very assertive, and you may not like that. It may help you to know she is routinely pretty (very) and skinny. But she's not what we used to call stuck-up, and she tries hard not to be so pretty. She dresses like shit, in my opinion, though her friends never mention it. She has blond hair (of course). Her major is — well, you don't care and I don't either. She was hospitalized for a while in high school for some kind of psychological thing I don't understand, and I'm not sure if that's important or not. I can't figure out whether she's attracted to either of the boys or, for that matter, to Joss. (I put that in to satisfy the last e-mailer.) She can be pretty abrupt, but not so much as —

Jocelyn. Joss is my favorite in this group, not that I should have a favorite or say so if I do. She would not, at first, seem all that comely to you, but before long you will wonder why you didn't notice what a wonder she is. I said she was abrupt, which is true, but not the whole truth, since it's more like she hasn't any filters: things just spill out. She's unguarded. That'd be bad in some people. She's not as skinny as Katie, goes up and down some. (I know you regard these comments on the women as riotously sexist, but wait: I'll tell you about the men, too. That'll even things out.) Finally, Joss is deeply committed to this scheme, probably more even than —

Cobb. As I mentioned above, Cobb is the prettiest of the lot. Like Katie, he absolutely does not care about that. You'll be thinking that if he didn't want his looks to speak so prominently, he could disfigure himself. I suppose so, but he hasn't done that. Also like Katie, Cobb dresses as badly as he can and slouches. Beyond his looks, there's lots to say about Cobb. He's the most adventurous of the bunch, reckless. I don't want to launch into facile analyses of his heedlessness, though I've often wondered if he isn't somehow suicidal. He talks too much. He's the most conventionally pleasant of the lot, tries not to be, and is also the most sensitive to sentiment: music, stories of the oppressed, touch. He cries sometimes, often. Certainly more than —

Brad. Brad is the quietest of the quartet, though he's not in the least shy. I'm not sure why he's so quiet. One possibility is that he is unusually secure, able to slide into place without any felt need to assert or announce himself. Maybe that's it. Anyhow, I'd like to have someone like Brad in my life, since he is immediately likeable, likeable in conventional ways, I suppose, though that's not a bad thing, since there are good reasons for the conventional being constructed as it is. We all have pretty good instincts about all this: people you lean into when you talk, hope to be around without knowing quite how to explain that need or wanting to acknowledge it. Brad is not at all handsome, not much of anything physically, apart from looking younger than he is [twenty-one, you remember], a lot younger. Maybe fifteen or sixteen. He doesn't seem to react to this in any way, isn't defensive in choosing how he dresses or acts. Maybe Brad is the most secure of the lot. He may also be the most dangerous.

I didn't mention what you'd likely first notice about some of these young people, the very things you can't help seeing, but learn pretty soon not to make remarkable. "Mommy, that man has no foot!" That kind of thing. It's part of getting along in the world, and it doesn't seem to me hypocritical to pretend someone's glass eye isn't distracting or a sliding hairpiece isn't worthy of guffaws.

Katie has a limp, some sort of ankle injury sustained in high-school track and field. I'm not sure what event, perhaps the high jump, which would make sense. But I'm only guessing.

Cobb has real trouble with peripheral vision, which allows nasty friends to trick him easily, creeping up from either side and doing to him anything they want. As is not the case with Katie, Cobb is perfectly willing to talk about this defect. Problem is he seems to tell a different story every time: injury, congenital, optometrist mistake, not there at all. Some people think the last is the true story, that he invented the problem in a futile attempt to make himself interesting. His three friends take it seriously enough to try to dissuade him from driving or at least not being passengers when he is. Myself, I wouldn't want to be depending on him in lion country or on the battlefield.

Joss wears a hearing aide. Sometimes she does. In social situations. She doesn't wear one where you'd expect her to do so, in class, for instance. She says it makes some of her courses almost bearable if she has to guess at what has been said. She is forever running out of batteries.

Brad doesn't know it, but he has a bad heart, the routine physicals he's had from time to time being so perfunctory as to notice nothing so subtle. Only it's not subtle: he tires easily, gets chest pains, has to pause going up steps. I guess it's not hard to guess why he ignores these symptoms. You yourself have a little growth on your back that's not getting any smaller.

Chapter 3

Routine matters pulled them away from the library. Scheduled duties and plans of one sort and another. They noticed the irony: here we are about to dive headlong into unknown depths and — but first, some obligatory class-meetings and clothes-folding.

"So, why we doing this shit? Why not take off this very second?" Katie asked.

They all laughed.

"I think we're going to set about, this very night, planning our planlessness, throwing our hearts and minds, our lovely bodies, into the abyss. Right after we soak some in the most deadening humdrum we can find: making charts, consulting maps, calling for reservations."

"Right, Joss! I gotta first check my supply of clean underwear. Or maybe just ignore that? Eight o'clock. My place. That okay with you? Katie?"

"'My place,' Cobb. You forget we share?"

"How could I, with pictures of you up on every wall? Trophies. Certificates."

[That wasn't true, of course. There was a single picture of Brad, but it was small and unflattering, taken at a carnival photo booth. Just so you know: Brad and Cobb have one apartment, separate bedrooms; Joss and Katie don't share any space, are lodged in different buildings.]

* * *

So they agreed on meeting at Brad and Cobb's, promptly at eight. They seemed to be hoping that their comic acknowledgment of the absurdity — meetings, schedules — would purchase them some distance from the slog.

The apartment shared by Brad and Cobb was messier even than the general run of student digs, though one might suspect that there was some deliberation in the messiness, as if it issued from a pledge not to be neat, a pledge they both found difficult to honor. For one thing, everything was clean and the piles were single-leveled. Had they been truly careless, the mounds would have been bottomless, insect-ridden.

The walls were beige, the floor was off-white, the window opened up onto a quad that was tree-lined and....

[I am not trying to write a parody here. What I am doing is describing as best I can, all because I was strongly advised to describe and regard that advice as sage. But I'll quit now. (You'll be sorry to hear that before long I will vanish altogether — at least as far as you will be able to detect.)]

Nobody brought any beer or pretzels. Not that kind of a group. They weren't too long in sorting out details, particularly since they were anxious to have these details remain unsorted, spring up on them — without warning. They recognized the difference between welcoming danger and creating it, but they didn't seem keen on observing it.

* * *

"We could take off right now."

"And fall asleep about six hours later, Cobb. Crash. Die, you idiot — especially if you were behind the wheel," said Joss.

"Oh, yeah. Sorry."

"Sudden death would probably be just the thing for us," said Brad, "or a slow-motion car wreck. Let's get Cobb drunk and have him drive."

"If we're going to be searching without maps, we at least

have to think about what it is we don't know, don't even anticipate, right? That make any sense?"

Nobody responded, so Katie continued, "So, let's say we leave — well, postpone when for a second. Whenever it is, we'll just throw our shit in a bag and we're off. That okay? No maps, forgetting essential stuff."

"You know, if it's not violating our no-plan planning, I have a general idea of where we can point ourselves," said Joss.

"Right," they said, more agreeably than enthusiastically. "We need a compass point. Up or down, back or forth. That seems okay, not too regulated."

Joss looked uncomfortable, but continued. "A little more than a compass point, maybe. How about we head north, then east, toward the Donner Pass and then into Nevada, Highway U.S. 50?"

Nobody said anything, wriggled in their chairs but were silent, so she went on.

"I realize this looks like a whole lot more than just a compass point. I say all that because the Donner Pass is a sweet sounding place, not that I've been there. But I love the idea of the Donners. We could make them our guides."

"And Highway U.S.50?"

Joss smiled, "'The Loneliest Road in America,' they say on the infallible Internet, 566 km of the blank. Empty, calling to us. Just Google 'most remote long drives in America' and you'll see for yourselves. They say right there: 'road leading to and bypassing nothing.'"

Brad looked at her, frowning: "Nothing sounds good, exactly what we're seeking, right? I know I am."

Just as soon as Brad and Cobb were out the door, meandering together back to their apartment, the women having separated to do god knows what:

"I got another of those calls, Cobb. They're getting worse."

"What'd they say?"

"They said, 'Don't ever come our way, asshole. You do it once, that'll be it. One and done. We promise you that.'"

"You say anything?"

"Just like in the movies: 'Who is this?' 'Why are you calling?' 'What do you want with me?' 'You'd better stop.'"

"Right. That's just what I would say."

"Thanks, Cobb. You figure this is a prank?"

"Yes. No."

"You going to tell me to go to the police?"

"Yes — and not campus cops, either. But will you? Not a chance."

"The other thing to think about is getting out of here fast. We haven't told anybody, and I don't want to sit around while the stupid cops come up with nothing, make things worse by fiddling noisily in all the wrong corners. That'd just delay our descent into the maelstrom and set me up for fielding more of these phone calls. Worse, maybe. Besides, like you would, I secretly love these calls. Up to a point. Maybe they'll keep it up, though, track us, find out where we are, despite all our camouflage."

"We could leave right away — tomorrow?"

"Right — or the next day. Ask Katie and Joss. They seem to be okay with not waiting. You know, Cobb, I'm surprised it's not you getting these calls."

"Oh?"

"You know, the sex thing."

Cobb didn't pretend to misunderstand.

* * *

Katie and Joss were not subject to threatening calls. Instead, they received notes, not the horror-movie sort with words and letters carved out of newspapers and then glued onto cheap paper. These were computer-printed. They appeared first in their separate apartment mailboxes and then, just yesterday, under their doors. Disturbing notes directed at women, you're thinking, are not so uncommon.

Neither are follow-ups, such as rape or murder.

Joss and Katie had mentioned nothing about these notes to the boys — or the authorities. But they did tell one another.

"What's yours say?"

"It's a long one: 'Oh my, Kathleen. I am too shy to approach you directly but must have contact. I hope you know that I mean nothing in the least out of the way — or threatening. Believe me. If I could bring myself to have a face-to-face encounter, you must believe me that I would. I know I said, "believe me" twice, but I won't change that. I'm nervous, you see, not stupid, and I really do need you to think well of me. That's not something I'm just making up. That's all I live for. Really, that's the truth, Kathleen. If you have any humanity, you will give me a sign, a sign that you do not hate me. That's all I ask. And it is true when I say that I'm really not stupid or a creep either, despite what I know you think. I realize that you don't regard me at all and that this note makes things worse. I know that. Yours truly and with no confidence at all that what I must have will ever be granted.'"

"Don't regard me at all. Wow! That's upping the voltage from the ones before, isn't it?"

"Yeah, I guess. And I do love 'Kathleen,' especially since nobody's ever called me that, maybe because it's not my name. Makes me almost give in, you know, since he's such a honey and since I feel this need to prove that I do have some humanity — not much but some. I figure he's a savvy sort, knows how to frame his appeals so as to make them get right beneath the skin and wiggle."

"Didn't he have a signature of some kind before?"

"He usually signed them with multiple names — 'Jason, Freddy, Arthur, Clyde, Melvin.'"

"Jason seems most likely — or maybe that's what he wants you to think."

"I agree. Not much of a lead there; half the boys around are Jasons."

"Maybe it's Jason Voorhees. You know, from the movie."

"Probably. You know, if we could locate the bastard we could get him in a dark alley and kick the shit out of him. Pathetic asshole. What have you been hearing from 'Available Dude'?"

"I thought either he or his perversity had expired, but then a new one today, trying to be ever so tough:"

> *'Listen, babe, I told you to meet me at Flanagan's last Friday. I was perfectly clear. Flanagan's. Friday. You think I'm messing around? Well, you'd better think twice if you think that. I'll give you one more chance, make that one last chance. Flanagan's on Wednesday. You wonder how you'll recognize me? I'll be the handsome dude buying you drinks — many, many drinks. Your devoted slave,*
> *M.*
>
> *P.S. You know where Flanagan's is, I happen to know, so don't pretend you don't.'*

"You worried about it?"

"No. Well, enough to avoid Flanagan's, which of course I would anyhow."

"We could both go."

"Yeah. Or we could beat it the hell out of here before Wednesday."

"Yes! Tomorrow?"

"Why not. We wait around a month until Spring Break, it'll seem to us as if we're just treading old paths, no matter what we do or where we go."

"Tomorrow, it is. We should check with the boys."

"They'll be up for it. Besides, they'll do what we say."

* * *

Which was true enough, not that they were unusually compliant or even befogged by lust or affection. Lust or affection was probably there — who's to say for sure? — but their mutual willingness to being bossed depended partly on not recognizing that bossing was in the air and partly on being males, and thus less canny and quick than these two women — than any women.

[I know your ears pricked up at the mention of "lust," sagged a little at "affection," and then almost collapsed into your skull when I dropped the subject altogether. Just hang on. Later on, I may figure all that out. I'm as interested as you.]

Only thing was, Cobb remembered he had laundry to pick up in two days and Brad wanted to talk to Johnson. They said as much to Katie and Joss in the morning.

"Shit, Cobb. Wear what you have on," said Brad, who did live with him but didn't pay much attention to Cobb when he was dressed.

[That's unfair. I'm hoping to have more for us on this quartet's bodies, unclothed, but it's not like I can arrange to flash them. As I say, my wish is not anybody's command.]

"No, don't," said Katie. "You smell bad enough as it is."

"I always smell that way. It's my fancy cologne."

"Pickup your laundry this morning, Cobb," said Brad, now sorry he'd been brusque. "They're always early with stuff. You want, I can get it for you. Or you can wear my clothes, which you do half the time, anyhow."

"And that settles that," said Katie. "Now, Bradley old boy, why do you want to talk to Johnson?"

"I just wanted to tell him he was right. He'd been saying things all term that feed into just what we were talking about, what we are going to do. I figured it was only right to expose him to a little of our resolve. Not that I'd let him in on the details, like where we're going, especially since we don't have any fixed idea where we're going, scouting for chaos the way we are."

"You let loose that muddle on him, Brad, and he'll flunk your ass, just in case you're even close to passing as it is. But you mean," Katie said, "that what we're doing runs parallel to that warmed-over hippie shit he dishes out. Jack Kerouac and all. And I am sorry about the flunking comment. But do you yourself think that what we're setting out on is just stale '70s stuff?"

"Yeah. Only not Johnson's version."

"I got ya. I do hope what we're doing isn't within Johnson's ken. And it'd be fun to jab at him, but don't."

"How come?"

"He'll alert those what can track us down. He's no free spirit — as you know."

"I'll be slanted, murky and oblique. And we can elude the finest trackers, even if they are set loose. Anyhow, like I say, I'll be guarded, super-careful. Besides, we'll leave no tracks. Trust me. Brad the Discreet."

He wasn't.

"Holy shit, Brad. Why are you telling me all this? You can't just run off like that."

"Why not?"

"I guess you can. You just can't do it and blame it on me. Who you going with? Not by yourself?"

"Shit, Professor Johnson, we're not going to leave a note saying you drove us to it. I just wanted you to know."

"Shit. Don't do it, Brad, don't do anything like this. Wait'll next month and go to Ft. Lauderdale."

"What if someone had said that to Kerouac?"

"He'd been better off."

"Glad I came to talk to you."

"I'm not."

* * *

One final preliminary meeting:

"So, we going to walk our way to annihilation."

"We'd be in our sixties by the time we got within range of peril, Cobb," said Joss, "but that trip could be great, assuming we could find some way to eat."

"Seriously, though."

"Seriously, Cobb, you're the only one with a car."

"Don't think I'm being a shit, no more than usual, but it's — what would you say? — limited in size. You know that. Barely bigger than old VWs — four at most, and that's a push, as we've found several dozen times. We'd be ignoring the power of emptiness being so occupied with aching asses and stiff knees. And no use even thinking about luggage, not even toothbrushes and deodorant."

"What about your parents, Cobb? They're rich and must have a criminally big car."

"They do, change it every year but always huge. And, Katie, they live in Connecticut, where also is the car."

"Brad, you're the only one with parents right here, right there over where all the best cars are garaged, exotic Brentwood."

They decided to settle all details, every one and not just whose car, the very next morning at breakfast. That seemed reasonable, or, rather, arbitrary and completely wacky.

[I mean, why on earth couldn't they decide about a car, right there? Why would putting it off until morning be living on the edge? But none of them raised these objections, so I guess I should not.]

Chapter 4

Ready for some backfill, some solid foundational work? I wish I knew if you wanted more detailed information about these young people. I don't mean more penetrating insights into what the hell is wrong with them, but more narrative of their lives to this point, maybe including something on their parents and grandparents, their problems in high school, favorite tunes, times they shoplifted. I have a feeling I need something weightier, something, say, you would regard as substance before we watch together as they rocket out of control. I realize I can only guess about you and your desires. You're thinking I should trust my instincts as a writer. I have none. Also, even if I had, I'd have to make it all up, as I haven't been supplied with what you'd call lots of good information, hardly any, really nothing I would dignify with the name of information.

I have a motive in exposing my empty hand, since there's them what could easily provide such information. That's what we need. It's a question not just of what but of why. Otherwise we have a story without depth. I mean, what'd be the point?

Don't think I'm mocking you, suggesting you're seeking in print the complexity and interest your life sometimes lacks. That may be my own motivation — I wish I knew — but you're not just a rookie. You have read things before and written them, just as like. I'm in the presence of the real thing.

Which is not getting our story told, even the going-back-and-filling-in part of the story I was hoping would just come to me. It hasn't, but I do believe character flushing out is required here, so I will turn things over to my friend. Wish I had one.

You are interested in me, just where I come from and why? I think I can say, without fear of too much contradiction, that this subject is central. Anyhow, central or not — and it's not — it gives me something I can use, some actual material.

Just for starters, I am not omniscient. I don't want to scare you away, so I'll just say I wish I could control things better, maybe get the hell out of the way, let things take their course. But we all know there's never really an independent course for things to take. Somebody has fiddled. I don't mean to sound like John Calvin, but imaging that when we come to the cliff it's our decision whether to turn around screaming or hop on off — well, come on. I mean, how did you arrive at that precipice in the first place? Ever think of that? Me neither, but now you know who I am. Don't be judgmental.

Chapter 5

I'm thinking what you're thinking. We hardly had a fourth chapter — went by in a blink. What's the story with that?

I can't hide it. Even had I been flush with facts and ideas, could not have relayed them to you. Truth is I was ordered to cut that chapter short and, worse, devote this one, the sixth chapter, to a memo. That's what I said, a memo. It came from my boss. That's how she thinks of herself.

YOUR BOSS. YOUR POINT OF ORIGIN, ABSOLUTE AND ENGULFING ENERGY.

That too, yeah. Anyhow, this memo came and I thought it best....

YOU THOUGHT?

Well, that's just a way of putting it, you know, a way of allowing the reader in on things.

HELL, YOU AREN'T IN ON THINGS YOURSELF.

I have some autonomy, needless to say.

NONE.

I thought I did.

NONE.

Well, that's the shit.

REPRODUCE THE MEMO.

Right. No sort of framing, some context? It seems to me we're asking for confusion if you force me to plop this right in the readers' laps. I'm not rebelling, just asking. It's a point of view worth considering, even for you.

YOU BEING SNARKY?

I never understood too well what that word meant. You asking if I'm resisting your authority in some way, in which case the answer is an emphatic negative.

THEN THE MEMO.

Right, the memo and nothing but the memo. Here it is then.

NO NEED TO SAY, "HERE IT IS!" JUST PRESENT IT AND NOT ONE MORE WORD, NOT ONE, FROM YOU, OR YOU'LL WISH YOU'D NEVER BEEN CONCOCTED.

Memo: To Al

You are getting in the way of the tale you are assigned to tell, Al. I know you imagine readers are tuning in to you, but I'm very sorry to tell you that's not the case, even were you, you. Your interruptions are intended to be diverting and witty, I know, but they are simply prissy and self-important. Neither effect is what you should be after. In any case, it's not what readers are paying for. We (I) intend to give them just that, the satisfaction of their desires, the true market value. These four kids are remarkable, and I am going to do unimaginable things with and to them. Their minds and their bodies need to live before the reader, unfiltered by some buttinski who thinks he knows. I'm not saying you know nothing, Al, but your routine sadism won't serve here. Cut your comments by, say, 95%. Agreed? Agreed.

ILLIMITABLE.

I know better than to ask if a response from me should be inserted here or later. But which is it?

NOWHERE. NO RESPONSE IS PERMITTED. MOVE ON TO THE SIXTH CHAPTER AT ONCE. BY NOW, ANY REMAINING READERS WILL HAVE TO BE REMINDED AGAIN THAT THERE IS A STORY. SO TRY AND RE-CONNECT TO IT.

Artfully.

JUST RETELL THEM ABOUT THE FOUR, THEIR PLANS. DON'T WORRY ABOUT ART.

Okay. I'll leave that to Art's wife.

WHAT?

Get it, Art's wife?

I'M TAKING OVER.

No more jokes, I promise. I'll move right to that flashback I've been planning. Me and Art's missus!

I WONDER IF EXTINCTION IS IN THE CARDS.

Chapter 6

I won't say good-bye, exactly, though I know we will miss our drop-in-for-coffee relationship, chatting it up on the way to the mailbox, cutting the grass in tandem, sitting out and watching the sunset. But you heard what I heard, and let me tell you extinction is no joke. You think she meant it? Never mind. I know better than to offer temptations.

So, back we go to a few years prior to where we were, to a time when our four favorite 21-year-olds were only eighteen, just entering college at USC. Isolated from one another, from anybody. It's a big school, USC, making lots of money from this entering class (and all others) and not too concerned about kids being left out, terribly lonely.

It's early September 2014, Freshman Orientation Week at University of Southern Cal. It's a Thursday, 10 a.m., hot outside, which wouldn't matter to those inside, were there air-conditioning. The actual date is September 4, and freshman are strewn all over campus, along with some parents, those who cared enough to come along or were too ill-at-ease to avoid it. Our quartet was able to shed their parents, keen enough to realize the irrelevance of the old. I'd say maybe 25% of the students here in Taper Hall of Humanities, Room 106, have parents attached to them, parents embarrassed and in equal parts devastated by the loss of their kids and eager to throw them away. Taper Hall, Room 106 (a sort of auditorium) is right now home to those who are expecting to major in something like philosophy, art history, Slavic languages (shrewd vocational choices). Other nervous new arrivals are portioned out to other venues across campus, divided according to whatever they imagine their major is going to be, the undecideds all shuffled over to the football field. Our four are not in the least undecided. They know what they want and are confident in what awaits them. They're wrong, but that's of course.

Anyhow, here they are in Taper 106, not together. Don't know one another, like I say, and are not drawn together instantly by some magnetic generator or sexual tinglings they could not resist. They are not to meet, really what you'd call meet, until a few weeks later, and the four do not become even a loose unit until after Halloween.

Right now, they are sitting there trying not to look too bored. The auditorium itself doesn't repay close inspection, being more or less indistinguishable from all other school auditoriums, in every state and at every level: hard seats made to look but not be comfortable, radically insufficient leg room resulting from the drive to maximize seating whatever the cost, a bad speaker system and cackling microphone, a complex lighting arrangement nobody present can work, air-conditioning that is never adequate and in this particular case is not functioning at all.

"LA in September and no air-conditioning? What the fuck's this!" was the way Cobb reacted, leaning toward a young woman next to him, who responded with, "Yeah."

She was pretty enough, but Cobb barely looked at her. She looked plenty hard at Cobb.

The speaker, introduced as the something or other professor of English, in trying hard to be winning, all self-effacing and nudge-nudge-wink-wink. His name, this oldish and oafish professor, was James Kincaid, maybe still is, if he's alive, which I'd say was fifty-fifty. He began by taking off his jacket, big mistake. I couldn't make out his tie. It may have had popsicles on it. That's what it looked like, but that can't be, would be too corny even for this guy. He didn't take the tie off.

What he said might be playing some part in what happens later, so attend to as much of this as you can. It's abridged, if you can believe it.

* * *

Welcome to USC, the best university in this country in which to get lost. Getting lost is what you should go to college for — the only defensible reason for giving up four years of your life. You are secure and stable now — it's time to become insecure and unstable.

I love Los Angeles and especially USC, since both are labyrinthine and make no sense. But what I love most about this place are the mountains and forests just outside, inviting us all to get lost. Not falling-off-a-cliff lost, maybe, but these are wild mountains and they contain perilous surprises. They lure you away from the marked-out trails, make you throw away the maps — get some nettles in your knees, some brambles in your hair.

I can't understand going to college to follow a prescribed route to a prescribed job — unless all one wants out of life is retirement to a barbecue pit and golf in the mornings. You know what's going to happen, so why do it?

The philosopher Adam Phillips argues that we are all always in the process of inventing our lives, constructing them in ways that are of interest to us. We damned well better develop the capacity to narrate an open and mysterious future — or we may lose interest altogether.

Philips says that education, as ordinarily conceived, functions not to foster but to dampen curiosity. When we are very young, before the schools have got hold of us, we keep asking *Why?* not to get answers but to open up new territory in which questions can grow. Kids love questions for their own sake. Their idea is to extend the game, keep the mystery squirming. Kids change the rules midstream not to cheat, to win, but to keep the problem unsolved, defeat time. If you are devoted enough to the joys of curiosity, it'll never be bedtime, the party will endure forever.

Schools regulate curiosity to the point of almost killing it, rewarding not the curious but the compliant — those who submit themselves to the interests and dull lures of teachers, school boards, and all those who prize obedience. A true education isn't regulatory; it is a skilled provocation. A set of hints, oblique and twitchy.

It opens doors away from the terrible trap of the normal.

Normal. That's what I'm talking about. Being normal. The goal of standard education. I'm here to tell you to fly by those nets! Normal is nothing more than the stifling forms established by the status quo.

Our culture expends so much energy horrifying us about the non-normal. But what are the rewards for being normal? And what price do normal people pay for being normal?

Let's say that in this room the normal person is the A student, and let's define the A student as someone who is obedient to the script our culture devises. Of course, part of the script is the illusion that it does not exist, that those following it are ruggedly independent.

The A- student is asked to be smart, you say, and hard working, willing to sacrifice for her ideals, keep her priorities straight, and so forth. Yeah, sure. A- students, let's say, are simply very quick at figuring out what other people want them to do and very adept at doing it. These are students who, at about the third grade, are willing to sacrifice their own interests for those of the standard curriculum, willing to let others tell them what they ought to be interested in, to what degree, and for how long. Isn't it odd that anyone would manage to get As in every subject? For forty-eight minutes I'm profoundly interested in social studies, then — what's that you say? — "Stop it"? Okay, now I'll be profoundly interested in math for forty-eight minutes, then California history, then whatever it is you tell me.

This is what gets rewarded, this abject passivity.

Nothing in our educational system is more troubling than curiosity, and nothing generally gets attacked more resolutely. Curiosity is more likely to end you up in prison than at USC.

But hold on: things are not quite so dark.

The glorious thing is that you can still preserve curiosity in the midst of such a giant crushing machine as college. That none of you is, deep down, normal is a tribute to your ability to be secret agents, terrorists of the imagination. You pretend to obey and get the automatic, worthless As, as you nurture your own quiet abnormality, your secret freakishness. I know you have it in you to continue this subversive game and I honor you for it.

Long live the abnormal—and each one of you!

* * *

You with me? It should be clear by now that this is a participatory venture: you have to help or I'll never figure things out. Please. To be candid, my needs are great. I haven't mentioned them before this; being a coward, worrying that you might throw up your hands, leave. Then where would I be? As Humbert Humbert (second cousin, mother's side) says, "Imagine me; I shall not exist if you do not imagine me; try to discern the doe in me, trembling in the forest of my own iniquity; let's even smile a little. After all, there is no harm in smiling."

Chapter 7

Nothing of interest (to me) occurred in the first six or so weeks of this, their freshman term. The weather got a little better, though only imperceptibly, not that our friends would notice, weather not being uppermost in the minds of kids— or in yours. I hear you. "Speed it up!" No need to be rude.

Our four have not yet made contact with one another, though that day was not far off. And, rushing past stuff that is probably boring and, in any case, unknown to me, at last they did connect that first year, eventually moved in together, trading with other compliant students so as to be joined — Cobb and Brad in Trojan Hall, Room 236 and Joss and Katie right down the corridor, Room 242. And from that point to where we are now in our story was a full three years plus a little. They didn't remain in the dorms, of course; nobody does. Some kids move into apartments, some into fraternity/sorority lodgings, and some drop out. None of our three was so limp-brained as to go all Greek, so they found nearby apartments, close to where they worked, variously, at 32nd Street Market, the local cinema, the dry cleaners, the book store, the Dean's Office, the copy shop. No bars

Now we're back to where we were, they were, the morning after the night before, meeting at an early hour for breakfast.

They hadn't explicitly settled what time they'd be meeting or where, but somehow our four ended up together — 9 a.m. at Jacks 'N Joe. Serendipity, I guess, or the gods of narrative neatness.

"How'd you two know we'd be here?" this from Brad.

"Because it's closest and you're laziest," said Joss.

"But...."

"We talked, Brad, me and Katie did, so we'd not miss you guys or be without a plan, a very sensible plan, which we knew was beyond you two reckless youths."

"Oh," said Brad.

"Anyhow," Cobb ventured, "What's important is that we're all set, have no qualms, nothing concealed. We talked about it, me and Brad. We're all set. You got nothing to worry about from this quarter."

When nobody responded, he added, "Yessir. We're all set, couldn't be more so."

"What is it you're all set on, sweetie?" Joss had moved close in and was now only inches from Cobb's face, stroking his ears and neck in a parody of seduction.

"Maybe we should take this inside?" Katie wasn't laughing, seemed to be the only one noticing that they were still standing on the sidewalk there on Figueroa, blocking the door to Jacks 'N Joe.

The booth they found would have been a squeeze for four, had they not been so slight, three of them, so they wriggled in and passed around the befouled menus nested in befouled racks, not that there was anything fresh to be learned from them.

"So, Brad, what do *You* suppose we're set on?" Katie was looking around the room as she spoke.

Before Brad could speak, Cobb laughed, "We did talk but only about male stuff, sex, and decided to make no plans, not a one — about sex OR our trip. So we got nothing set, nothing figured out. All we can offer is what you see before you."

Brad, who actually seemed to have something figured out, looked square at Katie and spoke without hesitating, though he was turning a menu over and over in his hands as he talked. "Okay, how's this: I'll call my mom right now, tell her to meet me at eleven — that okay? — with the car. Then I'll drive her back and return, pick you guys up, and we're off. Drive to—oh hell, let's say Davis. We could barge in on Troy and Julie, stay with them tonight? You guys can call them. You can do that while I get the car and you're packing and checking it twice."

Katie almost smiled. "That'll launch us, seems like, but into what? We want more in our heads than just Davis? That's what I meant. Once we have the car and have established the time and done the packing, then what? By the way, pack so as not to be unprepared for snowy evenings, which they all will be, if we get to any altitude. But beyond thermal underwear and ear muffs, what?"

Nobody said anything for a minute, then Joss: "I think Katie's right. We all know we're good at details and can get ourselves toothbrushed up for an excursion in nothing flat. But this excursion...."

That's when the waiter came up, looking grim — stood there tapping his pencil on a pad. "Yeah?"

"You been here most recently, Cobb. What's good?"

"Roo's Favorite is what I usually get, Joss."

Joss looked at the menu, looked at Cobb, then: "Yogurt, granola, and fruit — please."

Cobb, true to his word, got what he usually got, Brad and Katie both going for the Dakine French Toast Combo.

"Cobb, how come you ain't fat? Pancakes laced with chocolate chips, topped with whipped cream. What are you, six years old?"

Cobb just stared at Joss, then grinned.

Brad drew everyone's attention by some silent means. He was looking still at his glop-stained menu, not responding to their stares. Then he put it carefully back in the rack and looked up. "I see what Katie and Joss are saying. Cobb and I — well, we just assumed you'd let us in on it — whatever 'it' is — reveal it gradually as we went along, leaking it out so we could understand."

He paused, but nobody seemed to think he was finished.

"Besides, I think we avoid the big questions because — well, not because we're focused on details. I thought the big questions were going to be approached in the doing. I thought the idea was to allow the articulation to be unfinished, really unstarted. I thought we were going to let the experience itself, whatever it turns out to be, speak through us, maybe even redefine us — if that's not too pretentious."

Now he was finished. The other three looked at him, all serious now. Nobody seemed interested in being a smart-ass, so they had a chance to think.

The food came, and they glommed right in.

"Brad nails it," said Joss, finally. "We can do what I said earlier. Remember? Cross the Sierras, Donner Pass, U.S. 50 in Nevada? Or we can set off aimlessly. Problem with aimless is.... I seem to be talking too much."

Nobody thought she was babbling, or wrong. At least nobody said so. Finally, Katie spoke, the boys knowing they weren't expected to weigh in.

"If we catch the dribbles we've let fall so far, seems to me we have Brad getting the car, collecting us all at about eleven, make that noon, wheeling on up to Davis to Troy and Julie's for the night, and then over east. Maybe Donner Pass area and U.S. Route 50 in Nevada. Maybe not. Beyond that, open and empty, rough water, and banjo music."

Two cups of coffee for Cobb, one for Brad, a breakfast tea for Katie, just water for Joss. There you have it.

* * *

At 12:14, Brad pulled up in front of his apartment on Vermont. Cobb was ready to take off, even had his stuff all clomped in one bag, sitting down in the front area where all the buzzers were. Katie and Joss were already in the car, one in front and one in back, waving madly.

Cobb grabbed his bag and then tripped over something

just as he was trying to open the super-heavy door, balancing a mug, a bag, and some papers. He lurched forward two or three steps, trying to get his feet under him and avert his front-leaning topple. Ended up saving the mug (though not its contents), his bag, and the papers, sacrificing his forehead and nose, both of which hit the cement walk with some force and even more friction when he slid forward.

He came up bleeding spectacularly, warding off anticipated condolences and trying hard to do something with his face.

"Get a rag, somebody. Christ, Cobb. You break your nose? You got blood all over your T-shirt."

"Nah. Just a scratch." Then he did reach up and wiggle his nose-bone. "Really, just.... I'll be fine. I'll get it stopped before I get in, though. A Prius? Bigger-sized, which I didn't know existed, but a Prius? Your parents are really...."

"They're among the aware and conscientious rich. I know, Cobb. Even if it gives us not a hell of a lot more room than your car. Don't worry about the upholstery. Just get in back and try not to bleed on Katie."

He did, holding to his nose some cloth he had dug out of his bag, cloth that turned out to be underpants.

"Hope those aren't your only clean ones, Cobb, or I'm saying right now I'm not sharing the back seat with you beyond Bakersfield."

So, with only that single misstep behind them, off they took from Vermont Avenue, headed right down to the 10. Nobody noticed the stranger there on the curb. To be fair, he didn't seem to be seeking their attention.

So, it was the ten to downtown, then the 110 to the Five, beginning a long slog through the valley and, at last, climbing the mountains starting outside La Canada, up over The Grapevine, not that high, by any reasonable standards, but high enough to freeze in the winter and cause hellish backups. Brad, doing the first shift behind the wheel, had checked the weather, though it was a warm February and no chance of getting much below 40, even up there, which was now "up here."

"I know some good car games."

"Great, Joss. Let 'em roll."

"I'm going to have wild times, and I'm taking along my Attitude."

"My Bum."

"My Cocktail Shaker."

"My Dumb Roommate."

"My Ebullience."

"My, ah—

That seemed to be more than enough of that, so they put in some sing-along CDs which got them up the road a couple dozen miles. But such merriment soon grew irksome, so they put in an audio book.

Cormac McCarthy's *The Road.* The perfect choice, though nobody could remember who had chosen it. Maybe Brad's parents left it there.

Almost at once, the voice on the CDs, and the father and little boy he ventriloquized, mesmerized them and held their hearts. No one spoke, though in time they were making soft noises now and then. The engulfing power of the book, they would have said, came from somewhere in the deep fears of all of us, emerging from that point where terror and faith mingle. It had little to do with the post-apocalyptic setting or the nightmare world of death the Dad and child were struggling inside. It wasn't, clearly, a question of navigating this world successfully, of trying to get somewhere. There were no destinations left. The father did hope to reach the sea, though he knew all along the sea held out no more life than did the stricken land.

When the two reach the lifeless ocean, though, they do achieve the most that any of us can manage, frolicking on the front porch of nothing. The little boy, encouraged by a father who now knows no separation from his son, throws himself naked into the icy waveless waters, crying at all he has lost, but refusing to flinch as he becomes one with the emptiness and asserts what earlier writers would have called an absurd freedom. But what the small family creates, right then, there on the beach, flies much higher than any negative freedom. They merge, the boy and the man, become one. They are the all. In the terms they use, they now truly possess the fire they are carrying within.

* * *

> *"You have to carry the fire," the father tells his small son.*
> *"I don't know how to."*
> *"Yes, you do."*
> *"Is it real? The fire?"*
> *"Yes it is."*
> *"Where is it? I don't know where it is."*
> *"Yes you do. It's inside you. It always was there. I can see it."*

* * *

To arrive at this point, however, they first have to descend not only below the point of safety but below sanity altogether:

> *He started down the rough wooden steps. He ducked his head and then flicked the lighter and swung the flame out over the darkness like an offering. Coldness and damp. An ungodly stench. He could see part of a stone wall. Clay floor. An old mattress darkly stained. He crouched and stepped down again and held out the light.*
>
> *Huddled against the back wall were naked people, male and female, all trying to hide, shielding their faces with their hands. On*
> *the mattress lay a man with his legs gone to the hip and the stumps of them blackened*

and burnt. The smell was hideous.
"Jesus," he whispered.
Then one by one they turned and blinked in the pitiful light. "Help us," they whispered. "Please help us."

* * *

The world has moved beyond any thought that help might come, to an arctic stillness. Even so. the father and his more courageous son keep moving through the static terror. They evade nothing that they experience, joining together, across years andnightmares, embarking at the same stop.

"What would you do if I died?" the boy asks.
"If you died I would want to die too."
"So you could be with me?"
"Yes. So I could be with you."
"Okay."

Chapter 8

They pulled into yet another Rest Stop, about their fifth — California knowing just where to place, if not maintain, them. They all wanted to get to the end of the CD, not so much to get it over with as to give themselves a moment in which to pretend to recover. They foresaw that the last parts would be more than they could let in, that they would be wrapped around something they did not want to characterize — or suffer to escape.

* * *

Just take me with you.
I can't.
Please, Papa.
I can't. I can't hold my son dead in my arms. I thought I could but I can't.
You said you wouldn't ever leave me.
I know. I'm sorry. You have my whole heart. You always did. You're the best guy. You always were. If I'm not here you can still talk to me. You can talk to me and I'll talk to you. You'll see.

* * *

If you looked from the front seat over the edge and straight into the back, right then it would appear that Cobb and Joss were sleeping, drawn away from one another, facing their clouded windows, motionless. Surely their eyes were shut.

Look closer: they seem not to be breathing. In the front, Brad and Katie are staring ahead, though not quite directly ahead. They are focused on the CD player, not even the speakers but the player itself, its dashboard cover, as if they are hoping so hard for something, not so much for more of that voice but for a chance to hear better, deeper, to find inside the plastic slot the very fire the little boy is carrying, the fire that allows him to outlast his father, to outlast them all.

Finally, they realized they had to find a way out of all this. It doesn't matter which of them spoke first or what was said. They had nowhere to go, but soon found themselves at Troy and Julie's apartment house on J Street, a short hike from campus.

They managed, severally, to shake themselves free, make their way to the door, the buzzer, up stairs designed to admit only skinny children, and immediately onto couches, beers in hand.

They explained their mission, the determination to keep clear of all plans. Somehow, Troy and Julie ignored what could well have sounded to them self-congratulatory.

"You want to get away from all security, abandon awareness, ditch protections?"

"Well," Katie started, but Troy interrupted.

"You want to hurt yourself, there's some S/M parlors nearby. Julie has coupons."

That shut everybody up, for maybe ten seconds. All six seemed loaded with comments, waiting only to slot them in where they'd have some chance of being heard.

Finally, Troy began again. "Sorry. I do think I see. Like those strange ice-climbers Krakauer writes about. They deliberately put themselves in danger, seeking out more and more fragile icicles to cling to. If they make it, manage not to plunge and die, they can't even brag about it, since it's not known mountains with fixed altitudes they are conquering but shifting fields of impossibility. I guess it must be one hell of a rush."

"A rush?" somebody or everybody said, as if they had been insulted.

"Sorry. I guess you'd all be saying your pain and risk opened a gate into a new form of being, not a more authentic one, but a transformed and transcendent self."

"Shut up, Troy. You sound sarcastic," Julie said, sounding sarcastic herself.

Brad took up the slack. "We're not on some kind of spiritual quest. In a way, we want to experience something negative. We feel as if we're zombies and figure anything is bound to be better than routine. Maybe not better, just less padded and sanded down."

That seemed to take the air out of all the more ponderous pronouncements his trio of friends may have been pumping up, so they settled in for tidbit talk, pizza, and rounds of "Cards Against Humanity."

They almost made it into their sleeping bags when Troy again raised the issue: "But somehow fear has to be part of this. No?"

Nobody spoke for a minute. Then Cobb.

"It is for me. I mean, I have trouble remembering fear, what it is, even more than with most sensations. I can recall and even re-feel things like joy, sadness."

"Lust," Troy said.

Cobb ignored him. "For instance, I can re-experiece, get back to, that moment in 'Jaws' where they are comparing macho-scars and things turn amusing, or the nasty-comedy of the real estate lady who worries that safety measures will be bad for business. What I can't enter into is what matters. You all know."

"The shark. The biting. The sudden emergence from below."

"Right. That's it. From below. Our deep certainty that what is in the darkness has but one goal, is rising up to get you, like the ground when you are falling."

Chasing Nightmares

* * *

Next morning, they ran out to buy six person's worth of pastries and coffee, small thanks for a night's lodging, brought them back for their group breakfast, downed them quickly, said affectionate good-byes, and then took off down the street. Turned a couple of blocks, Brad did, then parked.

"So, now —?" he asked.

"Do we want to pursue our earlier idea? Eastward toward Reno, Donner Pass?"

"Maybe, Katie, but are we trapping ourselves into stale ideas of what'd be fresh?"

"Could be, Joss, but we might also fall into a predictable mode of rejecting something just because it's been mentioned previously."

The boys were keeping still, awaiting instructions.

Finally, the girls seemed to know without speaking just what would work, or, in this case, what would not.

"Lassen Volcanic Park." Didn't matter which one said it. Both knew.

"Mt. Shasta?" said Cobb.

"That's not the same place. Mt. Shasta is north of the park, west, too, a little. Just our kind of place. Renewal for those what can afford it. Home of spiritual hot-tubbing, get your insides transformed. Massages, too, ranging from voodoo cleansing to the traditional ass grinding."

Joss grimaced, but then relented. "Okay. What the hell makes the difference?"

So they headed north, some hours later found themselves just short of the actual mountain of the spirit, pulled into a helpful gas station doubling as a tourist information bureau. They were more than ready for wild goose chases, blind alleys, but found nothing of the kind, and were terribly disappointed.

Brochures flew right into their hands, brochures designed less to attract than to weed out: personal retreats (no group clutter), guaranteeing for those who were on the inside already "a visionary transformational healing touch," laid on by one Blanda Hossacha, "your own personal spiritual guide."

"What does Blanda promise," asked Katie, "or is it wrong to inquire too closely?"

"Not at all," Joss said, "Blanda is not in the business of concealing. Here's what she says: 'Discover the full and vital life you always knew was waiting for you! Lay bare your own unique powers and abilities. The world awaits you, yearns for you.'"

"You're making this up?" Cobb's was only half a question.

"Ha!" Joss said. "That question just proves how parched and empty you are. Yes, you. You, above all, Cobb, need Blanda balsamic blandishments. You'll start with visionary craniosacral and deep tissue massage."

"Is that it?" Cobb said on cue.

"It? How long since your last craniosacrality experience? Just open yourself and all your zippers to the.... But I do wrong to paraphrase. Blanda has a way with words: 'Then let the Healing Springs purify you and free you from the old.'"

"Free me from the old what? Never mind. If I were worth Blanda's time, I wouldn't have to ask. So, tell me something I can wrap my small head around: what do we do in them there springs? I trust this isn't some adventure where we discover ourselves by shedding our garments?"

"How can you be so literal-minded, Cobb! Actually, that point is not clear. At least not to me. Perhaps Blanda will be speaking more directly to others: 'Journey on a special vision quest (guided) to open up the greatest possibility for your contribution to Life itself.' Life is capitalized, you'll be glad to hear."

"So, as to nudity?"

"I'll admit, she doesn't spell that out, perhaps that'll be

revealed only on the vision quest, you know, as we develop our possibilities. Maybe undies-optional. That a deal-breaker for you, Cobb?"

"Do we have to climb the fucking mountain?"

"Just put yourself in Blanda's hands, Cobb."

"Yourself and your dick," said Joss.

Brad cut this off: "The copy I have says, 'As the sun sets, we close with a prayer of gratitude and a celebratory feast.' Maybe we can skip to the feast. I'm hungry."

But they couldn't do that, as Blanda had established limited hours in which she ministered and properly scheduled sequences therein, so they postponed food and put their spirits into Blanda's custody for the full ride, $755 for the quartet. There were four others along — parents and a young kid, maybe twelve-years-old, and a nondescript fellow who appeared to have wandered in by mistake and could think of no exit lines. Our four spent their time, most of it, trying hard to concentrate on whatever was not going on right at the moment: Would they hike? Would they pray? Would they strip?

As it developed, hiking was featured, though just a short stroll, the praying was done solo by Blanda, and the stripping never arose as a possibility. Damn!

[Try not to be disappointed.]

The feast featured humus and lots of it, along with coordinate grains and leaves. Our four were anxious to mix with the others a little, friendly-like, avoiding easy sarcasms, just in case those others were true believers.

Cobb ended up talking with the little boy, name of Pran, if you can believe it. In fact, that's what the kid said: "Pran, if you can fucking believe it." Good start and things sailed along from there. All Cobb had to do was grin and agree; Pran was an instant ally.

"So, why are you here?"

Cobb wasn't the sort to consider his responses, or his

audience. "Be fucked if I know. We're trying to do the oddest things we can, kid, putting ourselves where we wouldn't want to be, where nobody'd want to be."

"You should join up with my asshole parents, Clod."

"It's Cobb, Bran."

It was a match made in heaven.

The others developed relationships less memorable. Brad and Katie took on the parents, with predictable results: back and forth, both sides trying not to recognize that life was floating by and they had no handholds. Joss was left with the mysterious stranger, probably not the one from the Twain story---

[Who turns out to be Satan, I think.]

"You enjoying this?" Joss tried.

"Am I supposed to?"

"Well, I'm not requiring it of you. Just wondered if you were tuned into something I was missing."

"Why would you wonder that?"

"Look, if you're just going to rebound questions at me, hell with it."

"Sorry. No, I don't enjoy this. Not sure how I got sucked into it. This sort of thing happens to me a lot. Practically all the time. It's an occupational hazard."

There didn't seem to be anything to say to that, nothing that Joss wanted to venture anyhow. For some reason, she knew better than to give him an opening onto his "occupation," so they stared at the floor together, waiting for the others.

It was still fresh and pretty outside after the post-feast meet-and-shuffle was ended, so our four reconvened. Decided on a walk.

[Destination of course unknown.]

Cobb and Katie ended up setting off in one direction, Brad and Joss the other — exactly opposite. It occurred to Cobb they could easily reunite — just reverse course or yell. He was about to mention that, then noticed Katie limping pretty badly alongside him. He turned around, thought about touching Katie, rejected that idea as worse than stupid. He simultaneously considered trying to match his steps to hers.

Katie wondered how long it had been since she and Cobb had been together alone. At one point, they may have dated. She seemed unable to remember. Yes, surely they had: twice maybe, three times? Year or two earlier. Strange that nothing came back to her. Dates? Had they had sex? She could call to mind Cobb's body in some detail, but that didn't clinch the matter, as he was careless about such displays. Anyhow, who gave a shit? She certainly did, at least right at the moment, wished she didn't. Nothing could be more dismally predictable than lusting after Cobb. And, for now, the issue was conversation, not coitus.

"Well, Cobb, you feel washed clean?"

"In the blood of the lamb. Or, I guess, in the spiritual floods on the mountain."

"Fits better."

"Katie, can I ask you something?"

"No."

"I deserved that. I have that bad habit, don't I? I mean, I keep saying things like 'Can I ask you a question?'"

He smiled.

Katie stared at him.

"Well, here goes. Do you like me?"

"Holy shit, Cobb. We spend about 60% of our lives together."

"So do my parents, and they detest one another, would resort to homicide if they weren't so lazy."

"Oh. First, let me reverse things: do you like me?"

"Why should the male have the lead in this play, Katie? But yes, yes I do. You are very likeable — more than that. Saying you're likeable is a dodge. Yes, *I* like *you*."

"Uh-huh."

"It's not easy to say. I admire you, maybe take you for granted, to tell the truth."

"I see."

"I don't know you at all."

"Okay. Ball's definitely in my court. I think you are beautiful beyond belief, Cobb, and it's hard not to let that interfere with knowing what else I feel. Truth is I take you for granted, too, like pleasant wallpaper — if we had wallpaper. In a way, I do depend on you, find my eyes seeking you out, wanting to hear you speak. Still and all, I don't know how much independence you have, how much you exist as a separable being, at least in my head. So, in a way, no, I do not."

"Uh huh."

"Are you hurt?"

"I don't know. Yes."

"Well, I don't want to lie. Tell me — while I collect myself — more about where I am in your head, forgetting whether you know me or not."

"I think about you a lot, wish I were more like you. I think you are integral, if you know what I mean. Not that you have integrity...."

"Thanks."

He looked hard at her. "I think you have a kind of chorus inside you, like in Greek plays, which echoes back to you what you are and keeps you from saying anything false or even shaky."

"The chorus didn't help old Oedipus."

"That's because he was tainted. Don't condescend to me, Katie. I know some things. You are not tainted."

She looked at him in a way he couldn't decipher. She didn't say anything for a minute, and then, only "Let's try ascending this little hill. Unless you have other plans, Mister Man."

Cobb thought she was telling him the conversation was over, not begging off but declaring herself off-limits.

"Maybe I would like you, Cobb, if I knew what that meant, if I knew what was in me that likes or doesn't. When I say I don't know you, that makes it seem as if the only opaque element in that equation were you, when it's the idea of 'me' that I should be wondering about. Who says there is a 'me' and not just a lot of impermanent scripts?

Anyhow, I have no right to hurt you or to hide behind highfallutin babble about who is I and who is you and who is real, and such sophomoric shit. I think the honest truth is, dear Cobb, that I'm worrying that I might love you, love you so much. That'd be a lot more than I could take, so it's easier not to like you. Don't say anything or I'll be so sorry I said such a thing I'll knee you in the nuts."

Cobb didn't grin or writhe. He stopped her climbing with one hand on her shoulder and with the other stroked her forehead. Then he released her, saying only, "Okay, Katie. I won't say anything much, not wanting my balls squashed." He paused, then, "I hear you and won't step into the place your generous heart opened. I won't. But you can hear me calling, I know. Now I'll shut up."

Katie took his hand, made it seem as if she needed steadying on their mini-climb.

They conquered their little hill, watched the now-visible stars for a bit, and then headed back to the B&B, arriving to find themselves first-comers. Not having a good way to rev up again, the two of them, and having less idea what it was they'd be starting, they decided to read aloud to one another, poems they knew well or had in books they'd carted along or could call up on their I-phones. They were both looking for poems they figured would be especially fitting to the occasion, not knowing what "the occasion" was.

* * *

JAMES R. KINCAID

I lost a World — the other day!
Has Anybody found?
You'll know it by the Row of Stars
Around its forehead bound.
A Rich man — might not notice it —
Yet — to my frugal Eye,
Of more Esteem than Ducats —
Oh find it — Sir — for me!

* * *

Nature's first green is gold,
Her hardest hue to hold.
Her early leaf's a flower;
But only so an hour.
Then leaf subsides to leaf,
So Eden sank to grief,
So dawn goes down to day
Nothing gold can stay.

You did not come,
And marching Time drew on, and wore me numb.
Yet less for loss of your dear presence there
Than that I thus found lacking in your make
That high compassion which can overbear
Reluctance for pure loving kindness' sake
Grieved I, when, as the hope-hour stroked its sum,
You did not come.

You love not me,
And love alone can lend you loyalty;
I know and knew it. But, unto the store
Of human deeds divine in all but name,
Was it not worth a little hour or more
To add yet this: Once you, a woman, came
To soothe a time-torn man; even though it be
You love not me.

* * *

That, oddly, from Katie. It was Cobb's turn. And he did manage to start:

Though nothing can bring back the hour
Of splendor in the grass, of glory in the flower,
We will grieve not, rather....

He paused and then began sobbing, trying hard to stop, even when it was clear he could not. "Nothing can bring back. Nothing."

This was too much for Katie. "Oh, Cobb. Oh, honey. It's just the poems. Why on earth did we light on such gloom? Agents of depression, Cobb. It's just the poems."

"Yeah," he managed to gulp out, meaning "No."

Katie knew. "Oh, Cobb. I do like you right now, and I didn't mean the loving part as a high-sounding excuse. Really. I do like you. Of course I do. Not 'of course.' And not just 'right now,' as if it were a mistake I'd later erase. You are tender and beautiful. Not just beautiful. I mean that you are sensitive and willing to take chances."

"Thank you, Katie. I didn't mean to extract avowals from you, for sure not by crying like a — by crying. And I don't mean to make things worse by saying that. We're okay, you'n me."

That seemed to do it, be enough to release them from the trap both would have given anything were it somehow to be sprung.

This all had taken a good long time, yet Joss and Brad had not returned. Wasn't like they had been gone all that long, so their companions were not disturbed, not at all. It was more like things were edging toward that territory.

Not wanting to think about such alien topics as security and reasonable precautions, Katie and Cobb decided to separate and plunge into their paperbacks. Perhaps to pass the time or create a diversion, they both hit at once on the same idea:

"We should get rid of all our electronics. Right? Damn right! Yes!"

They seemed to be led to that denunciatory vow by recognizing, first, that they weren't using Kindles for reading but plain old paper.

"Get rid of laptops — did we bring any? — and...."

"Phones!" Katie said. "Why do we have them, if not as a hedge against exactly what it is we want to encounter."

Cobb nodded.

"Once our wanderers return, we'll spring this on them, our joint plan, the result of our intimate collaboration."

Soon as she said it, Katie was sorry. But she didn't retract it, make things worse.

It was a couple hours later when Joss and Brad laughed their way through the door and into the room they all were sharing. Neither Katie nor Cobb said anything, asked anything, though my guess is they were as curious as the suicidal cat.

What had they been doing? What made them so cheered-up, nearly raucous?

Katie and Cobb were so occupied thinking of what they didn't want to be thinking about, they forgot to mention their idea about losing the phones, and pads.

Next morning, though, they'd bring it up. Both went to bed making that vow.

Chapter 9

Next morning the odd-man-out from the night before was there at breakfast, the New Age family with the irreverent kid having made an early start for San Francisco (according to the whispering B&B operator). There, she said, the family had planned a visit (which they wished could be longer) with such interesting and talented in so many ways cousins they hadn't seen in ever so long, not since Lydia had graduated back in....

The stranger didn't take a separate table, plopped right down with them, occupying more than his share of the space, what with his flaring elbows, and commenced to eat in silence. Cobb it was who decided to charm him into speech.

"Headed out today?" Cobb tried.

"Are you?"

Cobb didn't miss a beat. "We're undecided. Thought we'd let you cast the deciding vote. Stay or leave? We're conflicted. Help us, please."

"Oh, I'll help you," said the stranger, keeping his eyes on the granola.

That was too much even for Cobb, so they all fell silent, trying not to hurry through the baked goods or find reasons to crouch.

* * *

Once they made it to the car. "Lassen, right? The National Park. Isn't that what we were thinking, jointly, having developed a corporate mind and no longer in any way separable, joined solidly at the ass-bone?"

Joss's comment hung in the stale Prius air. Katie and Cobb, sitting front to back (shotgun and right-rear), both figured the other should be the one to rescue the situation, drive them all away from unseemly images of asses, Brad- and Joss-asses in particular. But they were, instead, linked closely in wondering why Brad and Joss, after an evening both knew (imagined?) had developed into sexual congress, arranged the car seating in such a way, trying to make it seem casual.

So, nobody uttered a sound, until Joss picked up on her own suggestion: "I know I speak for all when I say, 'Lassen it is!'"

Nobody argued.

Brad, who was driving, turned to Katie. "The people at the spa thingy recommended a place to stay at Hart Creek, not far, they said."

"Not far from what?" Cobb said.

Nobody answered him.

"Well," Katie said, happy to clutch any reason for making noise, "we got us a guide book, outdated, and a regular old paper map, neatly folded, thank you Brad, and phones, which will expedite getting the choicest reservations, which reminds me — sorry for the garbles."

"What? Hart Creek reminds you? You been there?" Joss said.

"No, I mean the phones. Having phones with us, me and Cobb decided, is like swimming the English Channel with water wings — or some more apt analogy."

She turned around to look at Cobb, hoping to enlist him in this campaign, perhaps also to heal something. He didn't meet her glance but did give forth a sound that might have signaled assent.

Joss picked it up right away. "Hell, yes. Why didn't we think of it! Good for you and Cobb. So you didn't waste all of last evening, like we thought you had, me and Brad. How do you propose we get rid of all that shit? Just take a hammer to them? Anybody know how best to do this?"

Cobb, worried that he'd seemed sullen, said the first thing popping into his head: "Let's get to the park — Lassen, I mean — and find a very remote spot and bury them, deep, you know."

It's likely that everyone else regarded that scheme as a trifle unsatisfactory, but everyone also seemed to sense something about Cobb, didn't want to rain on his parade.

So, they started out on the twisty back roads that would, even with the bad navigation they had been counting on, lead them to Hart Creek and to someplace called Hereford Ranch — something or other.

"You should have brought your ukulele, Cobb," said somebody. "We could sing old favorites."

"You know what we actually could do?" Joss said.

Before anyone could take her up on whatever it was, Brad interrupted. "Would you look at that? A hitchhiker. Always very dangerous to stop for these axe-murderers, right?"

"Should we do it?" Katie said, not really raising a question.

So they did. Pulled over and reversed, so the moocher could catch up. Turned out to be no stranger at all, but the man from the night before, the one they had chatted with — only they hadn't — and gotten to know — only they hadn't — at the feast.

There was no room for him, but Joss scrunched over to the middle and Cobb mashed himself against the right door, the stranger taking up much more than the space left vacant. Waiting longer would not make them into a neat package, so Brad locked the doors from his command post, got out of the gravel and onto the main road, driving even more slowly now and waiting for someone to start a conversation.

Nobody did, so he said what he knew at the time was lame. "Did you enjoy your stay at the spa?"

Silence.

"I'm sorry," he continued, more amused than frustrated, "I was talking to you, Mr. Hitchhiker and sharer of our feast and breakfast."

"No," he said.

"No, what? You didn't enjoy your stay?"

Silence.

Katie turned — facing him from a few inches away, actually tilting her face and leaning in. "You pretending to be in some Thomas Harris novel, Mr. enigmatic violent man? You gonna chew off our faces?"

The guy smiled, looked like a smile. "Your faces are safe from me. I'm just going on down the road, you know. I am sure you know."

"You are sure? You think we have access to your route and destination? What the fuck do you mean?" Cobb asked, now almost angry, thinking about becoming angry.

"Why do you ask that?" the guy said.

"Look, asshole," Cobb said, "that's an easy game to play, if it is a game and not the only script you have, you pathetic creep."

The guy turned to look at Cobb and laughed. Seemed like.

"You can let me out about a half mile from here. A little road up there, actually goes right down to Lassen. But you knew that."

They did as he said, all four grateful to be shut of him, the exciting danger he might have contained also becoming a little boring. Or that's what they said.

"Well, next homicidal lunatic we befriend had better be more forthcoming or at least more challenging," said Brad.

"How did he know—?"

Nobody responded, though thoughts of menacing phone calls, inexplicable notes, webs of unwelcome knowledge threaded through the minds of each.

* * *

Before long, and too early for check-in, they arrived at Hart Creek and their spot, which turned out to be a farm doubling as a campground, home also to the world's most ardent sky-sailors, it said on a large sign that the walleyed desk clerk confirmed.

"It'll be another hour-two before we clear out the old sites. But then you're set. You all sailors, or just the boys? Not that girls don't make the best sailors, I always say, yes I do, and with reason."

"Oh, we're all about the same, as to our flying ability," said Cobb, a little sarcastically, figuring the checker-in was too dim to register it. He wasn't.

"I'm not sure we have anything, now I look — nothing that'd be suiting you four."

"He didn't mean anything," Brad said. "You know how it is with kids."

This, coming from a boy who looked less than fifteen, tickled the clerk back into his friendlies.

"Okay. Here we go, right here —" pointing to a chart hidden from all but him. "Come back in a bit and I'll get you established, assigned, to your site."

Site? They went ahead and signed in. Be back in a bit, we will. Nobody felt like extending things, so they let it go until they were out of range. Then —

"You realizing what I'm realizing, Katie?"

"I am, Joss. We got us a reglar ol campground here and not a classy motel like what we're used to and have ever right ta expeck."

"And us with no firewood, no sleepin bags, no bedroll, no blankits even, no nothing," said Joss.

"But exposing ourselves here at the Hart Creek Hmm-Hmm Campground and Slaughter House ought to give us what we want in the way of the unprotected and unembarrassed atmosphere."

"Naked unto the elements."

The boys felt excluded, had pretty near become used by

now to that feeling, so just waited for it to be over, veterans enough to know not to bite on the "naked" cue, maybe inserted just to trap them.

So, they headed off into the park, designed deliberately, it seemed, to discourage visitors. Once there, however, they encountered irresistibly friendly camp guides (both in breathing and brochure form) and uncrowded sweet-smelling trails, leading through thick pine groves, close by rocky cliffs, by cascading streams, paths pushing them downhill and then steeply up again.

Cobb was reading from a guide they'd picked up from Ranger Rick, part of which outlined "Dangers in Lassen Park."

"Let's head right for them!" Katie said.

"Right!" Cobb said. "But wait."

"Wait for what?" Brad asked. "That hitchhiker guy going to show up and do his enigma routine on us at the end of the trail."

"At the end of the trail is a golden hmm and the sweet silver song of a lark!" sang Joss.

"And a man with a shiv and a heart that's dark" added Cobb, trying to disguise his extraordinary singing voice.

"Okay, Edmund Hillary lovers," said Brad, "here's the official list of dangers, spine-chilling and therefore inviting. Wanta hear it?"

"Only if they include directions and maps, so we can locate the finest menaces without much trouble," said Katie.

"Well," Brad said, "you won't be disappointed. I'll start with the tamest and work upwards to the perils I know you seek."

Silence.

"Here we go. Falling off one of the cliffs put there for the special use and enjoyment of the sky-sailors."

"Whee!"

"Poison oak."

"No!"

"Getting Lost. General injuries. Falling somewhere other

than over a cliff's edge. Tripping on roots and rocks. Wounding yourself with your own implements [I think they mean axes and fire-making aides]. Spider bites. Cuts and scrapes. Sudden attacks of sneezing, homesickness, digestive upsets. Birds shitting on you."

"I love you, Brad, and the way you stick to the script. I'd never have thought of these issues, none of them, catastrophic as they must be — will be. Now I am armed and ready."

"Sounds to me like they're making fun of us, and all the defenseless tenderfoots, omitting the most common and terrible traps and counting the same thing twice — falling and injuries, for instance," said Cobb. "I mean, how is falling an injury if you ain't hurt?"

"Anybody but you'd see," said Joss, before she thought. "Falling is a euphemism for fatal 3,000 foot, whoopsie-daisy, plunging death, the old curtain-closer."

Cobb was determined to register nothing in his face.

Brad stepped in pretty quickly. "Then there's mountain lions, only some question exists as to whether there are all that many left, or any."

"But you can never be sure," said Katie.

"I hope not," Brad continued. "Bears, of course."

"And that they do have. Yes, they do," said Katie.

"Grizzly and Kodiak and Panda," said Joss.

Cobb did know something about bears, having a morbid and unproductive fascination with their habitat and habits, especially their habit of attacking and devouring humans. "You know how many fatal bear attacks there are per year in Lassen — oh, I mean, in all the national parks — oh, I mean, in all the country?"

"How many, Cobb?"

"Much closer to zero than to one. More dangerous than sharks" — another of his fascinations — "but not much. Many more people die from vending machines tipping over on them."

Everyone pretended to be astounded. Wow, Cobb!

Back to Brad. "The top danger, and our main attraction, is, of course, the volcanic activity. Not, just to anticipate your questions, that eruptions are likely to threaten current visitors, though those walking around here in 300,000 B.C. had plenty of that to contend with. We need only be aware that the heat generated by what's bubbling deep below us causes — well, we'll see."

"At least tell us where to go so we can experience those non-eruptive dangers," said Katie. "Seems to me I know about those simmering scorchers from classes or from outdoorsy sorts back at USC. You know who I mean."

"They say," Brad went on, "that the pretty babbling brooks might have scalding temperatures attending them. You'll be badly wanting to dangle your feet in them, take a plunge, but, says this excellent guide, don't you do it."

This comic routine had run its course long before it ended, so they turned to hiking, trying to find trails or passways not so annoyingly over-marked with signs to help the uncertain, protect the stumbling.

Following a sudden inspiration, they climbed a rocky hillside, looking for what they might, in a pinch, regard as "remote" and finally found a shallow cave, too shallow to house hermits, bears, or anything much larger than a smallish goat, were cave-goats given to hanging out at Lassen.

The land there was hardscrabble, though, so they hauled themselves to the ground above the cave, which was conveniently mossy and easy to uncover. Perfect! They carefully removed the top moss and dirt, dug down about a foot — would like to have gone deeper, but didn't want to spend more time on a dumb project — and put their phones right there, shoveled back the dirt and managed to replace the moss in such a way that nobody, they told themselves, would ever, ever, ever....

Then they slid back down, tried to remove signs of their

climbing, and resumed their wander, hoping to find the delirium of empty confusion, hard to accomplish what with the unavoidable signs, posted warnings, and leveled pathways.

They finally gave up their hope of getting lost and dutifully slogged over to an area that would have been exciting, had the name not so insistently told you how exciting it was: "Bumpass Hell Trail."

They found themselves, after a few weak jokes on their failure as explorers of the horrendous, separated, in no danger of being long lost, but out of hearing range.

The idea of dangling feet, babbling brooks, sylvan glory: that had lodged in each of their heads. But it was only Cobb who gave it much heed.

He recognized that you couldn't find nihilistic oneness by disobeying routine cautions from a book, charging dutifully at the earmarked prohibitions. All the same....

So, there he was, his feet on a rock just above such an innocent-looking cauldron, musing and, he realized, very happy. He wasn't usually one to be aware of his feelings, especially those that might be positive, so he was slow to allow it to settle into his mind.

All this time he was so hypnotized, so astonished he could look inward, that he lost contact with his surroundings. He wasn't aware that he had moved, wasn't aware of what might be around or behind him, when he suddenly found himself sliding downward toward the stream.

He was still thinking of what it meant to be happy, when his left foot hit a rock just above the brook, hit it and held, and his right foot slipped into the scalding water. It hurt so badly he didn't have a chance to scream; no instinct hit him except to get his foot the hell out of there. He managed to do that by shifting his weight to the left, elevating the burned toes and heel, instep and ankle.

That was good. What wasn't so good was that his leftward lurch caused him, only for a second, to lose his balance and start to topple. He caught himself, but only by throwing his left hand out and into the stream.

Now he did scream.

The first thing that came to join the pain in his mind then was the hitchhiker/spa guy. But that was ridiculous. Had he been shoved, he would have sensed it, seen it. He knew, though, even while offering himself these reassurances, that the combination of his reverie and diseased eyesight made thinking on it futile.

By then his mates were with him, all three.

Brad was first to make contact, scurrying down the rocks and almost into the water himself. He took it all in with one quick look, gently gathered Cobb into his arms and hoisted him quickly up the grade, finally into a grassy spot. Feeling his friend's arms, Cobb shut his eyes and concentrated on making no noise.

Joss and Katie saw what Brad was doing, got out of the way of the climb, joined their friends in the grass.

Brad didn't know what he was saying, but he knew what he was doing. "Oh, honey. Goddamn. It looks like shit." He didn't tell Cobb it'd be all right. He didn't think it would be all right. Still, he carefully removed the shoe, much paler than the other, from Cobb's well-cooked foot, thought about removing the sock and decided against it. Then he took out his knife and cut the pants leg, carefully holding it back away from the skin, then hiked up the sleeve of Cobb's shirt above the seared hand, so the salve they didn't yet have might be applied. At least the clothes wouldn't chafe and peel back even more flesh. But it must hurt horribly. Goddamn.

He kissed Cobb's head.

By this time, plans began to formulate themselves. Joss had a thin sweatshirt they could cut into a wrapping for the fast-blistering hand. They took off Cobb's sock, as gently as they were able but not without eliciting screams, at first partly stifled and then full-throat. The bared foot looked even worse than the hand, the skin now purpling as high as the bottom of the calf.

They then seemed paralyzed. There wasn't any way they could carry Cobb across rough ground, and a litter was beyond their devising.

Cobb had opened his eyes and he had seen.

"I can walk. Maybe if we had more socks — you know. Don't put them on but kind of wrap?"

Of course they had no spare socks. But they had the socks they were wearing, and they managed to cover the scalded foot with several of these (one from each). Then they cut away the top of Cobb's bleached shoe, removed the laces, and slid it over the sock bulk, so that he could almost make it along the trail by himself, leaning first on one and then the other of his unburned companions. Cobb did irregularly well, even tried to lighten the gloom by telling some very bad jokes. The rest seemed more bothered by trying to walk like My Son John from Deeddle Deeddle Dumpling.

But here was Cobb going on and on: "So, this guy goes into a doctor's office. 'Doctor, doctor, help me. I broke my arm in two places.' 'Ah,' said the doctor, 'then what you gotta do is, you gotta stay out of both them places.'"

"We can slow down, Cobb."

"No need." There was plenty of need, but he wasn't going to admit it.

By now, the over-marked, gentled trail was welcome, designed for the old and fat and now serving the halt and lame. Coming round a slight bend, Joss was the first to notice what became suddenly visible to all: flesh spilling out of a carcass.

They stopped to examine. It turned out to be a deer. Not all that surprising, a dead deer, but this one had been gutted, disemboweled with what must have been a deliberate and cruel knife slice from under the throat straight to the anus.

Nothing to be done here. But they seemed unable to leave, to keep themselves from trying to recreate a scene none of them wanted to be near.

Finally, Katie spoke: "Hunters?" Then answered her own question. "Why, if they wanted the deer or the meat or something, would they do that?"

Joss tried to pull them back. "One thing for sure. All this blood and shit is going to draw things we don't want to be around. Maybe it has already. I suggest we get the hell out."

CHAPTER 10

Nobody said what they all were thinking. This was bear country; that much of the Lassen Alarms list was reliable. These black bears were not all that dangerous, but they also weren't all that safe, especially if you stood between them and dinner, which sure as shit this deer would be.

Maybe Cobb's terrible pain kept him from entering their unspoken agreement to avoid saying what they all knew.

"Jesus. Bears. Or Mountain lions. We block the way to this thing, they'll eat us instead or attack, thinking we're competitors and much easier to get at. There'll be nowhere we can go to get away from them. I guess that's what we want though? Find a trap with no exit. Well, here we are."

"Ah, Cobb," Brad said. "Damn you." Then he thought more. "We'll be okay — just get the hell out of here, and now."

They all felt the truth in that and started wobbling and hobbling down the trail, hoping to put distance between themselves, the big animals and the big animals' meals.

They turned a couple of bends and, at Joss's urging, started singing, rather, they started arguing about what song to sing.

"How about some oldies?" Katie was saying. "We all know...."

That's when they all noticed the brown animal, right in the middle of the trail, looking at them.

They stopped, naturally enough, and stared at the thing, who returned the favor. Then it began to advance on them, waddling as it came, moving slowly, and taking up very little of the path. A small thing, a bear cub.

Their first instinct was to welcome it, lure it in so as to pet and cuddle. That impulse didn't last long.

"Fucking hell!" Katie said. "The mother's got to be close behind — or somewhere about. Even worse than blocking a bear from food is...."

No need to say more.

Of course they didn't know where the mother might be — close, for sure, but was she trailing her cub, to the left, to the right, behind them and advancing? Meanwhile, the cub kept up its steady tremble and bob toward them.

"Follow me," Joss said. She started forward very slowly, right toward the cub, who neither slowed its progress nor changed course, sure didn't beat it off into the rocks, which may have been Joss's hope.

They had formed a single line behind her, and when Joss came within petting distance of the cub, they bunched together, edging as close to the side of the path where the cub wasn't as they could. It seemed as if they stopped breathing altogether. The cub paused and looked at them with no expression they could read. Inching forward, they made it even with and then past the baby, trying hard to imagine what they could do to keep the animal calm. Of course they had no idea but figured a quiet slither might work.

Anyhow, that's what they executed, managing after what seemed half a day to maneuver Cobb, bringing up the rear, a few feet past the worst danger. They hoped. They then started gradually picking up speed, when Cobb stumbled a little and let out something like a yip.

His yipping didn't bring upon them any instant, furry death, so they all turned, resolutely moving forward, away from the little bear. About ninety seconds later, they heard a rustle behind.

The cub was following them. Should they yell at it, throw something? They were all thinking about initiating a discussion on these very points, when a loud noise barreled down at them from up the hill, just a little behind where they'd stopped to consider, right ahead of the cub.

They seemed to know there was little point in running. At least, they didn't run. Not for maybe three seconds. Then they did, Brad watching Cobb, ready to offer him an arm or a back.

The mama bear was huge, they supposed, though they weren't calculating either its size or its relation to the little thing. What they saw was that it hit the path, maybe fifty yards behind them and moving fast in their direction. Joss, who was the only one glancing backwards, saw that the cub was running toward them, too, somehow ahead of the mother. Little idiot!

Joss finally turned around, ready to feel the claws and teeth, death by hugging, when she heard a huffing noise right there, then again. She couldn't help herself, stopped to watch with fascination the cub retreating, bobbling back toward its mother. She must have called it, Joss thought, and then, in a minute said so to the others, still running as best they could.

"I think we're okay now and can stop torturing Cobb."

They didn't stop for a bit, then did, maybe imagining group cohesiveness trumped the likelihood of being mauled. Nobody wanted to talk about close calls, so just took turns inquiring after the state of Cobb's wounded parts and finally made it back, wobbly but whole, to their very friendly campground.

The camp operators did have salve and bandages, would take no money for them, and even treated Cobb's wounds, recommended that they try and avoid both boiling brooks and bears next time. They then suggested that Cobb be taken without delay to a proper doctor. Cobb, predictably, would have none of it.

His friends all wanted to inquire more closely into what had happened, the details of Cobb's accident, but felt it would be cruel, since surely he'd just tripped, clumsy as he was.

They knew the truth, though. He wasn't all that clumsy, so there was considerable temptation they were fighting against.

Finally, Katie: "Cobb, was it slippery there?"

He looked at Katie, as if relieved. "Not at all. I remember thinking as I was sliding that I'd been pushed, seemed to feel something behind me, though I didn't see a thing. But, then, I wouldn't see it. How a pusher would know about my eyes is a mystery, though not as much a mystery as several others we've draped around us. Anyhow, thanks. I wanted to say all that and felt stupid bringing it up. Promise you won't fuss over me. Love that phrase, my mother's favorite. I used to hate it. I guess I didn't know then."

Cobb stopped, seemed to feel that there was no more to be said. The rest seemed to accept that verdict and kept quiet.

Having no sleeping bags, no blankets or pillows, they decided they'd rely on woodland skills drawn from James Fennimore Cooper novels and make themselves comfortable under the stars. Luckily, there were pine trees all around, which meant pine fronds, which meant lush and fragrant comfort, once the branches were stacked and fluffed up. Only it meant no such thing, turned out. It meant uneven, scratchy, protruding jags, impossible to rest on, much less sleep. Dirt was much to be preferred, and there was plenty of that, most of it rock-infested, but some areas not too bad, if you didn't expect a lot.

About one a.m., nobody asleep, they decided to take ninety-minute shifts on the reclining passenger-side seat in the Prius, ninety minutes being hellish but better than nothing — maybe.

At some point in the night, Katie and Joss lit out pretty much at the same time for the nice latrines that weren't to be found. The women decorously squatted apart, turned backwards, and then tucked and zippered while they talked.

"Katie, I know you're wondering what happened between me and Brad."

"How do you know that?"

"Because I'm wondering what happened between you and Cobb."

"Nothing. We talked. I made him feel like shit. I'm very good at that."

"He's maybe very good at being wounded."

"Maybe." After a beat. "I don't think so."

"Yeah. But aren't you wondering what happened between me and Brad? That's the point at which we launched this intimate woman-talk."

"You're going to say, 'Nothing,' which is fine by me."

"No."

"No what?"

"I'm not going to say nothing happened."

"Okay. Let's go back to pretending we can sleep."

And they did.

* * *

Next morning, much earlier than they would have chosen, they found themselves awake and ready to start a new day, not fresh but determined. It wasn't clear even later which one noticed first that they had an alien camper invading their site, still asleep inside the very sort of comfortable sleeping bag they now wished they had brought along. Making things odder, this particular invader was female, judging by the hair spilling out. She wasn't quite on top of where Brad had been twisting and turning, but pretty close.

The four stood there staring at her, a silent attention which could well be what awakened her. Anyhow, something did, and she slowly yawned, stretched, and wiggled her way out of the bag, took her time standing up, dressed only in underwear. She looked around, reached back and scratched herself under her bra strap, and then slowly dug into her sleeping bag, rooting around for something, turned out to be clothes.

She got them out and shook them but didn't put them on,

just stood there, looking out at the landscape or something in it. Finally, she did turn to the group, all huddled together, and stared at them. It was about twelve degrees out, freezing the small birds and the improbably unclothed — but she didn't seem to notice, care.

"Well, hello there!" said Katie.

"Hi!" she said, advancing on them, to shake hands, it turned out.

"We're Joss, Katie, Brad, and Cobb."

"I'm Missy. Silly name, I know — though friends tell me I make it worse by apologizing. Tells you something about the friends I have. I've been thinking about dumping the lot of them, finding a fresh batch. I think you'd suit."

"I think we would," said Cobb, who seemed fully responsive to the beauty of this near-nude woman, perhaps a year or two older than our quartet.

"Too bad I have to head back to work, which I'll probably be late for. How far is it to the office? That's where I left my car before not finding my campsite, which is why I squatted in yours. I guess the signs'll show me. They're everywhere, annoying."

"We thought so, too," said Cobb. "Terrible if you're dedicated to getting lost."

She looked at him as if she understood, which of course was impossible. Cobb beamed.

"Well, I'm off, guys. Are you okay?

The last was to Cobb, who had initiated a move toward her and stumbled.

There followed an explanation of Cobb's episode along the Bumpass Hell Trail, followed by a display of his hand and foot (slowly uncovered) to this woman, still unnamed, who said she'd had some experience with "such things."

"They did a good job, but you should get to a clinic right away. Redding. Not that far. You could follow me. If you can keep up. I gotta hurry, but I go right past the place where they'll give you a tetanus shot and play with your ass while they're at it. They'll enjoy it — and you will, too."

They were pretty much gathered up and took only a minute to file in behind their new friend, still partially clad. They weren't far from the cars and quickly piled in.

Joss no sooner was seat-belted than she slipped out, went to the other car, and signaled to Missy to wait, roll down her window: "It's none of my concern, but do you work in your skivvies?"

"Shit! Thanks." She got out, dressed in about twelve seconds, and they were on their way.

* * *

Missy pointed out the window to the clinic and waved good-bye. Cobb was torn between following her and proceeding to treatment. The other three were not torn.

The aide attending him, very quickly, too, put some greasy stuff on the gauze they had applied and gently lifted it, trying and failing to keep it from peeling back flesh and general gunk. Once cleared of debris, the foot-ankle-leg were not just one color — they'd all expected fire-engine — but a sickening mixture of that with yellow and a horrid brown, even some white.

"Good!" said the aide. "Now, let's see that hand."

Cobb seemed to misunderstand, started to try and get off the stool.

"Cobb, sit your ass down!" Joss yelled, much too loud.

The aide pretended not to notice. "You're fine. Now, your hand."

This time it worked. Cobb's hand looked better, once unveiled, than his foot. At least it was more or less all one color, hot scarlet.

"Umm," the aide said.

"That bad?" someone asked, not Cobb.

"Oh, no. Looks like only second-degree. It'll be good as new in a few weeks."

"And the leg is better than that?" Brad asked. Cobb looked

at Brad, then at the aide, as if he had no particular stake in the outcome.

"Well, you can see for yourself," said the aide, who seemed offended.

That was more than enough for Joss: "What can we see, dimwit? You said it was good. But what does that mean?"

Aide snapped back to usual. "I meant it was a good sign that it wasn't any worse. It's third degree but no sign of infection. Still, we recommend strongly that this boy — Cobb — receive a tetanus shot, just to be safe. And it'll be important to change his bandages once every...."

Three of those in attendance paid careful attention to what she said. You know who was daydreaming.

"How is it going to be for walking?" Brad asked.

"Walking? Well, he'll be the best judge of that. A few careful steps. Going to the bathroom and short distances inside. I'll give you a sheet on bathing and that sort of thing."

"Hiking okay, right?" Cobb said. Seems he had been listening after all. "We're going up to the Donner Pass."

Aide looked at him, smiled, sure that he was kidding. The others knew better. So they took the sheet on bathing, all the good advice, and then trotted to the general information desk for help in locating the best store in town for outdoor enthusiasts like them.

And there they were, before you could say, "Hiking?"

"You got stuff that'll pad feet real well?"

"We do. What's your particular requirement? Bunions? Ingrowns? Cosmetic issues?" Couldn't tell if he was kidding.

They told him.

"If you got the money—cause they's pretty pricey — I'd suggest getting these boots over here." He went to the boot section and they followed.

"Let me see," said the clerk, cheerily. Cobb obliged, and the clerk seemed easy with it — not a problem, see this every day.

"If you can afford it, these are what you want, get a size and a half too big, you know, and wrap the hell out of this here one's foot and ankle. Get the wrapping that's over there, green box, and do it every night."

* * *

They decided to splurge, not only on the boots but on a motel right there in Redding, not too sure what else to do, needing time to get away from the plots being forced on them by accident, time, and the pressures of fear. The fear was hard to locate, but its presence did not seem to be inconsistent with their pledge. They wouldn't have put it this way, but perhaps they were concerned that the fear they wanted to embrace would have nothing to do with them.

* * *

They found a German restaurant, one of the dozens in Redding. Cobb executed a bad imitation of skipping up the walk to the front door, dancing badly in his new and huge boots.

"You mind sharing?"

Nobody said anything.

"Sorry, but Laura-Ann put a single diner at a table for six. Laura-Ann's new, you see, but she shoulda known better than that, new or not. I mean, how much brains does it take to subtract one from six?"

She looked as if she expected an answer. Receiving none, she led them to the table, promising she'd not add yet another to the six-seater, even if a single showed up, which wasn't all that likely, no offense (to the diner already seated).

The diner, who at first looked a little like their campground friend but wasn't, wasn't even female, it turned out, rose and welcomed them: "I'm Sal."

Sal wasn't from Redding, didn't know anything about the Donner Pass, hadn't read Viktor Shlovsky, and how bout them Warriors! That exhausted their attempts at making four into five.

Perhaps because of the awkward silences flooding them, Sal bolted his food, asked for his check, and beat it the hell out of there.

"You think we drove him away?"

"Well, if that birdbrain Laura-Ann hadn't set him here in the first place...."

They made it through dinner — sausages, potatoes, beer, sauerkraut, strudel, and other surprises — without talking more about the seating arrangements, about Cobb's foot, or about any plans for the morrow.

At the closest local motel, a lackluster chain place they landed at before they noticed what they were doing and could scout out a nice grubby ma-and-pa spot, the clerk assigned them two rooms without bothering to determine their preferences. So, they did as directed, a bad habit that seemed to be gaining ground on them. As they snaked around the littered walks, they realized their rooms were widely removed, probably the clerk's decisive stroke for decency.

Brad and Cobb hadn't been together since the fireman's carry, the kiss, and the "honey." Maybe neither knew where to start. Anyhow, they undressed and showered, found fresh underwear, and looked at the one bed, a king-sized.

"I guess we're cuddled up as one," Cobb said.

Brad stared at him.

"I'm sorry," Cobb said. "Look, Brad. I know. I really do know. You saved me back there. I knew all along you would. I knew."

"Cobb, I didn't want you hurt. I don't want you hurt."

"That's okay."

"It isn't."

And they climbed into bed, Brad being extra careful not to shuffle around, bounce, or do anything that might put pressure on the multicolored limbs of his companion.

His companion. Funny how neither used any word to specify what that meant, go more steps down that path. Perhaps they knew where it led, where they were already.

* * *

Brad woke first next morning, slithered out of bed carefully, found one shoe but not the other, his pants but not his shirt. That'd have to do. He felt his way to the door, having first, stealthily, slid opened a dark closet, then tripped a little, recovered and slithered ahead heel-first, ghosted his hand onto the door knob, twisted it the wrong way, not so quietly, looked round and tried to make out the form of Cobb on the bed, detected no movement, tripped again, and finally edged himself outside, realizing just as soon as the door clicked that his little plastic door-opening key-card was tucked safely in his unfound shirt.

Worse, when he reached in his head for the number of the room assigned to Joss and Katie, it was not there. What to do? Of course he could limp his way to the office and ask for the number, also warm up a little there and maybe get some free coffee. But he was shirtless and had lodged in his mind the notion that the clerk was part of the Decency Police and might misdirect him, knowing he was up to no good.

Just then, the adjacent room door he was facing opened suddenly, revealing a young woman, who started to step out, registered his presence, about three feet away, and his unshod foot, recoiled quickly and, damn it all, yipped, but much softer than you'd expect a yip would be.

"No, no. I'm sorry. I'm not an intruder, not dangerous. I locked myself out of the room right there. My roommate's injured, you see."

She stared at him with what may have been curiosity. Didn't seem to be alarmed. "I'm sorry about your roommate. Can I help? Do you need something? He have wounds? Is it a 'he?'"

Brad felt his tongue expand. That seems unlikely, but somehow he couldn't get it to form words. She seemed to sense that and stepped up to the plate.

"Nice outfit, though."

That did it. "Ain't it, though? Chosen especially for this occasion. And the season."

"Just for me? You shouldnta. And Jesus, yes — you must have shivers inside your shivers."

Tongue swelled again.

"You were probably going out to get something for your hurt friend, right?"

"Well, actually...." Brad didn't know how much to tell her, thought about giving her the full version, decided against that, and settled on, "I was hoping to let him sleep, roust up the other two in our group, get some breakfast, and see what the hell we're doing today."

She seemed interested. "So, there are four of you, right? I figured as much."

"Yeah."

"Making it up as you go along?"

He sensed some movement behind her, bodies in her room, lots of them, more than seemed reasonable.

"Pretty much," he said.

The bodies materialized. Five of them, all male, all big or bigger. She didn't introduce them. They just stood there, flanking her and staring at him. They seemed to wear no expression, impersonating stone effigies.

"I need to get to my friends. Hope I didn't wake you all up."

The five hulks turned as if on cue and went back in, shut the door. The girl, who may have been what you'd call pretty, stayed behind, moved out from the door a little. Brad backed up some. He didn't know why.

She looked straight at him, unblinking. He'd used his exit

line, but he didn't exit.

Finally: "You guys must be well-heeled, getting two rooms for four people."

Well-heeled? His grandma used that phrase, his grandma and a character in a Sinclair Lewis novel he'd read for class.

"We probably intended to pile four people into one room, but the clerk gave us two keys, seemed to disapprove of the idea of mixing us up — our other pair is female. I guess it's understandable, what he did."

Just then it struck him that he was being rude, that this here very female was bunking with a full quintet of companions, maybe more. He felt a quiver of an impulse to apologize but was saved by his customary reticence and a sense that he had no idea what apologetic words might fit.

"When we stay at a motel," she said, smiling, "which isn't often, we book for two people, just two, one room, you know — and then the other four join us, don't even have to sneak. We're not wealthy."

She didn't say, "like you assholes," but she might as well have done so.

Brad mumbled his way to an ending, wobbled unevenly to the front desk, and then discovered that the old man there would not disclose what he desperately needed to know, the whereabouts of Joss and Katie.

Nothing for it but to circle back and rouse Cobb. He touched the door so softly that the effect was more like a zephyr floating by than a knock. Nothing happened for a few seconds, but at least the strange economizing bunch next door didn't emerge. That Cobb didn't emerge either hardly registered.

But then there he was, smiling, saying something, and nude.

"Shhh," Brad said. Then, noticing: "Cover yourself, idiot."

"Hi!" Cobb said.

"You'll get arrested. This place is run by Baptists." But he wasn't thinking of the ownership — or of Cobb's indecent exposure.

"Oh, yeah. Sorry to be careless, expose us both to arrest for exposing. Expose: get it, get it?" Cobb said. "I feel so much better. Fit and ready for anything."

"Good. Let's go back inside and you can tell me where Joss and Katie are."

They did, he did. Both males got themselves fully clothed, and they made it to breakfast, where it became clear that Katie and Joss had settled on what was to be done.

"I don't know how we made it through the night without your comforting presence," Katie started, but then shifted ground, maybe noticing that the boys seemed uneasy. In any case, she did lose the sarcasm and both women folded themselves into inquiries after Cobb's health and insincere expressions of interest in Brad's morning adventures.

Such twiddle carried them deep into the fake-egg, genuine (let's hope) sausage, pancakes, odd little bagels, and orange juice.

They managed to grab a table, pouncing on it just as a fierce-looking Mom and Pop Joss had been keeping tabs on finally stopped yelling at their small kids and left, not bothering to clean up very thoroughly. When they were seated, Brad looked around the room, relieved not to see the pack of squatters and their female leader, and then wondering why he had been worried.

"So, what do you think?" Katie asked, trying hard to make it sound like a genuine inquiry. "Where should we head today? Kilimanjaro, the Andes, Newfoundland?"

She didn't mean to look at Joss, but she did, even nodded slightly when Joss flashed her some sort of signal.

Cobb and Brad probably knew that the women were being kind, asking them to feel at home, though not so much at home that they'd suppose their views mattered.

Joss, naturally, was the first to bust through. "How about this? We get a cabin or something on the lake, maybe a step above a campsite, it being the height of the freeze season, and see what we can find there in the immediate area that'll threaten our security. Okay?"

Neither Brad nor Cobb was prepared for anything like this, nor did they have it in them to adjust quickly.

Cobb spoke first. "I thought we were going to do the Donner Pass, or something like that. Up there, the outdoors. We're not far. We could go back to Lassen, too, find us more bears."

"And more bubbling brooks," Joss said, before she thought.

Katie tried to cover. "And creepy strangers and disgusting deer remains and...."

Cobb interrupted. "That's okay, Katie. I know I fucked up. I am sorry—really. But these padded shoes, padded feet, I mean, are working great, and hiking'd be no problem."

Brad looked at Katie. Something seemed to pass between them. It was Joss who spoke, however, trying hard to be diplomatic.

"Donner Pass is a fine idea, Cobb, but let's scramble things. After all, we'd thought of Donner Pass a few days ago, which means it's hardened into a settled goal, a destination no longer fraught. Even the name has lost its resonance. The lake idea makes no sense and lets us postpone Donner Pass or quit on it altogether, suspend it in midair."

Neither boy objected, but neither understood.

"What lake?" Cobb finally asked.

"Oh, yeah. Lake Tahoe. The bigun. And it's got ever so many sideline attractions this time of year, including skiing and skiing."

"Oh." The boys had no idea what they were getting into, but, then, neither did the women.

CHAPTER 11

So, they did it, drove from Redding to the top of Lake Tahoe, right past ever so many charming towns, beauty spots, enticing spas, scenic overlooks, and adventures all plotted and planned, established by those who knew what independent travelers would be happy to pay for.

Minus computers and phones, they were like vacationers from the 1950s, depending on tour books, signs, and serendipity for information on where they might find the very sort of cabin-by-the-lake they sought.

They did, by Jesus, find the very thing, though, without a hitch. Katie seemed to have been assigned the task of occupying the males while Joss negotiated, booking a vacation cottage for an entire week. It'd be best, the women had decided, just to do it and not bother with explanations to their mates. As one day followed another, they could devise time-fillers, and neither Cobb nor Brad would notice that they were cemented in, finding risks only in menu choices and daring to swim in the local indoor pool too soon after lunch. Maybe after a week, the pace of Cobb's blistering would have slowed and they could get back to courting menace with a more mobile unit.

Neither boy had much to say as they unloaded, sprayed belongings about the cabin, and made lists of things to buy — groceries, more socks, board games.

* * *

"Are there hikes around here? There are big hills, one might say mountains. And we shouldn't pass up setting off into the snow without the right equipment or knowing what we're doing — hey!" This from Brad, who seemed more than a little uneasy, willing to leave things to Joss and Katie but now wondering what those "things" might be. When would they let him inside?

Before either woman could respond, Cobb cut in. "That'd be the very thing. And you nurses won't worry if we're in snow, since it's soft and will cushion even the cushions you've wrapped me in."

"That's stupid," Joss said.

Katie tried to be a little gentler, was obvious in doing so. "Maybe, Cobb, but even less predictable would be a Monopoly tournament, or that X-Rated Apples-to-Apples, which I happen to know is your very own personal favorite."

Brad looked as if he were edging in on agreement. If Cobb were, he sure didn't mean to do so.

"Games are good, but hiking's better. I saw a ranger station about a mile or so back there, and I intend, all by myself, to drive there and get information on the best forbidden outings, hikes to disguised precipices, cave-ins-about-to-happen, bear dens, piranha ponds."

"Rabbit lairs, sparrow nests!" Katie added, sliding over and kissing Cobb, who seemed to think she was advancing to punch him and was flinching. By the time he caught on, Katie had ended her mission and was back on the other side of the kitchen table.

Nobody could think of a good reason — any reason — to try and deter Cobb from going in quest of trail guides, so go he did, leaving them with a chance to conspire openly.

Soon as Cobb was safely away on his errand, Joss said, "You realize what's up, right, Brad?"

Her tone was laced with doubt, but Brad didn't seem to be insulted. "You want to buy time so Cobb can heal — at least get better than he is now."

Neither bothered to assent, so Brad continued, "How long?"

"A week. That's what we rented for."

"Okay. How we going to convince Cobb not to set off, even on his own? He's dead sure he's fine."

"We're inventive sorts, right? Besides, the hours just melt away when you're deep into board games, which we'll go into town and purchase soon as we have a car again."

"Town?"

"There's a little village about six-seven miles down the lake."

Just then, they heard something outside, thought they did. Couldn't be Cobb returning this fast. Maybe he forgot something. Changed his mind.

It wasn't Cobb.

The woman from back at the Redding motel. Didn't seem to knock, was just there inside the front door, looking around, as if she were a prospective buyer at one of those Sunday open-houses staged by Realtors.

"What the fuck are you thinking?" Joss yelled.

"Hi! Can we do something for you?" That from Katie.

The woman stared at them, then smiled winningly. "Thanks so much. Yes, you sure can do something for us. Yes, you can."

Us?

Then there were five other figures in the room, filling it up, not advancing but leaving no vacant space. Brad and Katie and Joss felt jammed, squeezed into corners.

Nobody said anything, gave no indication of speaking ever.

Brad felt it was up to him. After all, he had been the one to initiate contact back there at the motel. "You need to get out. We have an injured friend with us and really have no time to — party."

The strangers didn't react at all, not so's you'd notice. They didn't do anything directly menacing, but there they were, stolid and expressionless.

"What the hell do you want? You ain't out of here in the next thirty seconds we're calling the — cops."

The pause seemed to take the edge off Joss's threat. Whether it was her faltering bravado or something else, the invaders seemed to expand their territory, edging forward. Certainly, they gave no sign of leaving, of doing anything at all apart from settling the ground they had claimed.

It was much like a standoff lifted from an old Western. Who's gonna draw first?

The smiling woman broke the silence, if not the tension: "Don't you all worry, now. We're used to keeping out of the way. You won't even notice we're around — not hardly at all."

There seemed no point in asking all the necessary questions: who were they, how did they find them, what did they want? And other questions, too: were they predators, would they use them in lousy ways, would they leave in peace, never leave?

It was Katie who first thought of Cobb. His goofy mission, searching for hiking maps they couldn't use, had at least removed him from this strange invasion. If there were some way to get word to him, he could bring help, bring the authorities who would get rid of these pests. Exterminators with weapons that worked.

At least warn him, keep him from walking right into whatever it was these six threatened. She didn't fool herself that it was not a threat, and she worried especially about Cobb. That made no sense, as he was, for now, the only one out of range, but nonetheless her mind was occupying itself with schemes: a sign surreptitiously draped off the front porch or in a window, marks in the gravel, smoke signals.

At least, she thought, what they had now was a stalemate.

Then she thought of Joss, about eighteen inches from her elbow, standing there quivering. Katie could not see the quivering but was dead sure it was there and accelerating.

"Look, we don't mean to be unfriendly, but we have things to do and we're going to do them. We have rented this place, and need for you to leave. Actually, we do mean to be unfriendly. Get the fuck out or we'll call the manager here, the police, and the private whoop-ass corps we employ."

For a moment, nobody seemed to react at all. The six trespassers remained impassive. They didn't seem to exchange signals, didn't look at one another, didn't look anywhere at all.

Finally, Brad: "Okay. I'm going for the manager." He had been standing in the kitchen; now he started toward the front door. Two of the invading males, without seeming to change position, blocked his way. Brad kept going, tried to, but the pair who didn't seem to be moving before this point now moved, grabbing him roughly, lifting him off the ground and holding him there.

Brad tried freeing his arms to throw punches, then tried kicking, all of which landed him on the floor, being kicked himself.

The smiling woman, grinning more broadly now, spoke to Joss and Katie as if she wished she had a megaphone: "You two buddies of mine, what do you say we do the womanly thing and go to the kitchen, make us a pot of tea, talk over the events of the day and sort out which of these six hunks we want to bed. Make that seven. You got another one hid away, I know. The pick of the litter."

"Up yours!" Joss said, moving toward the advancing woman, who immediately drew from her waistband a gun, unmistakably. She didn't point it directly at Joss, let it dangle there at her side, as if it had appeared by accident.

"You have any scones, cookies, little sandwiches?" she asked, now using the gun to wave Joss to the kitchen, Katie, too.

Brad, who hadn't been hurt badly, tried to rise, got as far as his knees.

The one who had kicked now found a voice. "Hey, whatdya say we leave the girls alone by themselves, doing girl things — for now? We'll stay in here and talk about football, play drinking games. Right? You agree with that, doncha? That's what you been planning all along? Okay? You're the host."

He seemed to be waiting for Brad, who finally said, "I am doing nothing with you criminal fucks."

"Maybe if we told you our names, you'd like us better. Okay? It'll be easy for you, too, as well as more comfortable, since we're all named the same. Really, the same name. I am not lying, never do. The same name. Ain't that the most divine coincidence? You guess what that name is. C'mon. That'll be our icebreaker."

When Brad was silent: "Guess now, c'mon. It'll be fun. You really do need to guess. And you'll enjoy it, too. We all will. It'll entertain us and that's required of you. After all, you sent out the invitations, offering — what was it you said? — 'Entertainment provided by the host.' Those were your very words. We naturally took that as a promise. We haven't the slightest doubt you'll honor it. Common courtesy, which we have naturally come to expect. We are confident you'll provide just that. Yes, you will."

Brad, still on his knees, remained silent, tried to rise. The speaker giggled a little and pulled both fists together to slam the fleshy mallet into Brad's right ear, sending him flying hard into the front edge of the sofa.

"Let's see. We want to reassure you that we do not make hasty judgments, and we never have. Anyone who says we have has interested motives. Now, don't you go judging us hastily. Or start in making personal comments. We understand, no need to explain, that you do so habitually just to ward off the unkind remarks of those who are themselves trying to ward off other unkind remarks. It's a vicious circle, quite vicious. You fear that we are going to remark on how pathetically young you appear, freakishly so. You are so afraid we will call you names, unkind names — 'littl'un,' 'kiddo,' 'tootsie' — and then ask you embarrassing questions about puberty and bodily secrets that are none of our business, though that's not quite true. You fear we will tell you right to your face, your not really handsome face, that you are a gawky twelve-year-old, not cute, but freaky. We won't do that. We will refer to you with all the respect you deserve and some you do not. You are twenty-one, as the crow flies. Your birthday is November 7, which means your parents were doing the filthy thing in the dull February twilight, right there on the couch, forty minutes after finishing a better-than-they-were-used-to dinner (meat pies from Stouffer's, water in jelly glasses, Little Debbie cakes, no coffee) having too little interest in one another to think they could maintain the proper heat until bedtime. You have often imagined the scene, wish you could have been present with a video camera."

"Your name, and a very appropriate name it is, is Brad. No need to shake hands. We'll take the will for the deed. Our name is — c'mon, guess."

"Wilfred," Brad said, as loudly as he could. It seemed somehow important not to reveal the depth of his pain.

"Isn't that remarkable? I can hardly believe it, would not believe it did I not possess unmistakable evidence, the evidence of the senses. Goodness me. You hit it. A sign, for sure, a clear sign, straight from God. We are divinely appointed to be together, us multiple Wilfreds and you, at present a single Brad, but not single for long, not Brad for long."

Brad remained silent, trying to think of what to do, wondering about the women in the kitchen, wondering about Cobb.

"Okay, Brad — is that short for Bradley, Bradford,

Octavius? You won't tell us? That makes it more fun, but not as much fun as the upcoming game. You told us we could play any game we liked, remember? You are a good host, a fine host, an accommodating host! Now, Bradley, the game we are willing to play, since you are really the one who suggested it, is jacks, a pastime for the whole family and not just little girls, not at all. I know you have always loved it, jacks, but worried until this very moment that it was a game played mainly or only by pretty little girls in dresses at recess, little girls in very short dresses carelessly kneeling on the playground dirt, tempting boys like you to peek up and up and up and up. Careless girls. Naughty Brad. Am I right, Bradford?"

Brad, feeling no fear but understanding that he now had only the one role to play, said, "No."

"Bradley continues to worry that jacks are not so much naughty as sissy. He thinks jacks are beneath him, threaten his ever-so-evident masculinity. Bradley is living in a strange land, a hostile land pulled right out of the nineteenth century, and he is begging us to roust him forward. Bradley wouldn't object if we rousted him forward by his manly testicles, right here and now. Right, Bradley?"

"Wrong."

"Bradley has reached into his deepest parts, found his true unisexual self, and has cast his vote for the come-one-come-all game of jacks, finally accepting that his gender identification is too rock-solid to crumble, even if he has to slip on panties and a little sun dress, squat here in the dirt — the carpet will do — and proceed."

Brad thought he heard something outside, kept himself from looking up, decided he'd been wrong and that he should concentrate on finding delaying tactics, designed to hold off what was coming. He didn't think these idiots were designing to kill them, but he did allow that idea, formed in a set of images, to take up lodging in his head.

"So, Mr. B, you are free to stand and sort through your

belongings for your finest dress — cocktail dress, formal gown, revealing frock — and frillies. A bathing suit — one or two-piece, would not be unseemly. However, you can go barefoot if you must. We want you to be yourself. You are yourself, right, Brad?"

Brad did stand up, which caused the circle around him to close ever so slightly. Seeing but the one descent, he started down it: "Jacks it is."

* * *

Meanwhile, in the kitchen, the conversation took a course more conventional, a parody of the conventiona.

"You do have tea, several varieties, British, Irish, and, native, I hardly need to ask, two domesticated nesting birdies like you are and don't I know it. I even have a good idea where they are, those bags, I'll bet, though I am not the one, no, to rise up and get then myself. My mother didn't raise no rude miss, let me tell you. Did your mothers raise rude little misses, fucking abominable sluts without manners whose only occupation is thinking of themselves? I'll not hear such slander. You are among the redeemed. So, I'll just sit right here and entertain you with amusing anecdotes while you make the preparations. I believe the fine china is way up there, on the highest shelf, stretchy-roo, but I'll admit, with some embarrassment, I know not the location of the linens — napkins and such like, you know, doilies. You have some secrets, even from an old friend like me. Such an old friend that, were I ever so sure of the exact location of that hiding place, I would pretend to be ignorant, knowing the proper duties of a guest, a lady guest, a proper lady guest. A friend of long standing. That's what friends do."

Joss seemed ready to take her chances with the pistol, but Katie put a hand on her thigh under the table.

"I'll put the water on," Katie chirped.

"Goody! You do that."

Pause.

"In fact," Katie said, "Since we girlies are bound to be kind to but still protective of our men folk, bozos that they be, I'll put on a never-handy saucepan in addition to our more suitable teapot. We're nothing if not generous to our fellas, little as they deserve it."

"You are a thoughtful wee hostess, Katie. Please do just that, not that we'll be thanked for it — not by men like these, club-wielding Neanderthals."

"But we'll feel that warm inner glow that dollies like us live for," Katie said, now up and behind smiley girl and trying hard to stare down Joss, who may not have seen what she was up to.

Their captor seemed utterly clueless, at least that was the pose she maintained. It was vital that Katie and Joss read her well, but they were having no luck making her legible. When she spoke next, things got no easier.

"Do you girls, friends-o-mine, know any good jokes? I always say you can tell a lot about a person by asking them, ever so politely, to tell their very favorite jokes, using whatever props they find necessary to maximizing its effect. I will be receptive, ready to receive as well as give."

Silence.

"Tell us yours, Joss, while Katie, who is clearly the more domesticated, not to say refined, of the two, sets the table."

Joss glared but then seemed to recognize what Brad and Katie had come to earlier. Then she blurted out, "It is only when a mosquito lands on your testicles that you come to see that some problems can be solved without violence."

The stranger lost her smile, actually started twitching. Maybe she was on her way to convulsions — but no such luck.

She got up for a glass of water, seemed to gain some stability, and, once reseated, turned to Katie: "Now your favorite, but not like that one, I trust. After all, even polite guests have rights, have limits, set by decent society, Christian society."

Katie, not ordinarily a joke-teller, started raking in her memory, thinking of her embarrassing father, and finally found one: "Two hunters are out in the woods when one of them suddenly hits the ground. He doesn't seem to be breathing and his eyes are glazed. The other guy whips out his phone, calls the emergency number, and screams, 'I think my friend is dead! Collapsed. What can I do?' The operator says 'Calm down. I can help. First, let's make sure he's dead.' There is a silence, then a gun shot is heard. Back on the phone, the guy says, 'Okay, now what?'"

"Oh my precious lord, you two are depraved. I must say. Depraved. I don't think I can stay with you. Had I not been so well brought-up and educated, so deeply imbued with a positive and multipurpose aversion to indelicacy, I would be out of here in less time than it takes to fuck a 5-year-old."

Katie and Joss were looking at one another, hoping some useful communication might develop.

Stranger continued: "Would you like to hear mine, my favorite? I don't pretend it has the poise and balance, the exquisite sophistication of yours, but, for what it's worth, it is my own. So—?"

She was interrupted by a ghastly moan, followed immediately by loud cries from the other room.

* * *

Just minutes earlier, the game of jacks had begun, pitting Brad against one of the Wilfreds. The rules were clear and, very soon, familiar. Brad must have played the game on just such playground outings as the tormentors had outlined.

"You go first, Brad. I'm sure you're a champeen."

Brad scattered the jacks, bounced the ball. "Onsies," he called, picking up a jack and grabbing the ball before it collided with the floor a second time.

The closest Wilfred seemed totally absorbed in watching Brad's moves, eager to match him, acquiring in the process a skill that would serve him well in life.

But while Brad reached "foursies" without the slightest difficulty, Wilfred's ball bounced twice at that point. "Shit!" he said, but softly and smiling.

"You get to collect your winnings now," said a second Wilfred, handing Brad a razor blade and a small receptacle.

"What?"

"Go ahead!"

The losing Wilfred held his arm out to Brad, palm up.

Brad saw what was offered but substituted a lesser grade school penalty, wetting two fingers and bringing them down with a smack on Wilfred's wrist. Giving forth a yowl suitable for real pain, Wilfred made a move, clearly to get to Brad, but was restrained by another.

"Okay, Brad. Remove one article of clothing. That's what the winner does, you know, according to time-honored practices we would not dream of violating. And there is reason for it, of course: the victor now has the opportunity to play without irksome and uncomfortable restraints."

"Can't I...?"

"No, no — we appreciate your sportsmanship, but we play by the rules and insist you allow us to do this. Really, you must allow us to do this. It'd be wrong, more than wrong — immoral, indecent — were we to ignore the rules. We're very earnest jacks enthusiasts and we respect its tradition and its hallowed history. We'd no sooner bend the rules, than we would go down on our mothers. Or yours."

Brad took off a shoe.

The other Wilfreds seemed eager to do well in the game, probably they were, but none seemed to be especially well-coordinated, were possessed of so little skill, in fact, that only the first of them had climbed even to the low pinnacle of "foursies." Within a few rounds, they all had red marks on their wrists. Brad had no clothes at all.

Finally, as was inevitable, one of the Wilfreds managed to win. It wasn't a fair win; he had roughly jostled Brad on his way to catch the bounced ball. Brad mentioned the interference but to no avail: "Wilfred here is in charge of appeals. What say you, Wilfred? All was fair, within the rules, kosher? There you have it. Don't be a selfish sally, Bradley. We didn't throw tantrums when you won seventy-odd games consecutively, now did we? Without murmur, we endured with a smile your sickeningly lustful assaults on our wrists and other parts we won't mention."

Brad noticed the razor blade and the small gray boxes being passed toward the front.

"Give us your arm, Brad. I promise not to strike it, not to descend to the ruffian level you have occupied."

"What's with the razor blade?"

"Only fun, Brad, fun. You've heard of rubbing salt in the wound? I believe it's Biblical. It's Biblical, right, Wilfred?"

From that point, they made sure Brad lost four games running, the first penalty being only a little nip and a pass with the saltshaker, growing into a three-finger cut, opening a fold of skin, layered then with salt, and pressed in harder and harder.

Thus the scream.

* * *

Smiley girl reacted to the noise by grinning more broadly, lifting her chin slightly, brushing back her hair with her left hand, and, with the other, reaching behind her toward her ass. When both Katie and Joss rose, their chairs clanging back noisily, the right hand snaked around to the front, to shoulder level. It all seemed casual, this production of the gun, still not exactly leveled at either of the girls.

"C'mon, girlfriends, resume your seats. The boys are enjoying themselves doing boy things. You know how it is: put 'em in a room together and they revert to 7-year-olds. We've all learned long ago to ignore this harmless boyish fun. We overlook it. That's what girls do. That's what you will do. As always."

Joss and Katie had stopped when the gun appeared, but both seemed ready to move again, move toward Brad.

"Ignore them, do."

They didn't

"Ignore them! Sit! Now!"

They didn't. The gun then did come up, swayed back and forth between them in imitation of old movie gunslingers: "Y'all jist line up aginst the bar and we won't have no trouble. You over thar. I'm talkin to you, too."

As Joss started to get up, the gun advanced closer to her head, almost touching it. "You just rest yourself, honey, my dearest Joss. I will be the one to fetch the tea and strainers. Leave it to me. I will produce individual units, and not just any old cups and saucers neither. Everything designed for our very own individual tastes and needs. Very elegant. Just the thing for our Tea Party, our comic Alice party, our Mad Tea Party."

Gun girl then relaxed, lowered the weapon and started giggling, giggled right through the next scream, even more harrowing than the last.

* * *

This slice was from Brad's right thigh, the side closest the front. Four Wilfreds were now required to hold him down, while the fifth, the smallest among them (though all were giants) pretended to be undecided about the butchering point, playing with Brad's nipples and then, for what seemed like forever, his testicles and then his penis. Then he switched over to the thigh, waved the razor aloft, pretended to pocket it (just kidding!), and then carefully layered off a filet slightly larger than the last, applying salt, then, even more vigorously. He waited a few seconds and then grabbed more salt from a dainty, flower-embroidered bag and rubbed it in, probably as hard as he could.

Brad almost broke away from his human bonds and did manage to free one leg enough to land a reasonably incapacitating kick right into the groin of the monster attached, now not, to his right leg.

As the gods of the virtuous (or blind luck) would have it, Joss entered the room right in the midst of this chaos and....

* * *

Just seconds before, back in the kitchen, Joss had caught on to what Katie was doing, smiled at their nightmare companion sitting across from her and asked if, there being nobody here but us girls, she didn't think it was time for true confessions, just the thing for post-tea conversations among girlfriends. "So, sweethearts, let's each talk about our very best sexual or near-sexual experience, sorting through our mental files and finding the one, the one among many hundreds, modestly speaking, that stands out, stands up, perhaps I should say?"

If Sadistic Sally wasn't shocked, she managed a fine simulation. "Well, I never, ever.... Whatever did I do that would make you think...?"

"Okay. You don't cotton to that topic? I'm flexible. Worst sex? Most recent sex? Largest number of participants? Most dangerous venue?"

"I had no idea you were that kind of girl. And if I'd known, why...."

She had no chance to complete the sentence, tell them exactly what by god she would have done, had she known she was cast among the fallen. She kept making noises, gasps that quickly became shrieks, even louder than Brad's. She reached behind her, clawing desperately with both hands at her back, trying at first to rise and then collapsing hard into her place setting and, shortly thereafter, into the tea service itself, flapping like a snared pigeon and scattering cups, pots, and silverware.

Katie stood with the open teapot in her hand, teeth set, ready to use the kettle as a club if necessary. What she felt at that moment, gentle Katie, was regret that she had missed her target, the head and face, had gone too low and scalded only the neck and back of the demon.

She quickly reached for the intruder's gun, ready to hack off a hand were there any resistance. There was none, so she grabbed it, the first she had ever held, rotated it so it pointed straight away from her, and turned to follow Joss into the torture den.

* * *

Before any of the Wilfreds could disarm Joss, even move toward her, she let fly with the boiling water in the saucepan. She had no time to aim carefully, but she did target the guy farthest away from Brad, managing to soak his left arm and torso and, even better, the side of his face. She had thrown from reasonably close range, but not as on-top-of-the-target as Katie had been. As a happy consequence, she managed to damage two others, and not just a little.

Only the one was disabled by the boiling water, joining the apparently identical Wilfred Brad had put out of commission with his kick. But that left three, all of whom took a step toward Joss. And then they stopped, froze.

They were looking at Katie, who had the gun and was pointing it at something close enough to a human target they weren't sure, any of them, if any further advance on their part might not result in getting shot. Pretty clearly, they didn't care a hoot for one another, but Katie's wobbly aiming made it uncertain if they themselves might not end up the focus of her shifting sites.

Nobody spoke for a minute. It may have occurred to

the Wilfreds that a flanking movement should have been the answer — but no use trying it here: the room was far too small to permit of any but a single-file advance.

As they were considering, Joss moved to the kicked-and-still-writhing Wilfred, clonked him decisively on the head with the saucepan. Certainly not a fatal blow, but enough to draw from the victim not only a yelp but, immediately thereafter, sobs and tears, howls of protest choked out between shrill snuffles: "Why'd you go and do that for? I ain't done nuthin to you. You broke my head, you very mean person."

The still-upright and less-damaged pair looked at one another, seemed to reach a decision. "Put down the gun, girlie. You won — this round."

That was far too much for Joss. "This round? Stop that B-movie shit or we'll just shoot you right here. No question it'd be self-defense — and we have the wounds to prove it. Plus, you are too stupid to be alive." She glanced over at Brad, still naked, sitting with his back resting on the wall and his hands straight out, as if beseeching, waiting for help he knew would never leave the station.

He hadn't reacted to what Joss had said. He was slumped forward, heaving, not with sobs but with jerking efforts to get his breath.

The Wilfreds, left without their absurdist script, could only glare and pretend to ignore Joss's words.

Katie stepped partway into the kitchen and kicked the chair holding what had been the smiler, now bunched over and whimpering. She somehow made it to her feet, though, and then past Katie, who was halfway into the main room, gun still at ready, more or less.

The maimed and the growling Wilfreds also began stirring. They were not quick, but they were now compliant. As they approached the front door, bunched tightly together, Katie and Joss took up their position mid-room and tried to look steely and by god don't fuck with us.

The six were out and gone before either Joss or Katie had a chance to come up with good send-off lines. They also didn't think of what might happen if their visitors turned on them. Wilfreds and maiden didn't leave without some final words, but what they said, or one of them said, didn't seem sufficient cause for homicide.

"It's been great. See you soon."

CHAPTER 12

Then they drove away. At least, they must have done so. By the time any of the group thought to look and see, suddenly struck with the notion that it might be well to have car description handy, a license plate number — it was too late.

"That was smart!" said Joss, but her mind was now on Brad, and she looked for Katie, just to form a team. Katie had left the room right away—looking for the necessary first aid materials, hoping they might have them. Joss knew where her friend had gone without inquiring and turned to doing all she could to comfort Brad, who did seem to be aware of her presence, if only dimly. He was still gasping a little, but his breath may have been coming a bit easier.

Just then, Cobb entered, all aglow, brandishing some paper. He was about to spurt our glad tidings, when he noticed, first, the watery mess, and then the mess that was his buddy. He dropped the papers and was on Brad's left side at once.

"Ah, Jesus. You're bleeding like shit. Ah, fuck. Brad, you okay? Don't answer. We're going to fix you up."

He glanced at Joss, who frowned, changed her mind, nodded.

Cobb at least shut up, just stared at Brad for a tic and put his hand gently to his friend's cheek, then his hair, stroking and muttering something, maybe just meaningless sounds.

Here came Katie, finally, with a pretty impressive haul of bandages, antiseptic, tape, and other usefuls. They applied them as neatly as they could, after patting first a little and then a little more, hoping to stop the bleeding. They kept at it, even when all their most deliberate work didn't stop the blood coming. Perhaps the flow slowed some, almost enough to make them feel they could handle this, that enough wrapping, clean enough bandaging, and lots of hope would do the rest.

They wanted to head off to a clinic or hospital or whatever was in this lakeside retreat straight away. Brad, however, no longer stunned and with his breath returned, declared loudly that he was certain he didn't need that — not now, at any rate — and that they should not lose a minute getting to the cops. He looked so little-boy-lost, so comically defiant, now upright and pointing at something or just using his finger to emphasize his avowals. A keynote speaker at a political convention.

A naked keynote speaker. Perhaps it was that, his sad vulnerability, the way this shy boy's armor had been ripped from him, that made them, finally, agree. It was a dumb thing to do, all realized, but it was required. Somehow it occurred to none of them that these necessary errands might be combined, that the clinic would be able, in a pinch, to get in touch with the police. But it's hard to think straight when you've just been delivered exactly the very nightmare you were yearning for. When that happens there's little left to hope for. You want to move on. But where?

* * *

The police, located through the kindly offices of a gas station/stop-for-snacks woman, did not brush them off, took down everything they said and, in their own good time, asked questions anyone would be comforted to know they were asking.

Description of the car? License? No? That's okay. You were

under terrible pressure. We'll proceed without any of that just fine.

Of course they could not proceed just fine, could hardly proceed at all with the descriptions they had of the Wilfreds and their moll. Try their best, the four could not, among them, differentiate the male attackers or even give a very telling composite. One was a little smaller than the others, maybe, but all were larger than they first seemed to be. Maybe, oh, 6'5", heavy-set but not fat. Strangely blank looking and not just their faces.

They did better with the woman, but even that report was embarrassingly generic: medium height, medium-length hair — blondish, medium-sized features, medium pretty.

What they did remember was the way the Wilfreds and the woman had popped up again like repulsive memories, the way they drew their lines from a Samuel Beckett play, the way they tortured and enjoyed it, the way they ministered to fears and hopes.

Officer Johnson — "Fred," a smiler, too — had invited them into his office, asked for their beverage preferences — "Coffee all round? Cokes?" — and only gradually slid into official business, even then more like someone at the Chamber of Commerce than a cop. "You like our village here? We do our damndest — ha, ha. It ain't New York. It ain't even Reno, but...."

At very long last, they had a chance to explain. And did. Fred looked pained.

"Well, this is a serious crime, a set of serious crimes. Trespassing, assault, assault with a deadly weapon. A long list. Maybe a hate crime, too?"

"Huh?"

"Not being bigoted, you understand, but do you have any reason to feel these might have been Muslims or Islamists, resenting your, you know, Christian ways?"

"No."

"Well, you've given us plenty to go on. Welcome to call us any time to check on progress, though of course we'll alert you at the first break in the case. Naturally, we'll proceed at once to your place to gather physical evidence."

Nobody said anything, so the kindly officer continued: "You know — fingerprints, personal belongings they may have left behind, other telltale signals evident to the trained police eye."

The quartet seemed to know they were being shuffled off, getting strokes in place of protection, but the police did one thing for them, made them find within themselves the resolve not to run. It may indeed have been the presence of these officials, their promise to patrol outside their cottage and "keep a sharp eye out for anything suspicious" (they really did say that), but that's unlikely. It's not that they talked about it, but they seemed to know and to agree: first, their enemies would expect them to hightail it and would rely on what were obviously first-rate tracking systems; second, they wanted to run their own course into nightmares and not have it set out for them and then be chased along it.

As they were leaving the station, Joss called a halt, then a huddle: "You mind if I ask these Barney Fifes where we might get guns?"

It was so unlike Joss to ask anyone's opinion, they hardly had time to call up their deeply felt, if routine, distaste for gun-owners, the NRA, and so forth. It appeared as if everyone nodded, more or less.

The cop behind the desk seemed unruffled by the question, told them there were two options, one requiring a waiting period and background checks, the other not, depending on whether they were willing to cross the state line into Nevada.

"And a clinic to treat Brad — this boy here?"

He told them about that, too. And that's where they headed.

* * *

At the clinic, they were informed, though politely, that they'd have "only about a half hour before we close" to get treatment for Brad, Joss offering only a mild reprimand ("And if he were bleeding more profusely, like to death?"). Katie and Joss then drew apart to confer. They didn't even hide what they were doing from Brad and Cobb, who took it in stride.

"You thinking what I'm thinking, Katie?"

"That these guns aren't for show. That we'll use them."

"You and I better know how to do it."

"YouTube? Maybe at an Apple store or someplace with public computers?"

"Right. Or maybe the gun-shop fellow."

"Yeah. You think they'll come back to the house?"

"No."

"Me, either. They won't need to."

"Cobb is going to force us to hike, and Brad won't say no to him."

"He won't say no, period."

"You think so? I don't understand him, Katie. Do you?"

"Not at all. Sorry I said that about him being acquiescent. Didn't mean to suggest I knew. I think he's a little mysterious."

Joss stared at her, wondering if there were more she might say, remaining mute.

"Joss, I think we need to get to the gun-shop before we hike. Cobb won't like it, I guess, but he'll do it. Don't you think? It's maybe not quite that he's still back in high school, running for most-likeable-in-the-class, but...."

"He works hard at resisting what everyone is sure he must be. I think he has more to him, but that's part of it. He's more reckless than would come simply from trying to be reckless."

"Yeah? Well, we got shit tons to deal with, then. Not that I'm all that stable myself, Joss. But you knew that."

"I did, Katie, I just sure as Moses did."

* * *

Brad and Cobb were right where they had left them, grew a little more alert as the women settled back in, and tried not to look too wonderingly at them. Brad was in terrible pain still and wanted so badly to do a better job hiding it than he could quite manage. Three *People* magazines later, a boy in a gown appeared and called out "Chad?"

It was all downhill from there, stationed in a room for twenty minutes — "We have no rules against friends accompanying, but there's really not sufficient space" — then hustled to another, then a third, before a distracted doctor (doctor, they assumed) came in and began examining the correct arm and then the wrong thigh. Finally got oriented.

"How in god's name did you get these? They look surgical. Holy hell! Lucky they're not deep. What are those crystals?"

She put her finger to the gauze she was using to daub the cuts, looked at it, then licked. "Salt and lots of it. How'd that happen? Must hurt like blue blazes. Here, let's first wash things out."

So much a babbler was she, so self-absorbed, that she didn't wait for answers to her questions, which was lucky, as our four had neglected to plan that far ahead. They had been protectively sketchy with the cops, hiding the details of the torture, the game of jacks romp, for instance. Nothing about the motel meeting.

Within ten minutes, Brad's wounds had been rewashed and rebound, secured by advice on replenishing, drinking lots of water, and — repeated several times and insistently — resting!

* * *

Joss and Katie wasted no time. Just as soon as they were hustled out of the surgery — "Sorry! Closing time!" — they issued instructions to their wounded mates.

"We're soon heading off up and around the Lake, eventually over to wide-open Nevada, by way of the resplendent village of North Lake Tahoe. Yes, we are. First, though, before we do anything else, we need to find a shop where we know you boys will equip yourselves for the time of your rip-roaring lives. Then, we'll do not one damn thing for a day or two."

As they had foreknown, Cobb objected, drawing forth one of his ranger-fed printed schemes guaranteed to lead them into pointless peril.

Katie took her turn: "That's the very thing, Cobb. And we'll count on you to be the guide, bad as you are at it. First things first, though. We're going to get guns. Joss and I feel sure we aren't shut of that Sadistic Sextet, and we know you're way ahead of us. You and Brad were the ones who said we didn't have to worry about life in our cabin, that away from that coziness, though, lay in wait this murderous field of revulsion. Thus, as you say, guns."

Neither Brad not Cobb was fooled, but neither said so. Brad was brightening by the minute, the light coming back into his eyes. It was not a kindly light, seemed to be fueled by some fire he was set on keeping secret, but it gave him a new way of appearing in the world, beginning to replace the unbearable picture of their defeated friend, crying and nude driven into their minds.

Threading their way up the one main road and around the lake took much longer than they had allotted, but finally there they were, inside the extermination shop, facing a smiling proprietor, alerted to their coming by a tinkling bell hung atop the door. It could have been a candy store, so cheerily was it lit and decorated.

"You sell to little kids?" Cobb asked, smiling, of course.

The guy got it: "I blame it on my dainty and oh-so-cute

wife, only she isn't dainty nor cute — and she isn't my wife."

They didn't pick up on the hilarity, asked him for recommendations — "No, not hunting, just self-protection" — and swallowed whole the single endorsement he offered. "This'll blow the head off any intruder, disembowel him at the same time. Just what you're looking for."

"It's not an assault weapon, is it?" Cobb couldn't keep his programmed liberal unease from leaking.

"It's a handgun, son, not a rifle. Sorry. I see what you are asking. Nope, it's just the thing the Democratic Party will be a long time banning, way down on their list."

Good enough for them. Four of them? Yes, he just happened to have four — and enough ammunition to hold off a determined siege.

* * *

Nothing for it now but to trail on back to the cabin.

Despite the confident reassurances they were piling on one another, they were each surreptitiously checking out with their glances the area in front of the house, the roof, and what they could see of the sides, not much, as it was pretty heavily, if irregularly, wooded. Once inside, they found reasons to visit all the rooms, the back porch, and as much of the within-reach territory as seemed justifiable.

Cobb was all for heading for high ground right then, but Katie knew she could get him to withdraw the idea gracefully, nothing more than significant eye contact required. Turned out that didn't work worth a shit, so she had to say:

"How about, it being so late afternoonish and this being February, we give it a rest, give us a rest, until tomorrow. I know Joss and I can sure use it."

Master stroke to lay it on the two who least needed time to heal. Neither boy was consumed by a need to prove his manhood, but neither was entirely free of that stain.

111

Joss knew it was her job to add more weight to Katie's good sense.

"We also got this here deck of cards I smuggled into my pack, knowing we needed to hone our skills a bit before heading down to South Lake Tahoe, which, as you sharps know very well, is for gamblers what Indianapolis is for car mechanics."

All three looked at her quizzically, as if she were an experienced actress unaccountably flubbing her lines.

"I mean, car racers or their essential greasers and lubers and other assistants. It takes a team, you know. Here's my plan. We stay here and play games. If poker doesn't suit your needs, we can find or invent others."

It wasn't clear that Brad reacted to this at all, but the other three certainly did. It was Brad who spoke:

"I need to say something." He stopped there and gave no indication of proceeding at all. He did give an indication of tearing up.

"I haven't thanked you all for saving my life, Joss and Katie. No melodrama going on here in what I'm saying, you know. I mean, I don't want to be slushy. But they were going to skin me, flay me alive. You both.... Thank you."

Nobody knew how to break the silence, so Brad did.

"Thank you, my friends. I love you."

No hugs, no mutual avowals.

* * *

So, games it was, varieties of poker, actually only two varieties of poker, not because they could master no more but because the seven-card stud and the Texas-hold-em varieties absorbed them pretty fully. They did fiddle with blackjack, but only Joss didn't already have under her belt some experience (family-time, round the table) with that game, so they focused on the unfamiliar.

By the time they were sufficiently schooled — and fed — it was a little late for launching the not-so-twiddling trip down to South Lake Tahoe. But they were wild youths on the lam, constrained by nothing, so they followed their impulse and took the necessary time, much more than they reckoned on, to get there. They hauled into the first casino across the line, found a modestly-priced poker table, and sat down, Brad did, the other three clustering round in a consultative pack that drew frowns from the dealer and stronger ones from the fellow players.

The committee-meeting arrangement turned out to be all-for-show, as Brad made the decisions and managed to keep his tally just a little below zero. Only once did he relax his impassivity, when Cobb left to hail the drink woman and the hefty half-sober high-roller next to Brad toppled from his stool and kept his balance only by half-punching, half-clutching Brad's thigh, right where the pain had not been stilled.

Brad let go with a "Gaaa" sound, all the more shattering for being muted, then turned all his energies to reassuring his sweetly apologetic neighbor, and then the companions of his heart, that he couldn't be better, was just dandy, and would try to keep himself from imagining he could fill any more inside straights.

The evening had not given them anything they wanted. Somehow, though, they felt more clarity, more purpose. So far, the expedition had been a debacle, sure, and up ahead seemed to be nothing they were hoping for, nothing.

They had sauntered into the room of the absurd and not flinched. They had not asked for directions, and had, none of them, felt cheated. It was what it was, and each of them began to believe that it was them. In a way, all that agreement added up to no more than an illusion, a fatheaded fantasy. In another way, it was as powerfully real as anything they would ever encounter.

Chapter 13

They knew, all of them, that sensible plans were not going to be followed, even discussed, so nobody bothered giving them headroom. Still, there was a difference between abandoning oneself to existential openness and sticking one's noggin dead into the oven. They sensed that.

What happened next morning was that Katie and Brad woke first, slipped quietly out of their rooms, and found themselves skulking together in the kitchen.

"You'll let me change your dressings, right?"

Brad would — and did.

"Let's go out on the deck, Katie, talk a bit while Genghis Khan and Bloody Mary are arming themselves for the day ahead. I think it's heated, at least closed in."

They crept out the door and ended up side by side on the none-too-clean (or comfortable) porch-swing-rocker combo, a device which managed neither to swing nor rock very well, driving away anyone settling in with hopes of giving over a few hours to sloth. Katie put a hand on Brad's new-bandaged arm, being careful to miss the wound and careful, too, not to imagine him as he had been so very recently, damaged and naked.

But she couldn't help herself, and there was that very image, minus the damage. She knew she had to block it out, so she didn't, leaned over and kissed Brad on the mouth, not slowly and not in a chummy way. Brad certainly responded but didn't much shift his swing-position. They both planted their feet to stop the quasi-rocking, though.

It may have been Katie's sudden awareness of what she was wearing (shorty pajamas with ruffles, a gift from her mother— "I know they're old-fashioned, but they're cute!") and nothing else, but she managed to pull back.

Brad started rocking again, said, "Thanks."

"It wasn't a charity mission, Brad."

"Yeah, like I'm so irresistible here in my skivvies." He looked down to check, saw he was fully dressed.

Skivvies was too close to naked, was too close to tears and torture, so Katie moved on. "I know you're okay to hike, Brad, or will pretend to be. A shortish stroll would be just the thing, then some prolonged touristing down here on the flat, some boat rides or non-wetting lake fun, tame snow frolics, more raking-in-the-dough at the casinos. But we both know what will happen."

"That reasonable course won't be followed," he said, "not with Cobb straining at the bit."

"And Joss."

"Yeah."

Katie looked over at him again, trying to keep her hands and face to herself and failing, but not in major ways. This time, Brad did lean over pulled her to him and hugged, with his head beside hers, not on it.

"Jesus, Brad, a girl's not safe within twenty feet of you."

"Or Cobb?"

"Cobb's too busy trying to be gorgeous to act on it."

Brad looked puzzled.

"I'm sorry. That's unfair. And untrue. Let's stop talking about sex or we'll end engaging in it, waking the other two, and landing both of us square in a whole heap of trouble."

"We wouldn't want that."

"Oh, yes! Yes, we would. I would. But we must stifle our desires, moderate our transports, and think of the greater good."

That seemed to do it, pull them away from the only reasonable course of action open to them.

They both looked straight ahead, rock-swinging more deliberately, not considering that such pumping motion might not be the best antidote to whatever it was tingling them. But they resisted and snapped back to the sensibles.

"Okay, Katie, I know Cobb has this extreme hike planned, the very one the ranger warned against, of course. He was about ready to take off last night in the snow, engage us in midnight high-altitude frolics. How can we deflect that idea? No chance that he'll forget it, but maybe we can find a way to disguise a sensible activity as even more dangerous. That might do it."

"You expecting us to be sensible, even pretend to be?"

"I'm expecting us to care a little about Cobb's terrible injuries."

As soon as it was out of his mouth, Brad wanted it back, wanted to rescind his accusation, about as unfair as any could be. He hurried to erase the clouds and gathering tears from Katie's face.

"Ah, shit, Katie. I know you would never ever hurt Cobb — or anyone — even in a joke. I was just riding my one-track, the way I always do."

She smiled and touched his cheek — in a buddy-buddy way, she hoped. "You're a dearie, Brad, yes you are. Cobb loves you almost as much as I do — and Joss too."

Brad just stared at her, so Katie frowned and went on.

"Here's a start on the idea you had about disguising what's a little safer as a little wilder. Since Cobb spilled all that to you last evening, we could say it now counts as laying out a schedule, the sort of neat, predictive schedule we're pledged to ignore. According to his fucking maps and guides, there'd be nothing for us except obedience, right? And.... You with me?"

"Brilliant, Katie."

He might have added, "Only it won't work," but he was busy helping Katie from the swing and into the kitchen, but first into his arms.

***

Not five minutes until the other two had joined them, Cobb in full hiking regalia and with his hand nicely bandaged (how did he do that?) and Joss in jammies even skimpier than Katie's, only half covering what she presumably did not want to wave in the breeze. It may seem odd but so it was that the boys were much more conventionally modest than the women. They now and then arranged demonstrations to show that it was not so. But it was.

Not twenty seconds into the Cheerios and granola, Cobb did the expected:

"Okay. Looks clear out, so...." Only then did he check to see what actually was "out" and saw it was, by Jesus, snowing. "Oh! Only light and fluffy. It'll stop by midmorning. I checked."

They knew he had not, let it pass.

"So, how about Freel Peak, fellow Sherpas? It ain't the most demanding stroll in the continental U.S., but it's about as good as we can do here in the neighborhood. You can see for yourself."

Here he drew out the maps and guides, almost toppling the milk on them, at least two of his companions wishing he had, and then drawing in a deep breath, getting ready to explain fully.

Brad looked pointedly at Katie, who knew he was telling her to jump in, without delay and with both feet.

"Maps and guides, Cobb? I mean, what's with laying out the day in a set of instructions? How about the unplanned, the dedication to the daft?"

"I thought about that very thing, Katie. It worried me, worries me. But, how about this?"

Cobb glanced round the table, a certainty of impending triumph swelling his heart and sinking his friends'.

"I'm with you all the way to hell, buddies, and I agree

that, if we were to stick to the plans and maps, sure. Nothing but a well-marked trail and no consequences more threatening than sweat. But — you all see where I'm going."

They did, but Cobb couldn't resist: "You all see that where I'm going is just where none of us knows where we'll be going."

* * *

So, off they went, up Oneida Street and then, following the signs (which Cobb reminded them would soon be only laughable cautions) up a very rough road, partly plowed, it seemed, but only partly. They had put a bunch of rocks in the trunk, figuring the weight would do them better than snow tires. Even so, they did a fair amount of sliding and skidding.

They made it to a gate and a signpost (visible, even in the snow) for Armstrong Pass. There was no place to park, so they did, and proceeded, as directed, finding just in front of them a fork, a wide and pleasant-looking path to the right and a narrow, mean-looking thing to the left.

Our four naturally went left, on a route that took them within minutes to a creek identified on Cobb's irritating map as "Trout Creek."

The snow had, probably on Cobb's signal, pretty near stopped and then stopped altogether. But that didn't make fording the creek any easier. There was a log there, hardly constituting a footbridge, but the only thing available, wading being out of the question. They might have made a carrier thing and carted Cobb over, but that didn't occur to them and Cobb would never have tolerated it. Anyhow, they just walked on right across the log, wobbling and semaphore-waving but without soaking.

On the other side, they started up — and up and up. Trouble was, there were clear marks in the snow of considerable traffic, even a posted notice for mountain bikers. Worse, the forest around them was out-and-out snow-covered sylvan, just begging for those original photographs everyone's vacationing relatives send back. And the upward trail, as trails have a habit of doing, sometimes dropped gently and did not demand skills honed in the Himalayas.

None of the hikers said a word in the first hour, sure that Cobb would bare his fangs and strike before long.

A little ways on and up again, they came upon another sign, "Armstrong Pass," which could only be reached via the TRT (Tahoe Rim Trail). They had no compass, naturally, but the now-visible sun signaled that they were headed either north or west, or somewhere in-between.

Cobb seemed satisfied with sticking to the trail, so they slogged along amidst more conventional beauty, this time in the form of juniper forests.

"This is what I brung you for," Cobb called back over his shoulder: "Monty Python! The Miracle of the Juniper Bush!"

They all laughed agreeably.

The trail seemed to level off. Actually, it dipped and rose some, but not much, so that they did nothing more than glide along it.

"You guys want to rest?" Cobb had stopped and was turned, facing them.

Nobody seemed to know what to say, so Joss offered: "Sure, Cobb, this trail is about as challenging as an escalator ride at the mall. We're exhausted."

Cobb grinned, but nobody was fooled. He knew Joss was right, which did nothing to temper his hurt.

"I could use some water and a sit-down," Brad said, more or less on top of whatever Katie was saying.

Cobb joined them all squatting in the cold snow, so cold it might have frozen their asses but wouldn't wet them.

"You're wondering why I called you all together. Sorry. So, here's what's what, unless somebody wants to find a precipice and jump off. We have a good climb and then some tame switchbacks up ahead. Those'll take us to a saddle, but while we're getting there we'll have what they say are 'stunning vistas and views of Desolation Wilderness.' You're going to tell me that 'vistas and views' is redundant and that if it were either desolate or a genuine wilderness, it would be something more than a posted sighting on a directed outing."

Everybody tried to look cheery and knowing.

Cobb surprised them. "I know you are all worried about my feet, my feet and hand. I know that."

He paused. "I know that."

Whatever was holding them together seemed to tighten.

"Okay," Cobb went on, "we will, before long, following orders as we've been doing, find ourselves at a saddle top, from which point is visible, for the first time on our journey, Lake Tahoe itself. But we've seen that and won't even glance in its direction."

He paused to look at the sky, then back at his friends, reaching round to adjust something, scratch something.

"Our scenic trail will continue beyond the saddle, going north or northwest, but not with us on it. We are nothing if not trail-ignorers. We're turning our backs on the trail, striking out south, and finding a way to lose ourselves grappling with Freel Peak, which is sign-free and rocky and 1200 feet above safety. There may be pines here and there as we thrash and stumble and fall, but they will offer us nothing in the way of stability or assurance of any sort, so don't think it."

They hummed assent, put away the canteens, went off to pee, and reassembled, once again to follow Cobb, at least to the point of disintegration.

Just as they should, they turned right off the TNT and faced a steep collection of mean-looking scarps, no trail anywhere they could locate, and much more snow now they were trail-free.

An hour later, having slogged through ever-deepening snow, they had gained a fair amount of altitude at the price of losing solid ground, entering cliffs that offered less and less in the way of clear contours or good footholds.

Just as things were moving beyond impossible, Cobb, who had inexplicably spun round, hissed at the rest of them: "Wait. I saw something, something over there, below us, I think."

Badly balanced as each was on a rock or trying to get on a rock, they risked a lot by turning quickly. But they did — and saw nothing.

"Just wait," Cobb muttered, snakelike, "down there to the right, quite a ways, in those boulders and stuff."

Well, down to the right was nothing but boulders, so that was no help.

The others were soon thinking that Cobb was right, had spotted something. They were also thinking this something had come on them not really by surprise, that they had left their sanctuary only to expose themselves to their tormentors in open and desperate territory, miles from help, utterly defenseless.

Not quite defenseless. They had not forgotten the guns they had purchased or neglected to file them in a handy spot inside belts, underpants, or bra straps. Ammunition was nearly as handy, and each began the process of loading up, right then.

Cobb saw what they were doing. "I don't think so — looked like a single climber, a small one. I know it's hard to judge at this distance, but it seemed to me no more than a kid, maybe. I could be wrong."

"A fucking decoy for the Wilfreds," said Joss, sounding more certain than she was, could possibly have been.

"Let's be quiet for a minute," said Cobb, "see what our target is before we start peppering it."

Chapter 14

It was quite a few minutes they waited. Nothing. Then, Cobb again, "Hi! Don't hide. We won't hurt you. Fuck, we're harmless."

No results, but, then, nobody but Cobb had expected any, had even seen the being he was trying to soothe. Was he making this up?

Silence for another five minutes, and then, unmistakably, a figure, a figure not belonging to any of the Wilfreds they had seen, a very small figure, just as Cobb had said. A small figure clad for summertime.

"Please," he called out, a thin voice, no whine in it.

When no one answered, he seemed to shrink back, but then re-straightened and repeated, "Please."

They all started scrambling back down the crags on this signal, this plea that contained no hope at all, was more of an admission than a cry.

"Careful about dislodging stones," Katie called.

"And don't scare him off!" Joss said. "He didn't seem too confident."

Perhaps he had so little confidence that he had lit out. At least, he wasn't where he should have been when Brad reached that spot. Katie, then Joss, then Cobb appeared shortly, all struck with the same obvious question and all but one not saying it. "Where'd he go?"

"We don't know, Cobb. Maybe if we weren't such a noisy avalanche army, he'd have stayed put." Joss was immediately sorry she'd said such a thing but right now was occupied worrying about this small figure she didn't believe in.

They were now perched on rocky crags, not sheer cliffs exactly, but certainly not a meadow, rendering spying tough to accomplish. So they shuffled around in the small declivity they were in, looking at blank stone walls, under small rocks, and, mostly, at one another. Finally, Brad climbed down, without handholds, another twenty feet, into what turned out to be a mini-cave, tucked into the hillside.

They could, however, hear him.

"Hi! My name is Brad."

Pause.

"That's okay. You don't need to talk. God, kid, you gotta be freezing. Here's my coat. Don't worry. Here, take it. I'm backing away."

Pause.

"What did you say? That's okay. You don't need to talk."

Pause.

"Jesus, kid, you got on tennis shoes. Your feet must be.... That's okay. I didn't mean to grab at you. That's okay."

Pause.

Then, keeping to the same stage whisper but drifting up to them, "Stay where you are. "

Slightly louder: "He's so scared and so cold."

All was silence from below for a minute, maybe more. Then, incomprehensibly,

"That's okay. I got more. Here."

More what?

"That's okay. Really, I got more. Got lots. Well, see for yourself."

Pause

"Did you say something? That's okay. Oh, Jesus. Poor honey."

Pause.

"No, no. See, I'm backing up."

Joss hissed in his direction, "Can we come down?"

"Not for a minute. He's so scared. I think he wants me to leave, but we can't do that. He's so little." After a pause, "He most be so cold."

Pause.

"My name is Brad. Don't be scared. What is your name?"

Pause.

"Rubber ducky, you're the one. You make bathtime lots of fun. Rubber ducky, I'm awfully fond of you — bo-dodie-oh-doe."

"What the hell's he doing?"

"Shhh."

Silence for a minute, then Brad again, somehow initiating a strange duet, then, achingly, it wasn't Brad singing, "Rubber ducky, you're — muddle — *Ustedhace el gran cantidad de* bathtime *de la diversion. El caucho Duckie, yo soy terriblemente carinoso deusted. ¡Vo hace de!*"

Silence for a bit. Then Brad's voice again. *"Minombrees Brad. ¿Comote llamas?"*

More silence, and then they thought they heard, *"Mojado!"*

No need to guess at what Brad was saying, "No, no, no. You are a person, a fine person, not an insult. I mean, *usted es una persona, una persona incredible.*"

Silence. Then Brad again:

Un nino se sube a un bus y le dice al chofer,
— ¿Cuanto cuesta el bus?
Y este le responde,
— Pues, 10 pesos.

Y el nino le dice: ¡Vale, que se bajentodosque lo compro!

"What the hell," Cobb started, but was shushed by Joss, who was, like Katie, stifling giggles, giggles that echoed those coming from below, the loudest sounds so far, though still muted and uncertain.

"Will somebody tell me what that was?"

Joss huffed, but Katie either knew better than to try and muzzle Cobb or simply was finding her kindest self. She yelled out, "Hey, kid! This is for you. Little boy gets on a bus, asks, 'How much is the bus?' the driver says, 'Ten pesos,' and the kid says, 'Everybody off. I'm buying the bus.'"

What sounded like laughter floated up from below, maybe just from Brad. They couldn't tell, but somehow they caught the signal that this foundling was now with them, with them all, their number up from four to five.

Or maybe they were hearing things.

"Can we come down?" Cobb called out.

"Give me a minute," came back.

Then, "*¿Hablas ingles? Mi Espanol es muymalo. Esunamierda.*"

Now the giggles were less tempered, almost to the edge of safety, "Yes, a little. But my English sucks worse even than your Spanish."

"*Amigo?*" Brad's voice.

No answer.

"That's okay. I won't hurt you. That's okay. You understand, yes? I just want to help you. I won't hurt you. I promise."

"I understand."

"Great, now tell me your real name, the name your parents gave you."

Silence.

"I'm sorry. I didn't mean.... What name do your friends call you?"

"Friends?"

"None of this is important anyhow. Look, now don't be scared, but I have three other people with me."

"I know."

"Of course you do. They're all good people, anxious to be your friends."

"Anxious?"

"They want to be your friends."

Silence.

"They won't hurt you."

"Okay."

"They're right up there, but you know that. Can I call them down?"

Silence.

"They won't hurt you. They have clothes you can have and more of those granola bars — that candy."

None of those waiting above could detect it, of course, but the boy looked straight at Brad, nodded uncertainly. What choice did he have?

"I know. I know," Brad said.

The boy kept his distance, which wasn't much to begin with, all the space the small irregular cave allowed. He didn't take his eyes off Brad even for an instant, as the big white boy let the others know that they'd first descend, he and the boy, to the base of the escarpment, where they had some room and could spread out. He didn't say, though they all heard it, that there the desperate kid would feel less threatened, not so much as if he'd been captured.

They all did make it down, cautiously, Cobb being slowest and hardly able to disguise his hobble when he made it to flat ground. It flashed through his mind that he was grateful for the presence of this small boy, this distraction. That thought made him feel so ashamed, he was the first to speak, despite having nothing to say.

"Hi, there. My name's Cobb. Very pleased to meet you."

The others looked at him as if he'd just pissed in the punch bowl. But then Cobb realized something, took off his coat, moved over to the boy, who was maybe too startled to protest, draped it round the kid's shoulders on top of Brad's, and then, unmistakably, hugged him.

The kid looked into Cobb's face, only a half-hand away. He may have hugged him back, a little. For sure, he said,

"Thank you," in the loudest voice he'd risked yet.

Cobb thought about unwrapping some of his multiple sock layers and protecting the kid's feet, but he knew none of the others would welcome that, least of all the kid, so he contented himself with a smile, and backed off.

Cobb's smile failed to draw forth more than a stare.

Time for Katie. She knelt before the boy, a move that might have been excessive but didn't seem so, reached up and patted his arm.

"My name is Katie — like the bug."

Whatever she might have meant could not have been clear, but the kid did smile.

"We are going to help you. I promise."

The kid neither moved closer nor drew away. Our quartet seemed to realize all at once that he'd been cajoled before, had learned that threats and blows were, at least, trustworthy. Words were not going to help. Somehow, this boy had been welcomed to life, maybe to America, with a whip. No kindness anywhere. Why should he find it here, with these big kids he'd followed, now ganging up on him?

"You were following us," Katie continued, but in a new and softer tone, "because you wanted us to help, right?"

The boy looked almost shocked, was quiet a minute, as if considering, then spoke, very clearly: "I have nowhere to go."

"Oh, Jesus!" Cobb said.

"He's found what we thought we were looking for," Joss said, almost crying, "the avenue to nothing. He's somehow kept moving, who knows how long or from where. He doesn't have hope, isn't going anywhere. He followed us not for any reason, thrusting himself, for all he knew, into the dragon's mouth."

She paused a minute, then, "Ah Bartleby! Ah Humanity!"

It didn't seem to any of them overblown or pompous. In fact, it seemed perfect, this echo of Melville's lawyer, who realizes the futility of good intentions, stares straight into the abyss.

The boy looked at Joss almost as if he recognized some kinship, knew what she was about. But that look quickly vanished, to be replaced, first, by blankness and then what may have been a dark certainty.

"Are you going to undress me?" It was just a question, expressing neither terror nor threat. It paralyzed them all.

Finally, Brad: "Nobody is ever going to do such things to you again. You hear me! Nobody is going to undress you or hit you or make you do terrible things. Nobody. Never. You hear me?"

He was shouting at the boy, angrily, mercilessly.

The boy didn't recoil, looked at Brad for a moment, and then began to cry as if all the tears in the world, from Adam on down, had been dammed up in him.

* * *

They made it off the mountain without much chatter — meeting no other waifs, criminals, or one disguised as the other — and soon found themselves back inside their housey sort of cabin. They all wanted to lose no time in finding ways to connect with their new ally or waif or dangerous intruder.

But there it was, they shortly saw — a sheet that'd been stuffed under the door, a little tough to read after they'd all walked on it. Too bad it had retained some legibility —no matter how much they might try to mis-see it.

> *"Hi there, you party animals, you! Out on the town? Now, why didn't you invite us to go along? Don't be shy. You'd be surprised how much fun we can be, if you treat us right."*

There was no time now to consider it. It was the Wilfred pack, was it? Well, fuck them. Issues of real moment had presented themselves, and they would deal with them first.

The boy, by this point, seemed, so far as they could detect, no more confident than he had ever been; perhaps he was resigned. Upon entering the house, he kept his eyes to the floor, as if looking round might be presumptuous, dangerous. Katie gentled him into the kitchen and a seat at the table. The boy didn't raise his eyes, seemed to be hoping for invisibility.

They knew enough not to disturb whatever equilibrium he had found, just set about laying before him enough food, first cold and then hot, to feed ten people, ten who had given up.

But the boy had not given up. Despairing he was, apparently without schemes or resources, but pretty clearly he was not about to stop.

Katie was trying hard to be focused on staying in the kitchen, fussing around without crossing the boundaries marking the child's limits, which seemed pretty tight. The other three shuffled into the front room.

Joss: "I wonder if he escaped or was abandoned?"

Brad: "He called himself a wetback. Maybe got cut loose from a farm, maybe ran away."

Cobb: "A farm? Oh, I see, migrant worker."

Cobb again: "But he's only, what, twelve, thirteen?"

Brad and Joss stared at him, not bothering to fill him in on the dark history of migrant workers.

Joss: "He had a strong reaction when you asked him about parents and being named by them."

Brad: "Yeah — who knows? Maybe it was the question, the assumption that we had the right to ask. Maybe the parents are dead, maybe a part of his problem in other ways."

Cobb: "He isn't going to tell us."

Joss: "No. Right now we're part of the stone wall he's been trying to climb — that's not right, not a wall but a torture chamber he's been crawling through. He's now waiting to see what sufferings we have for him."

Brad: "Let him eat and then, if he will, sleep."

Joss: "I see."

Cobb: "You can explain to him, Brad. Put him in the first bedroom there, ask him if he wants the door shut, promise him we'll stay away, playing Parcheesi, and he can join in whenever he wakes up or decides he wants to play. We'll start a new game and give him a head start."

Both stared at him, not disapprovingly.

Cobb: "That bedroom has its own toilet. He wouldn't have to come out into the other part of the...."

Cobb trailed off, and then went on: "I was going to suggest asking if he'd like to take a bath. No need to tell me."

Katie had been calling on all her brains and charm, trying to cajole the kid into eating the eggs, the ham, the microwaved pizza, the granola bars, the ice cream. The kid looked at her only once, maybe smiled, and accepted a pizza slice and two little carrots. Then he sat contemplating his plate — as if he were drawing on all his abilities to summon up resignation, accept the current trap. She went to the doorway, ordered the trio of gossipers onto the porch, and came back to the boy.

"You need to sleep. Don't argue now!"

The boy looked at her, this time did smile, unmistakably.

"We'll try to be quiet, but those two boys there, Brad and Cobb, are about as good at being quiet as they are at speaking Spanish."

The smile had disappeared. Was he being imprisoned? She seemed to be saying mean things about the big men. It was funny, too, but he'd learned that white peoples' funny never was.

Katie caught some of this, reminded herself not to be impatient, looked more closely at the wan, unlovely face before her, and nearly crumpled.

She waved to the boy to follow her, guided him into the front bedroom, pointed to the bed. "The toilet's over there, that room, if you want. Towel, too. That's the bed."

She smiled. He didn't.

She started to leave, and then turned.

"Oh honey. We'll love you. We'll save you."

Then she left. Who knew what she meant? She did. The boy did, too — but he was many miles away from believing.

Chapter 15

He slept for more than sixteen hours, never turning over. When he awoke, it was dark in the room, though he could sense the light behind the curtains, frustrated at being blocked and trying its best to enter.

He wasted no time trying to orient himself, started searching for an escape. The windows in the room were too small, even for him, same with the bathroom. He crept to the door and listened carefully. Silence — then not silence.

He turned around and retreated, crawled under the bed and tried to reduce his breathing to an undetectable level, to something beneath quiet.

He was no longer cold nor really hungry. He had forgotten hungry, but not cold; and it was not with him now. But he was no less alone.

He stayed there another hour, two. This was not a solution. This was not what he should be doing. This was nothing.

Like always, he had no choice. He crawled out, then, hitched in his belt and made sure he hadn't peed on or snotted any of the strange clothes. Then he walked to the door and into what he knew would be hell. Long ago, he'd heard about hell, found it interesting to hear about, and then had lived most of the last two years right there.

He stood outside the door, waiting.

He'd been so quiet that none of the four heard him and it was several tics before Brad noticed. With a motion of his hand, he asked the others to be quiet, careful.

They caught at once what he meant and obeyed. The boy understood that this was the conductor's initial beat, the start of some melody of pain and humiliation.

When all four looked at him, none with malice he could detect, he very nearly gave up the only defense he had. And when Katie came and — no kneeling this time — wrapped him in her arms and let him smell her woman smell, he felt lost as he never had before.

He knew he had to speak. "I thank you. I must be leaving now."

Even as he was saying it, he knew he could not escape, and he felt a different and stronger fear.

Katie kept him in her arms, but she did not speak, nor did any of the others.

"Okay," the boy said, hopeless, asking for no pity, for nothing.

"How about some dominoes?" Cobb asked. It was a ridiculous suggestion, also the very thing.

So, they did, the boy drawn into the game he either had known before or quickly mastered, the others wondering what they could do to cause things to advance, knowing that they were not the ones to advance anything.

All five seemed to be caged together. If so, there was no key.

* * *

While the child was sleeping the four had taken counsel earnestly, settled nothing, managed no more than a short-range agreement, very short-range. The unrelenting snow had given them the idea that they could track any invaders pretty easily. It also seemed to reduce their options for occupying the boy, calming and securing him, reduced them to dominoes or charades or skiing or.... They might as well have considered skydiving.

They knew that no white-folks pastime was coordinate with the life of your ordinary migrant worker, much less a kid whose life had been so terror-driven he might well be suicidal. Surely, there were things he had once found interesting, distracting. Maybe there had been happiness, at some point? But, even if that were true, how could they possibly locate that entry point? Was anything they could plan going to come near to consolation, even to the unfrightening? Maybe something familiar to him, something neutral, not involving pain. But what would that be?

"Are you going to undress me?" None of them mentioned his question, but it was inside all of them, ripping to shreds any easy notions of recreation, ways of finding what no one was heartless enough to call his comfort zone.

Some practical things did occur to them, gave them small lies they could grasp and then fling away. Clothes, food, medical check — that much was easy. Toys, games, electronics? Like sending a Hallmark card to death row. Getting him papers, making him legal? Maybe he was? Should they ask? What did they know of fixing it, if he even wanted it fixed? Getting him a gun? That made sense.

They talked about whether he might have encountered the Wilfreds clan, might have been drawn across their path up there in the rocks while following their trail. Was he allied with the enemy? They decided such ideas, such nightmare images, were pulling them away from where they needed to be headed.

They talked about some selfish things, though maybe all their talk was selfish, seeking formulae to rid themselves of responsibility under the guise of embracing it. But there seemed to be no virtue in ignoring Cobb's foot; Brad's mini-scalpings; Joss's developing sniffles; the pressing demands of laundry, groceries, more socks, more hope.

They all seem drawn most strongly to their earlier resolution to arm the kid, give him, not so much protection — it seemed too late for that — as a way to act. None of them wanted to push it past that point. Act how?

As a distracting footnote to genuine concerns, Brad, unlikely as it seems, had been the one to say what the other three felt obliged to rise above, school and their enrollments therein. "We got loops of wire around us, fellow freedom lovers, and we aren't liberating ourselves by ignoring them."

"Parents, taxes, rent, overdue library books, clinic appointments? Let's talk about lunch." Cobb knew he wasn't going to derail the talk, just thought it was his mission to try.

"Just about as bad," Joss said. "School. We intend to drop out?"

Nobody bothered to shout out their watchwords: "We are living outside intent! We are in the moment! We are Meursault on his way to the guillotine."

They tried not to look at Katie, failed. She was way ahead of them.

"I'll call Morris."

"That's it?" Cobb said. "Aren't we going to wiggle around and convince ourselves that this defeat is a triumph, that we aren't falling back into the mire?"

Brad smiled. "We can say we're clearing the way, finding new means of destroying all road-signs. Hell, Cobb, we've all been thinking of this, wondering how long they were going to blithely mark us absent and postpone any reckoning."

Joss looked at Cobb, then got up from her chair and plopped on his lap, running her fingers through his hair, probably a mean reenactment of a bad scene in a bad movie. There was nothing mocking in her tone: "Dear Cobb, my scalded sweetie, you know we can't create a universe. We'll carve out what we can, float while the air sustains us, lie a lot to ourselves but not to one another. That's what love is."

All this time the boy sat mute, registering nothing.

So Katie did call Morris, who was a Dean of some sort

and a longtime friend of Katie's parents. She said whatever occurred to her on the spot, offered the functionary a brew of quasi-truths, insinuations, and blatant lies. He sniffed it, and finally agreed that this was a prank, a harmless prank, and a set of accidents, and a medical emergency, and a favor to the family, and a chance to wave a banner proclaiming that he, Morris, was a friend to youth and a goddamn regular fellow.

They'd all get Incompletes and would have a full year (more on appeal) to turn them into their predictable A's.

* * *

They figured they could best ease the kid into their life by talking about food. Other topics seemed unsafe. He needed so many things, and a few of these they could give him, not things that mattered a lot. Most surely, he needed clothes, some way to keep from freezing if he went outside, went skiing, went hiking, went off on his own. But clothes seemed to suggest some terrible vulnerability to him.

Joss, the least likely, proposed the most likely solution, whispering to Katie. "We'll take him to the store, see if he'll pick anything. He won't, so we'll just buy him stuff, guess at sizes. He won't care about colors and style, won't care if things fit. We can't even hint at trying anything on, exposing him. He'll still think we're using him. He'll probably always think that."

So they agreed on clothes, and decided to gentle into that troubled area with easy talk about food.

"Hey, buddy, we're down to our last frozen pizza, and it's not one any of us likes anyhow — has kale on it. So, would you go with me to the store, help me carry things? We'll get anything you want."

It would have been better had Cobb not added the last bit, though he could not have held it back for the most lavish reward. He could see as well as any of them the walls surrounding the boy, but he could not keep himself from crashing against them.

"I can carry," said the boy.

When no one responded, he looked around, his face written over with uncertainty: "I can sweep up. Clean. I can carry."

Brad and Katie both started to respond, deferred, and then smiled at the boy, being careful not to move closer or offer what the kid would recognize as some sort of bribe.

Finally, it was Cobb who spoke. "That's good you can do those things. Right now I do need you to carry. Groceries. First, we go in the car. Get groceries. After groceries, clothes. Cheap clothes. Carry."

Maybe Cobb's idiotic attempt to transcend the language barrier — he also upped the volume, spoke very slowly — was what did it, but the boy smiled and, wonder of wonders: "Yes. We go car. Me carry."

It wasn't much of a breakthrough and it didn't last. But while it was there....

* * *

As soon as Cobb and the boy were out the door:

Joss: "At least this kid's ugly. Were he cute we just couldn't resist taking him home as a trophy."

Katie: "You wanta think of him as ugly? That help you, Joss, fine. We see right through you, of course."

Joss almost smiled.

Brad was just watching, used to doing little more than that. Waiting.

Katie: "No need saying it. We don't want to make him safe, since we all know what that'll entail. But giving him some chance to stay clear of starving and freezing isn't the same as sending him to prep school, teaching him lacrosse."

Joss: "Poor thing. He is what he is, but I have no idea what that is. Recall him crying so hard? Seemed to be part of his toughness. He didn't give a good shit whether we saw that or what we might think."

Katie: "Well, Cobb has good sense and will — what do

they say? — first do no harm. He also won't outfit him in rich kid shit."

Joss: "Rich kid shit is all Cobb knows."

Brad thought about letting that pass, didn't: "You don't mean that, Joss. There's a reason Cobb is the one trying to do the impossible with this kid."

Joss flinched a little but didn't protest. Finally, "You're right, Brad. He'll find a way to stay away from all the prickles this kid has grown, all the prickles and all the wounds. The wounds. I guess they're well matched there, too."

Katie sensed the impasse. "He'll not force Air Jordans on him, sure. I wonder what he will do, what conversations they'll have."

Joss wanted to agree: "I was going to say 'if they have any,' but you're right about Cobb. He'll find a way."

* * *

Cobb's immediate problem was locating something like a Target here in Lake Tahoe territory. He first looked for a phone booth, having seen people do such things in old movies: just flip the yellow pages. Then, he went looking for a gas station. It wasn't like Cobb to hide his dorkiness, to pretend he was in command, so he didn't.

"You know, buddy, what I was thinking? Do you?"

"I'm sorry."

"No, no. Do you know what I was thinking of doing?"

A wave of terror crossed the boy's face. Then he seemed to realize it was only Cobb.

"No, I don't know what you were thinking of doing."

"Well, what good are you?" Cobb didn't wink or even smile.

Maybe the kid smiled.

Cobb wasn't deterred. "You mind driving while I consider how to find the cheapest grocery and clothes place, really shitty clothes like I wear. Just stay on our side of the road — mostly."

Cobb found a driveway, hoped he wasn't disturbing anyone, thought briefly of the Wilfreds, and got out. He wasn't sure what the kid would do, but figured things couldn't be a lot worse. Cobb had no way of knowing things were already better, only a little, but that little was pure light.

The kid went around the back, Cobb the front. As he was grabbing the door handle, he spotted a gas station, the very place to get information. But he knew better. The station was only a few hundred yards away, far too close. Stopping right away would be responsible. He didn't want be all caretaker for this kid. He wanted to get out of the way, burden the boy with nothing. In the process, he would love the kid. He knew that. He also knew he could bury that, blow his affection into the empty air. He was thus resolved.

Neither said anything at all, Cobb pretending to fiddle in the glove compartment as the kid studied the instruments and handles. Within a shorter time than is possible, the kid had the car in reverse, slowly onto the main road, and then, none too slowly, spinning south toward — that was Cobb's job.

Neither said anything for a few minutes, but not because either was worried about the driving. One of them knew what he was doing, even if he had never done it before, which possibly he had not. Cobb somehow felt the kid's desperate competence, even tried whistling to show how at ease he was, remembering only a little too late that he didn't know how to whistle. The boy looked over at him, just a glance, but Cobb tried to freeze a smile, just to show how much he relied on the kid's driving skills, honed over — the last seven minutes.

Cobb waited another two or three minutes, spotted a gas station: "You wanta pull in there, Ace, just a short pit-stop. Don't worry. I ain't alerting the authorities — just want to ask directions to a place selling rotten food and stinky clothes."

"I will."

Cobb tried not to feel hurt at his failures. But what exactly was he failing to do?

The kid drove into the station, equipped with a snack shop, featuring every form of junk food known to man, known to Cobb, anyhow. He grabbed six or seven items, thought better of it and settled on pretzels, not even barbecue or cheese-coated. He hated pretzels, which he regarded as not even a single step above straw, and bought them so it would seem unprogrammed, not like a weapon.

By mutual silent agreement, shyness, habits of obedience and fear, the boy had stayed in the car while Cobb had gone in, got the information he wanted: there were Targets and K-Marts, one of each, anyhow, the guy was pretty sure, though possibly the K-Mart or maybe it was the Target, couldn't remember, had been forced to close, shoved out, you know, by those fucking boutiques for fucking Yuppies, located, almost for sure, way down in South Lake Tahoe, most an hour's drive, but can't miss it. Run over a couple those fucking Yuppies for me on the way. They use hiking poles just to walk along the road. Pay couple hundred bucks. Feed a family of six for a month. Run down a couple for me now. Tell 'em Evan sent you.

They'd been there in South Lake Tahoe before, at the casino — several lifetimes ago. Cobb had no trouble locating where they were — after near an hour driving, the guy being accurate about that — and left it to the driver, as silent as an experienced chauffeur, to find a store they could use.

"Sir?"

"Oh, please, buddy. You can do anything you want, and I don't blame you if you don't trust me, if you are disgusted by me. But please, please, please do not call me sir. Call me 'dickhead.'"

The kid looked at him sternly, giving no sign that he saw himself included in the joke. He may have felt that he was being given just another order he must obey and could not.

"What did you want to ask?"

"Is that okay? That store there? I don't know about stores, not too much."

Cobb tried not to show that he had heard. "Yeah, that one with the target, that being a store called, and I only learned this yesterday, T.A.R.G.E.T."

Even Cobb was embarrassed at releasing such an obvious plea for companionship, especially here and to this boy. The kid, however, read something in the remark, located something that made him feel sorry for the big guy, so badly armed for making war of any kind, even friendship war.

He looked at Cobb directly, didn't look away, and then suddenly made as if to punch him in the nose.

Cobb would gladly have absorbed just such a punch, but saw it for what it was, flinched wildly, and got out of the car.

Chapter 16

"If we do nothing else, we got to arm the kid. That's a necessary thing, and it is a thing we can do. Is the gun shop within walking distance?"

"I don't remember, Brad. I think so, but we don't want to be away when Cobb and our little fella return."

"I could go. It's not that far, not if I head north, cross that way. A mile or two," Joss said.

It snuck up on all of them, the certainty that they should not be splitting up, creating that scene resonating through all horror movies and all the horrors of life: "You go the basement; I'll check the attic."

Of course, Cobb and the kid were by themselves, but they did have a car, which, in a pinch, could be a fortress, or a weapon.

"Let's all go."

Before they left, feeling ashamed and scared, they took a step toward a declaration of authority, an authority they neither felt nor possessed. In bold letters and with a red marker, they made this sign:

So sorry we missed you!
Make yourselves at Home!
Back Soon — and Ready!

* * *

"What should we get, do you think? I mean, we gotta eat. I think we gotta eat. That's what I always heard, though most of what I heard when I was your age turned out to be wrong."

"That was wrong."

"What?" Cobb was genuinely mystified.

"You don't have to eat."

"Ah, Jesus, honey." It was the wrong door to enter but Cobb could not have chosen another for the life of him.

The kid said nothing, but was suddenly struck with the idea that he was painting himself as a pathetic little shit, making himself vulnerable, whining, being nothing more than a child. He wasn't starving. He could feed himself.

Only he couldn't, and he saw himself as a fool, a weak fool, if he pretended he knew how to survive, as if he could dig out hot pizza from a snowbank.

Cobb seemed to have but the one mode, the one set of weapons. He meant them as invitations, but the kid knew better. Still, what could he do?

"Let's do clothes first, kid. That way, the food we get, the kinds you and me like and who cares about the others, won't turn all mushy and attract flies while we're clothes shopping. Maybe."

Then he looked around the huge super-store and switched his plans.

"Oh shit, buddy. The clothes is way over thar, they is, and right here's the best groceries money can buy, or we can buy anyhow. We'll do food first, since we don't mind, you and me, about them setting around in the heat outside, about a little rotting and smelling — and we won't tell the others. You've noticed it's not like it's all hot, swimming weather, anyhow."

Cobb grabbed a basket, stuck another one in the hands of the boy. "Now, listen, Ace. I ain't gonna do this alone. I ain't able. It's more than I can handle. Up to you to get good stuff. Healthy stuff. Or just good stuff. Up to me, we'll have nothing but celery. You go that way, toward the bread and vegetables. I'm off to raid the canned peas."

Blah, blah, blah.

Cobb was determined to stay away from the kid and to occupy by himself as much time as it might take for the kid to basket more than a loaf of bread.

The kid, trapped as he surely was, felt it, thought for a bit, and decided that, of the many bad scripts he had, the one he disliked least was to obey what Cobb clearly wanted, since, in some small part of his heart, it was also what he wanted.

Cobb didn't know how to react. He had tried to be moderate himself, not embarrass the kid, who would choose nothing at all.

But twenty minutes later be damned if the boy didn't have a full cart, bread, to be sure, and canned goods, the cheapest variety, and soda crackers. Then Cobb's heart leapt up: four gallon bottles of soda (diet soda and sugar-stoked equally matched), bars of chocolate, even a giant (family) carton of mixed chips, all guaranteed to avoid giving you a single useful nutrient. Good!

* * *

Meanwhile:

"You want another, the same as you got before at Mel's? I know what that's, as that crook's been unloading those worthless popguns for several weeks now. Spots peace-loving tourists like you and hops them. No offense. Let me give him a call, though, be certain."

They looked at one another, thinking the same thing: yes, this was Looneyville.

He made the call, then:"Was I right? What do you think, young pretties?"

"You were right."

"Holy Jesus, yes. You should go into business for yourselves, yes you should, instincts like that. They don't come in every baby's package, I can tell you. So, what did that bastard Mel charge you for his defective toy shooters?"

Somehow they made it out of there with the gun and all their wits about them.

* * *

"I'm sure I know what you think about clothes, buddy. Now, do listen to me."

Cobb's voice was gentle but there was a seriousness in it the kid hadn't heard before and didn't at first know how to read.

"I will listen."

"I know you don't want to think about shit like clothes. I know that. I do know that. I don't like thinking about them myself. But — believe me now. I'm not trying to make you feel bad — or scared. You need clothes, though. You do."

Silence.

"Do you see that? Do you?"

Maybe a nod.

"You can't just freeze — or not change or anything. You can't."

He looked so scared.

"Nobody's going to undress. For sure, I'm not."

All at once, he changed. He didn't brighten, but it was no longer midnight.

"Let's just pick up some stuff—packages of stuff—you know: socks and gloves and a jacket and shirts."

The kid now did smile.

"You mocking me, kid? You making fun of me cause I need to make lists of clothes or I'll forget? You little asshole!"

Cobb felt he shouldn't have said that. He was wrong.

The kid turned around, walked ahead of Cobb, straight to the section of the store that'd work, just as if he'd been there many times before. Had he been in Targets in wherever he had been? Any store? Cobb looked closely for the first time at the kid's clothes, visible now that he had left both jackets in the car. He sure as shit needed more and new. Nothing seemed too ragged, apart from his tennis shoes. Maybe they could begin there.

The boy was tilting toward socks, T-shirts, jeans areas, but Cobb caught up and moved close: "Good. You're an experienced.... Never mind. We need to start over here."

He more or less shoved the kid into a chair in the shoe department, grabbed one of the metal measuring troughs he thought had disappeared in the second Roosevelt administration, measured, and then started to pull out boxes himself, and then thought better of it.

"Listen to me, Mr. Glub, we need you to be able to do several important things with us, for us. These things will demand different sorts of footwear—shoes. First is hiking boots. We didn't tell you, but we have big plans for these mountains, and those plans are nowhere without you."

He looked at the boy, who wore no expression, sat there as if he were inside some penal regimen, just starting. "C'mon, kid. Help me out a little."

The kid now looked at Cobb, somehow believed he understood what Cobb was aiming at.

Cobb waved the kid toward the stacks, pointed generally at the hiking boots, a wide variety, not surprising considering where they were, but still way beyond Cobb's expectations — or knowledge.

"What in fuck are these? Oh, sorry."

The kid looked at the shoes, at Cobb, and finally responded.

"These are $119 dollars. No."

Cobb had anticipated this, had something ready.

"I know, and I know that seems a lot, is a lot. Will you trust me, at least for a second, trust me to explain?"

"Yes."

Cobb hadn't expected this, but he really was a quick-adjuster, at least with kids. "Okay. I know it's a lot. I can guess what that must mean to you, how much it must seem like a fucking trap. But hear me, now, okay?"

"I already said okay."

Cobb laughed. "Sorry. You make me nervous."

Silence.

"We have in mind doing some stuff in the next few days, stuff we like and figure you will, too — hiking some more and, before that, maybe some skiing or sledding. We want you to be with us, that's the truth. We do. You cannot do hiking without boots and you cannot do skiing without boots...."

The kid interrupted: "And you can't do dominoes without boots."

Cobb knew he had misheard. Then, "You monstrous pecker-face!"

The kid laughed a little, then tugged the boots on, let Cobb lace them, stood up, took some paces. "Okay," he said.

Now ski boots, now tennis shoes, now socks and sweaters and fleece jackets and non-fleece jackets and gloves, even a ski mask. If Cobb hadn't known better, he'd have imagined the kid was enjoying this.

When they were done in this part of boy's wear, Cobb started quickly toward the utility wear section, only to have the boy shove in front of him, elbowing him deliberately, and pile into the cart what eventually added up to seven brightly colored and defiantly labeled T-shirts; two pairs of jeans; six-packs of undershirts, underpants, and socks (one each). He even picked up a bright green ski hat, looked at Cobb and then, without waiting for an answer, added it to the collection.

Cobb wasn't alert enough to decide whether this was all they needed, but he also didn't want to start rummaging through the cart, so he tried to appear bored. Moving his hands from the cart-handle, he let the kid push it, and didn't try to disguise the total charge, which alarmed even him. But what the hell.

Out the door, into the car, boy driving. Not a half-mile down the road, though, Cobb was struck with an inspiration:

"Turn around!"

"Huh?"

"Sorry. We need to go back. An emergency."

The kid looked at him, made no move to turn around, but he did slide the car over to the berm.

"I got plenty of things."

"Yeah, well, maybe you do, clothes horse, but I'm not talking about more socks. Just trust old Cobb. Even if you don't trust old Cobb, please circle back, circle back to Target, which at one time was called Gold Circle, which I'll bet you didn't know, but which is just one of the thousands of kernels of essential knowledge you'll find lodged in your head, if you stick with me. I really hope you will stick with me."

The boy stared at him. Cobb hadn't expected a response.

"Why?"

Cobb was startled, but, even through his fuddle, realized that this question marked some small advance, that the boy wasn't just assuming, knowing that they wanted him for nothing that wouldn't lead to grief.

"Well, there's lots of reasons. One is we'd feel like shit if we just waved bye-bye to you. That'd make us feel guilty. We don't want to feel guilty. Guilty is a rotten thing to feel."

"You're doing it again."

"What?"

"Talking like Sesame Street."

In what distant land had this forlorn child been able to find those sunny days? On our way to where the air is sweet — can you tell me how to get to Sesame Street? Cobb looked at him — undecipherable.

"Sorry," he said. "I wanted to be honest. Part of the reason is that we're thinking about ourselves. But that's not all. It really isn't. We don't want to corral you, make you do or be anything. We think it's just what people should do, those who can — try to give other people who have no chance at all — a chance. Some kind of chance, even if they fail. I said that stupidly."

"I know what you said."

"Okay, then."

"Okay."

They made their way back to Target, the kid restraining himself from giving voice to the puzzlement he had to be feeling. Parked, entered.

"Here's what we need. This'll be cheap as hell, too, so don't yell at me or hit me. We need more games and we need a book or two. You gotta be playing and you gotta be reading. No two ways about it. That's just common sense. We let you go without games and without books — hell, we might as well be crocodiles."

It was probably just too much trouble to argue or try to understand, so, a very short time later, the boy, green ski hat atop, started up again from the parking lot, this time not to return.

Chapter 17

The three back at the cabin were no longer able to disguise from themselves or one another how worried they had become. Cobb and the boy had been gone a long time, so long that anyone else would have suggested calling the sheriff, reporting them missing, doing the responsible thing or some responsible thing.

Just as their concern was about to bubble over, the boy swung the car smoothly into the elevated driveway, managing not to topple down the grades on either side and land them in the bushes. He got out quickly, heading round to the trunk to retrieve as many of their bags as he could handle.

The thoughts of those inside turned immediately to shielding Cobb and the boy from any hint that they had been worrying.

"Let's go into the kitchen, pretend we've been getting together some food and not planning an ambush."

"Let's not pretend, Katie. I'm hungry. Bet Brad is, too. Cobb always is, and the little kid has to be near starving."

The result was that Cobb and the boy entered to no one at all, an apparently empty house, surprising Cobb mightily and the boy not at all.

"You want me to take these out there, where we eat?"

Cobb had no time to answer, first, because the others had just then stormed into the room and, second, because the doorbell rang — then again.

Answering that clanging seemed to be the thing to do.

There before them were four hefties, all in suits, white shirts, ties, and no overcoats or jackets. Joss, who had answered the door, opened it cautiously, a few inches, scanned the strangers closely — decided no, not the Wilfreds — and then looked to find their car and its plates. No telling why she wanted their plates, harmless as she had decided they were. Still, so she did. And found no plates, no car.

"How'd you get here?" she asked, not in the least hospitably.

"The Lord sent us."

"Screw that," Joss said, laughing a little.

The four, all bunched together, now, as if on cue, let loose, smileless, a thousand-watt radiance, suitable for a gigantic stadium, the second coming, or, at the very least, an audience likely to be receptive.

Joss just stared at them, perhaps made as if to close the door, when the speaker stepped onto the transom, not threateningly, and purred, "If you'd allow us just a little of your time, just a little, a little for the Lord.... Why, hello, son."

The boy looked at the man, turned and went into his room, closing the door softly behind him.

It wasn't clear at what point the leader had made his way inside or how the others followed, but there they were.

Katie, perhaps sensing something offered, "Would you like a glass of water?"

"Why, that would be most kind," said the leader, who was fishing while he spoke, first, in his inside coat pocket and, then, in a large bag dangling at his side.

Cobb, who had considered following the kid and then rejected that bad idea, walked over to where the Lord's men were, looked intently and discovered that they probably were not all men. Two, at most.

"Would you please be seated?" he said. "We aren't loaded with chairs but there's that sofa over to your left."

Joss looked at Cobb as if he were an alien, but Brad and

Katie saw what he was up to, kept quiet. In any case, Cobb immediately went after each of the visitors in turn, directing them insistently to seats in various parts of the room, as widely spread as the space allowed.

No sooner were they plopped down and watered, than one of them began, a besuited female, besuited for sure, female probably.

"We are here to talk to you about damnation, bring to you His Holy Word on that subject."

"The first subject, the only subject we all should be hearing about, all of us, every one," said another.

"The subject that defines us and our future, our only just concern and the base of our being," put in a third.

"Yes, indeed. Maybe we should introduce ourselves now," said the one who had knocked, seemed to be in charge.

"We are the Trumpets of Gabriel, the Hosts, the Bringers of the News."

"Well, Trumpets, finish your water and go!"

They either didn't hear Joss or were simply programmed to ride right over any interruptions.

"You children of darkness have been tutored by Satan, the Fallen Prince, the angel of light turned darkness and your own sire. Down deep, you know all this. He has taught you very well, all the while half-concealing his tutoring. Worst of all, you have been a willing accomplice in this deception, trying to conceal the fact that he has pitched his tent right there inside your heart, letting on that he lives only in ancient stories and in the minds of fools and dullards."

No one replied, so he continued, standing first and sweeping his hand round and round in front of his ample body. "Such as us."

He smiled and then he stopped smiling. "We are responding to your sign. Your own sign. Your inviting sign. How could we not do so? How could we leave you as you were?"

"Pretty easy, I should think," said Katie, more irritated than apprehensive. "The sign was not addressed to you, not intended for those spreading the news, good or otherwise."

"I see," said the first woman. "What makes you think, fallen one, that our news is good news? You know better. You know that our statement to that effect is a way to reach your heart, bypassing your mind, tricking your Satanic watchdogs."

"Sister Joan has ever the best interests of our parishioners at heart, an important point to take note of, not that I need tell you that. Sister Joan's intentions speak for themselves. They go, as she says, straight to your sin-soaked hearts."

"Can we pause a minute, take a deep breath, try to get back to level, to something closer to sanity?" Brad didn't look angry, but he was.

"Retreat would be foolish — and sinful," said the leader. "You are now far from the peaceful shore, you know, yes you are, son."

"Very deeply stained with sin, sinking to...." sang Cobb, standing as he did so, striking a pose he knew was mocking, hoping to draw their ire to himself and away from Brad.

"I think it is time we advanced to the next level," said the leader, still standing but making no move toward any of them. "I feel the spirit inside me, and in a minute you will feel it, too. It is calling to me, calling to me. Do you hear it, sinners?"

His voice rose neither in pitch nor volume, but something did happen to his eyes, some new gleam. The other three rose as one, then reached toward the beige and cracked ceiling with their outstretched hands, as if they were seeking to claw something out of the plaster.

The leader called out, "You did wrong to mock the angels of Jehovah, the instruments of His divine wrath. That sign you posted was devised by Lucifer, operating through you, his oh-so willing disciples. It is his plan, but you are the ones who are its instrument, and are eager to execute it. His craft is never to be underestimated, and he is always at work, never resting. He is doing all this. Oh, yes! We accept that you are, in part, ignorant, made blind to the reach and horror you generate, so satisfied are you with the rewards he offers, ministering to your basest desires, the vilest parts of your physical and spiritual being. But it is You who have resigned your will and turned your back on your god. Yes. Admit it! Repent! You cannot save yourself. No. By now, you are being driven by the hell within. You have no will. You are helpless. Submit to god, to us!"

"Just get the fuck out!" somebody said. Didn't matter who.

"We can save you, cleanse you, rip away the foulness within, burn your wickedness away, show you how to find the blessedness that awaits you on the other side, just beyond pain and submission."

It was then that they started to chant something, kneeling together and addressing the carpet, fouled by pets of former careless renters. All four of those besieged, however, knew at once that their visitors wouldn't be kneeling for long, so they took the moment to find the kitchen, then a key, then a locked drawer, and then four of the guns. The fifth they had left in the kid's room. That was stupid, but they could correct it later.

As they came into the room to rout the invaders, they saw that the child had beaten them to it. He was standing just outside his door, decked out in some of his new clothes: new jeans, the hiking boots, a brilliant orange tee-shirt saying "I Ain't as Stupid as I Look," and the green hat. He was holding the gun on the gospel team, holding it steady, saying nothing.

"My child," said the leader, "It is you we specially seek, you we need."

"I'll kill you," said the boy. It was a new tone, at least to the ears of those wishing to be rescuers, and it stopped them cold.

Whatever rapturous trance may have been enveloping the four suited ones seemed no longer to have a hold on them. They looked at one another and then at the older tenants, each also pointing a gun. Then they straightened up, found a table on which to set their water glasses, now all empty, and moved toward the door.

"Let this be unto you...," began the leader.

"Don't say anything," said the child. "Go!"

They did just that, obeying both commands.

* * *

Katie suddenly ran to the window, then out the door and onto the porch. In less than a minute, she was back. Everyone was staring at her as if she'd just decided to do aerobics in the middle of a tornado.

"No license plate," she said, shaking her head. "Nothing. No car. They seem to have vanished — probably just ran off to another place housing the sin-soaked."

Even the kid seemed to understand.

The kid. He was expressionless and stationary, still pointing the gun at where the invaders had been. He noticed them all staring wide-eyed, looked back and then directed his eyes down at his gun.

"I didn't know where the bullets were."

"Son of a bitch. You saved our lives!" That was Joss, who took a step toward the boy, thought better of it.

The boy walked over to the group and held the gun out, butt-first, for anyone who might take it.

"No, that's yours, " Joss said. "Hell, you might need it several times a day, you stay with us. We're champion nightmare-attractors. Guaranteed."

"They were going to hurt you."

"You're right, kid. They weren't just your run-of-the-mill

Jehovah Witnesses. Like Joss says, we're maniac-magnets." Cobb stopped.

"We probably did you no favor dragging you into this. Visitors seem to stop by on us, vacationers from Hell, about every second day. They may all be part of the same family, but they assume different shapes. We didn't mean to do it, but we've stationed you inside whatever circle they want to invade."

The boy looked at Brad as if he were going to say something, perhaps contradict him. He did not.

They stood there, first-dance awkward, waiting for someone to effect a transition to — anything at all.

"I can cook."

Of all people to ease them out of awkwardness. But he did.

He walked over beside Cobb, who went with him into the kitchen. The others plopped their asses down, waiting for whatever might happen. What that was emerged in about fifteen minutes: Cobb with a platter of hefty sandwiches and a big smile.

"Chef Raymonde's special. He's now doing a soup to complement these finger foods, a soup made out of — well, I won't spoil the surprise."

The cooking kid gave no sign that he was joining them, so, very shortly, they all took what remained of their sandwiches out to the kitchen and squeezed around the small table, trying to create happy chatter. This was the time that would melt all distances, forge a natural union. They had that sense, all of them.

It did no such thing. The boy, prodded, was willing to eat the smallest of the sandwiches and had two servings of the tomato soup. Beyond that, nothing. He seemed to squeeze back into himself, stopped making eye contact. Finally, it became so clear he wanted out of there that Katie took pity.

"That was just the thing, that great food. Time for a nap for this sleepy time gal. You know what I mean and I'm sure you all feel the same. It's just what we need—after all this."

"A nap!" Joss began, and then stopped.

The boy didn't look up, but they knew. Cobb and Brad moved from their side of the table, pretending to have some errand in the front room. The boy, eyes still downcast, made his way to the kitchen arch, turned and said, "I'm sorry."

* * *

Once he was in his room, the others jammed back into the kitchen, trying to imagine that they could uncover the deep mysteries of the boy, the Evangelical Evils, and the Wilfreds, hoping somehow to find a story to counter what they deep down knew about their impotence and sustaining ignorance. After five minutes of aimless hard thinking, they decided without saying it to put all these things on hold, these things that mattered, and turn to what they could handle, routine activities for the next couple or so days.

"Couple or so?" Cobb protested.

"Make it just two, Cobb," Katie said, touching his good hand. "We can't have you slowing us down as we go off to reenact the Donner Party's fun time."

"You be okay for that yourself, Katie?"

"I don't know what it is, Joss, but I'm feeling really good walking now, lurching less. Think I'll take up ballroom dancing—instructor of."

"You'd be the top," said Brad, aimlessly.

"You lousy son of a bitch, Brad! Why don't you just do a fake hobble?" Joss was really pissed. Katie, Cobb, and Brad were beyond baffled.

Joss looked around, trying to read blank faces. Finally, "Didn't any of you get the brutal pun? Huh? Flop — flop?"

Cobb caught on first or was the first to speak: "Not *flop*,

Deefie, *top*! Brad said, "You're the *top*!" or some such, and you musta heard, 'You'd be a *flop*.' Says something about you, Joss."

Katie cut in, "And what it says, trumpets with horns double *forte,* is that you need new batteries. New Batteries!" she shouted.

"Ah fuck. All these years and I still don't know where that beeping is coming from. I am so sorry, Brad. I know you won't forgive me, but please don't poison my tea."

"I wondered about that beeping, too. At least it's not the smoke alarm. And you're right, Joss. I know how to carry a grudge, let it blossom and explode."

"So, go get the batteries, Joss. While you do, we'll finalize extraordinarily complex and impossible plans for our two-day vacation from peril and have you participating."

Then Cobb thought again. "I'll go with you."

Then again. "Even better, take our friend, who is doubtless listening in on what we're plotting."

* * *

But he wasn't and was probably frightened at the knock on his door. You couldn't tell by looking at him. Anyhow, Joss explained everything in more detail than was called for, asked him to drive her for batteries.

"Batteries?"

"My hearing aide. It helps me hear — these things do — but when the batteries start to fade they make these terrible binging noises, bothering not only me but everyone within miles. So, would you do it, drive me?"

"Yes."

Out the door, Joss forgot for a minute Cobb's tale of the kid's driving skills and started to the left side, corrected her error, and edged between the boy and the passenger door he was about to open.

He drove in silence straight to the close-by station, the one Cobb had ignored. Joss didn't move, wondered if they needed gas, looked over at the kid.

Finally, he said, "They will tell you how to find the battery store. It is not required that you buy gas or the stuff inside, candy. I don't want anything."

Joss nodded, got out and equipped herself with directions, re-entered, and spilled it all to the kid: "He said keep going straight along the way we're right now headed, about a mile, just about, maybe more, he didn't think so — but he was a stupid one, about as stupid as—"

"Me."

Joss was the only one of the group who wouldn't have hit him like a snake with apologies and assurances. All she did was look at him and crinkle her eyes. "If it's any comfort, you're not the only stupid one in the group."

"That is comfort."

Even Joss was startled by this, drew back a little and almost smiled.

They got to the jewelry store in just a few minutes.

"Want to come in with me? We could steal some diamonds."

"Good. I know a lot about stealing."

Joss felt as if she were being tested, which probably she was. "Bullshit! I'll bet you never even lifted a comb, which you fucking need, by the way."

He did smile now, seemed relieved that someone was insulting him. He knew his hair looked like shit, maybe thought about saying so, extending the banter. But what would that do, where would it go?

Inside, the over-courteous woman dropped a level on the fawning scale when she discovered they weren't customers, really, just battery shoppers. Joss noticed right away, being altogether too alert to snubs, real and less so.

"Maybe we'll get us an engagement ring while we're here? What do you think, honey?"

"I don't see anything that would be good, not for us." How could he know how to play these games?

Joss decided to push harder. "I expect they got dangles, too, you could hang some from those piercings of yours we all admire so."

The boy looked at her, as close to pleading as any look could be that was not: "Please."

Outside the store, she didn't apologize, seemed softer. Though she could find no way to transfer softening into words, she couldn't leave it there.

"Well, at least you're a terrific driver — and you don't have to wear these fucking ear-tinkles. I'll bet you can hear really well."

"I can hear well."

"See, what did I tell you?"

"I can hear real well if I turn toward you, this way. See?"

Joss saw, couldn't think of anything to say.

"I am sorry. I wasn't making fun of you. I am sorry you have to wear those in your ears."

"Do you have to turn to hear me? Your right ear isn't so strong?"

"It works okay. I mean, I am not crying about it. Sorry. I did not mean to be rude."

"That's okay. I like rude, you little shit."

Silence.

"What should I call you?" Joss asked just as they approached their driveway.

"That is your choice. It's all the same," the boy said, parking and opening his door quickly. This was the longest conversation he had allowed, and he seemed to regret it.

CHAPTER 18

The two days they had promised themselves, time to sway and sing, avoid thinking useful thoughts and facing necessary fears, had hardly begun when the doorbell rang. They were all sitting around in an after-breakfast mutual laze, the boy there with them, but as distant as he could be within the same room.

Nobody moved, so the boy felt he had to offer: "Should I answer it?"

For no reason at all, nobody responded, so he tried another: "Should I get the gun?"

Cobb hauled out a fake laugh, motioned the kid to stay put, and crept across to the window, snaking his head around and through the curtains.

"It's a kid. A girl."

"Anybody behind her? A car? Other people? Sure it's a kid?"

"It's a kid."

"Want to see what she wants, Cobb, or just drill her from the roof?"

"Okay, Joss, I'm on it." Then, "Hi, kid. You selling cookies or magazine subscriptions? We're on the lookout for either."

"No, sir. I'm Julie. How do you do? We are in the place over there—"she gestured vaguely behind her. "I saw a kid in your cabin, I thought, around here. He with you?"

"Hello, Julie. I'm Cobb. Yes, we do have a kid here, a boy. He's with us, you know — just as he should be."

Julie looked at Cobb as if she'd awakened a demonic maniac. Didn't retreat but seemed to be considering it.

Cobb decided to make matters worse. "You saw him, you say, and want to make his acquaintance, or something like that. Am I close?"

She smiled, maybe mistaking Cobb now for a rational being. "Yes, sir — Cobb. I'm staying over there with my parents, who are bad enough, and my uncle and aunt, who are worse."

"I get the idea."

"It's almighty shit boring, to tell the truth, so I thought I'd ask if the kid I saw wanted to do some video games or something — anything."

The boy had been watching all this, giving no indication of anything, certainly not of welcoming this stranger. Video games!

But he did get up from the remote sofa, crossed the empty space and stood in front of the girl, who had made it maybe five feet into the room. She was apparently the same height as he, within range of his years, and blindingly pretty, made all the more jolting by her attempt to disguise it with crummy jeans and a heavy jacket that looked none too clean. She had long hair, almost as messy as the boy's but much lighter, and she wore outsized glasses that did nothing to disguise her eyes — penetrating, emerald, flashing. Despite her poise and the "shit" she had dropped, surely as some sort of signal, she was heartbreakingly alone, unprotected. But they all knew she was in no danger from the boy. If there were peril, it would be his to face.

She made the first move, didn't quite shake his hand but touched it and said something to him so soft none of the biggies could make it out. Made them realize they shouldn't try, should leave these kids to find their way.

Whatever it was they said to one another — or she said, wasn't clear if he mumbled back — they gave no explanations, simply made their way to the kid's room and shut the door. No slamming but no welcome mat either.

Each of our four wanted so badly to peek, overhear, but all knew that the stakes were too high. They didn't have the bankroll that would allow them to participate. Good time to find distant chores to do.

Cobb and Katie made their way to the kitchen but could think of nothing to occupy themselves apart from hammering together yet more sandwiches for lunch, still a good three hours away. Joss and Brad jacketed themselves and went outside and then looked carefully around, as if they were sentries, which, in a way, they were.

Even close vigilance and skulking could occupy them for no more than fifteen minutes in the drilling cold, though, and they quickly saw the comedy in it.

"Feel like parents retreating to the bedrooms while kid and date neck in the parlor?"

"A fucking icy bedroom, Brad, and snowy as hell."

"We should be doing snow things with our kid, Joss, maybe a fort, snowman, snowball fight."

"I'm sorry I yelled at you, Brad."

"Is that a yes on the snowman?"

"You'd be easy to love, Brad."

"So grand at the games, so carefree together that it does seem a shame that you can't see a future with me," he sang, so slowly and sweetly he seemed inside the song, somehow, not repeating lyrics but finding them.

Joss was so near tears she felt she had to make a joke or lose something important. She couldn't find a joke, though, so what could she do but: "You'd be so easy to love, so easy to idolize, all others above—so worth the yearning for, so swell to keep the home fires burning for."

She couldn't have found another sound had she needed one to halt a firing squad. Brad sensed that. He put hands to either cheek, looked at her and said nothing. She managed not to cry.

"Well, Joss, should we get back inside where it's warm and where we're at least as competent as we are at doing whatever it is we're doing here?"

He thought she looked hurt, so: "I love you, Joss — and that's not saying anything that's news to you." He immediately realized he should have quit after the first four words. But it was okay. Joss had stopped listening at that very point.

"I suppose it should be part of our tunneling below the predictable to avoid declarations, but what the hell! And yes, we might as well head on back, put a halt to all this childish funny business."

"And start a mature version." Brad had no idea what he meant, figured Joss would. He was right.

* * *

They found themselves creeping across the front room and into the kitchen, wanting to detect without being detected.

"What in hell are you two doing?"

"Loading up the larder, Joss, advancing toward two score and ten sandwiches, just in case that young beauty in there has in mind dumping her very tedious extended family on us — or something. Shhhh."

The call for silence worked, allowed them to hear pretty clearly, coming from the bedroom, the sweetest ever:

"Oh the bulldog on the bank!"

Then—"C'mon, pig-face, your turn!"

"And the bullfrog in the pool!"

"The bulldog called the bullfrog

"A green old water fool!"

Giggles and more. The kitchen spies tried to keep themselves from edging into the other room — or from joining in.

Then— "Well, you green old water fool, do you feel like — mumble, mumble?"

Now they did steal, if not into the front room exactly, then to the very farthest reaches of the kitchen, hoping to believe what they were hearing, hoping for some true joy to connect with both kids. They knew they were now inside a sentimentality that could turn rancid. All the same....

Just then, they heard the kids emerging from the room, walking quickly — they wanted to run but were too polite — toward the door. And then: "Do you allow me to go outside?"

"Well, that depends," Cobb said. "Are you two going to get into trouble?"

"Yes," they both said.

"In that case, fine. Be sure you do!"

* * *

It was a good three hours, fun for the young kids and wonder and worry for the older ones. Finally, Joss, Brad, Katie, and Cobb gave up, piled on layers, and went out to investigate. Turns out the boy and his friend were right behind the house, somehow in a tree and armed with snowballs they let fly at the four biggies, just as soon as they all were around the corner and within peppering range.

Truth is, Brad had glanced up and seen them but wouldn't have given them away for anything. Fourteen hours later, seemed like, the older four were wearing out and were struck with a stab of let's-be-responsible-here they should have warded off. "You kids want to come in and warm up, have some hot chocolate?"

They didn't even have hot chocolate, and the kids had found ways to tunnel into much more warmth than was available indoors. Julie said as much — politely. The boy just looked cross, didn't say anything.

Katie to the rescue. "Okay. We'll leave you to your own devices. Come in when it's dark—or whenever the hell you want."

* * *

They kept themselves from checking, and it was well after dark when the boy knocked.

"Why you knocking, doofus? Where's Julie?"

"I am sorry. Julie returned home right over there."

"Did you lay plans for tomorrow?"

"I hope it is okay. I said I would see her tomorrow. Is that okay? She has to go back the day after."

"Yes, that is okay. Now go get changed and dried off and ready for the best hamburgers this side of the house next door."

He did change, came out in yet another new T-shirt (purple — "I'm Confused — Oh Wait! Maybe I'm Not,") and joined their burger-blast. He showed no signs of loosening, and if he were warmed it was only in a literal way. Somehow, the childlike happiness they were sure he had experienced that day seemed not only self-contained but tentative.

They managed to rope him into a few of the recent store-bought games they none of them knew or enjoyed a lot: too much time learning the rules and then pretending to compete with others they'd rather not beat. After a couple of hours, ready to call it a night, the boy asked if it were allowed for him to go to his room. "I like that book you let me buy," he said.

What were they going to say?

* * *

The next day dawned in John Greenleaf Whittier style — "The sun that brief December day rose cheerless over hills of grey." Or so said Katie.

No one needed to point out that it wasn't December, so Cobb did, but then smiled, trying, as they were all starting to see, not to win a nice-guy contest but to draw them away from being controlled by fear. If they were going to live free, live at all, they had to stop thinking of guarding themselves, much less of escape.

They were around the table, minus the kid.

"Should I get him, tell him that if he hopes to eat he'd better rouse his butt and get out here?"

Cobb was surprised when nobody raised eyebrows, snorted, so he went to the kid's room and knocked, expecting silence or repulse.

"Come in."

Come in? He heard wrong. Still, he opened the door and entered, into pitiful neatness, ready for inspection, arranged into geometric order appropriate for no kid ever who wasn't driven by punishment.

Cobb couldn't help himself. "Jesus, Half-Ass, where's the mess. Fuck things up a little."

The kid, dressed in yet another fresh outfit, looked at him blankly.

"Love your shirt. Suits you great, that puke blue color does!" Cobb said. It was yet another shirt with a slogan: "I AM in Shape. Big, Fat, Round Is a Shape!"

The kid looked down at his belly, smiled back. He was getting used to Cobb, maybe had run into Cobbs before, though they weren't all that common.

Cobb was anxious not to say more wrong things, so he stood staring. The kid didn't seem embarrassed, shifted gears smoothly: "I saw the washer in the garage. Do I have your okay to use it?"

"Sure. I think we need to get soap and stuff, you know, softener for fabrics, sheets of film, heavy duty this and that."

The kid did smile now. "You know a lot about it."

"I do. You have no idea. There's nothing I don't know."

"You don't know shit."

"Watch it, Richard head. Get it, get it?"

The kid stared at him. Finally, "You know why you have trouble with the girls?"

"What? Okay, why do I have trouble with the girls?"

"You stick with me and learn."

Cobb could not believe this. "I hope I can."

"You can — Cobb."

Cobb nodded, turned and left, the kid following, no longer talking or smiling. Maybe something had happened.

They settled in to breakfast, not exactly chatting easily, not chatting at all. But the silence was considerably less gruesome than usual. It didn't last long, in any case, as the doorbell dingled minutes later. The boy made as if to jump up, then looked around, clearly for permission. Nobody was dumb enough to grant it, so he went ahead, knowing who had come calling.

He opened the door and stepped aside.

Julie was decidedly less formal this time, barely gave them a "Hi!" in passing, beating it back to the kid's room.

"Well, I never!" said Katie, hands-on-hips, imitating some Bette Davis film or other.

"The youth of today!" said Brad.

Chapter 19

This time the kids stayed in the room for several hours, no giggling, no nothing. Brad took sandwiches to them at noon, but they treated him as if he were room-service, minus the tip. The others turned to board games, almost no talk about planning the future and what it might hold.

Just a little: "She goes back tomorrow," Katie said, "Damn it all!"

Nobody responded, though all were entertaining variations on the same thought, "Wonder where she's from. Wonder if...."

Impossible. What did they have in mind for the two? Going steady? Connubial bliss? How about happiness, friendship? Something other than whatever dark thing was waiting for the boy, possibly for Julie.

This was close to the point of no return, and they had reached it simultaneously. They glanced, turned back, pretended there was another path.

"Well," Joss said, knowing something had to be said, "Cobb reminded us we need laundry essentials. That'll solve most of our problems, give us just what we have every right to."

"Sure," Brad said.

"How about," Katie said, trying to brighten things, "we do nothing at all today, keep ourselves out of the way? Tomorrow, when he's alone again, so alone...."

She stopped, looked apologetic.

Everyone knew.

She resumed: "Tomorrow, we can go skiing, over at the snow park — over there somewhere. They have skiing."

"Oh, Katie," Joss said, and started crying, stopping herself fast when, without warning, Julie and her companion emerged, stood as if ready to make an announcement. Then they did:

"Attention, everyone!" They seemed to be speaking as one.

Not waiting for a response, the boy continued. "Please. Everyone in here. We have for you a reading."

Julie chimed in: "Hurry up! Doesn't matter where you sit, but you can't talk to one another. You have to listen. This is important."

They did hurry, sat, as astounded as if they'd all been asked to shed several years of their lives and join the two in what it was they had. It would float away tomorrow, but that didn't matter now.

The boy, appointed announcer, seemed to lose his careful reticence, even came within a whisker of hamming it up, of playing Alfalfa in the old, old sweet shows:

"And now we take you back to the days of yore, when Huck Finn lived, as in the book you bought me, *The Adventures of Huckleberry Finn.*"

Julie smiled at him, clearly lost in love or whatever better form of connection exists for the very young, and continued: "We pick up the action, just as Huck finds out some really important news. But, so you'll not be lost, dim-wits that we know you are, we will back up a little, so you can get it."

Then they started. No giggles, no overplaying, nothing between them and the novel, the hunted, haunted boy and his outcast, despised friend, both altogether beyond even a hope of safety. They alternated voices and passages in a way that made no ordinary sense, joining together without gender, sequence, or time.

It was not a professional reading, of course, but what it was counted, both for the audience and the speakers.

> "Well, I reckon you HAVE lived in the country. I thought maybe you was trying to hocus me again. What's your real name, now?"
>
> "George Peters, mum."
>
> "Well, try to remember it, George. Don't forget and tell me it's Elexander before you go, and then get out by saying it's George Elexander when I catch you. And don't go about women in that old calico. You do a girl tolerable poor, but you might fool men, maybe. Bless you, child, when you set out to thread a needle don't hold the thread still and fetch the needle up to it; hold the needle still and poke the thread at it; that's the way a woman most always does, but a man always does t'other way. And when you throw at a rat or anything, hitch yourself up on tiptoe and fetch your hand up over your head as awkward as you can, and miss your rat about six or seven foot. Throw stiff-armed from the shoulder, like there was a pivot there for it to turn on, like a girl; not from the wrist and elbow, with your arm out to one side, like a boy. And, mind you, when a girl tries to catch anything in her lap she throws her knees apart; she don't clap them together, the way you did when you catched the lump of lead. Why, I spotted you for a boy when you was threading the needle; and I contrived the other things just to make certain. Now trot along to your uncle, Sarah Mary Williams George Elexander Peters, and if you get into trouble you send word to Mrs. Judith Loftus, which is me, and I'll do what I can to get you out of it. Keep the river road all the way, and next time you tramp take shoes and socks with you. The river road's a rocky one, and your feet'll be in a condition when you get to Goshen, I reckon."

I went up the bank about fifty yards, and then I doubled on my tracks and slipped back to where my canoe was, a good piece below the house. I jumped in, and was off in a hurry. I went upstream far enough to make the head of the island, and then started across. I took off the sun-bonnet, for I didn't want no blinders on then. When I was about the middle I heard the clock begin to strike, so I stops and listens; the sound come faint over the water but clear — eleven. When I struck the head of the island I never waited to blow, though I was most winded, but I shoved right into the timber where my old camp used to be, and started a good fire there on a high and dry spot

Then I jumped in the canoe and dug out for our place, a mile and a half below, as hard as I could go. I landed, and slopped through the timber and up the ridge and into the cavern. There Jim laid, sound asleep on the ground. I roused him out and says:

"Git up and hump yourself, Jim! There ain't a minute to lose. They're after us!"

Jim never asked no questions, he never said a word; but the way he worked for the next half an hour showed about how he was scared. By the time everything we had in the world was on our raft, and she was ready to be shoved out from the willow cove where she was hid — we put out the campfire at the cavern the first thing, and didn't show a candle outside after that.

I took the canoe out from the shore a little piece, and took a look; but if there was a boat around I couldn't see it, for stars and shadows ain't good to see by. Then we got out the raft and slipped along down in the shade, past the foot of the island dead still — never saying a word.

* * *

The two stayed in character a minute, saying nothing, lost in the world of Huck and Jim. Then Julie turned away from the boy, as if pulled by an alien force, and bowed to the audience. She then glanced over at her leading man. The boy bowed. Wasn't as if they were overwhelmed with applause, which would have seemed corny to the older kids and insulting to the younger.

They bowed again, then dissolved, began giggling, kids again. With no explanations or permission-requests, they beat it out the front door, claiming their territory, forcing it open as they entered.

The four sat, not wanting to be stunned.

Finally, "What just happened?" Katie was speaking.

Nobody answered, reluctant to stamp it, make it too easily available to themselves or their friends.

"That section of the novel they read." Cobb broke the silence. "They telling us something?"

"Yes," Brad said.

Cobb waited and then went on, "That passage, though, the way it grows and grows, moves as fast as Huck is moving."

"It's the whole world right there," Brad said, not waiting for anyone to catch up with him. "Later on in the book, things get squirmy and Huck even fools with Jim, belittles him, and Twain seems to sink back and let go of the force he was riding. But here, right here, in this expanding minute, there is absolute truth, formed into a perfect and furious challenge."

He paused, looked at Katie and Joss, one of whom responded: "They are after US."

Nobody wanted to let it go, to leave the moment. Brad held onto it longest: "Huck doesn't make any vows or decide anything, he simply enters into an energy that takes over. They are after us. We know well enough about the "'They,' but the 'Us' is what cannot be screwed with. It cannot endure, but right there, right there it blazes through time."

Katie was touching her head as if in pain, but it wasn't pain: "Nothing that comes after can touch it or fulfill it. Huck's resolve is Jim's, and it holds even when the plot fails it."

"The plot and the world," Joss said. "They are after us, and only the They holds together."

"I hope our kid is inside our us," said Cobb, "even if that means they are after him as well. I think they are in any case, and maybe he'd not be much worse off catching hold."

There was nothing more to say, but the four felt not just educated but somehow reformed, given permission to reenter the vow that had begun all this and then nearly disappeared from their hearts.

* * *

They agreed to stay inside the house, outface boredom and find occupation in just about anything, counting backwards from a million, if need be. They would not be the invaders. That was not their role.

Brad gave them the script. "Remember that movie we loved so much, 'Bad News Bears'?"

Yes, they all remembered.

"They got it right. Big people ought to vacate the lives of little people. As Coach Buttermaker, or whatever, says to parents of his Little Leaguers, 'Get the hell out of the way and let them go at it. The kids know.'"

"And we big people have managed to move away — or been exiled," Katie said, "if that's not being sentimental."

Joss, of all people, jumped in, "Remember that other movie, *Magnolia?* The former Quiz Kid says, 'And no! It is not a mistake to confuse children with angels.'"

Still, as dinner-time (anyone's reasonable dinner-time) came and went and the hours slipped by, they had to work hard to ignore what was on everyone's mind. Ten, eleven, twelve, twelve-fifteen.

The door swung open and the boy started in, stepped back as if to announce himself, decided against it, and came on.

He looked around, gave no explanation for his late return, started back toward his room and then stopped, knew that wouldn't do.

"I am sorry to have been — to be — so late. We lost the time."

"Hell with that," said Cobb, "we just hope you had a great romp, a happy day."

"Thank you," he said. "Julie asked me to thank you, too, and to tell you she is sorry she could not be here to do it, but her parents — she called them a name."

Everyone looked expectant, hoping.

"Her F-ing parents."

"Her what?" Katie said. "Her fucking parents?"

The boy looked at Katie, expressionless.

"Yes. They came looking for her." He seemed about to say more.

Everyone rushed to rescue him, but rescue was not what he sought. He was holding out his arms, like a supplicant locked into a dead religion. He dropped his arms and stood frozen.

"Well, hell," Joss said, "Ain't like you can't keep in touch with Julie."

The other three looked hard at Joss, the boy actually flinching.

"Nah!" he said, started toward his room, stopped and, looking at nothing in particular, said, "Thank you. You agree that I can...."

"Yes." They echoed one another.

* * *

They watched him close the door.

They looked at nothing and then made their way to the kitchen, all talking too loudly, pretending, first, not to hear, then, not to recognize the sounds coming from his room.

Chapter 20

The next morning, they trickled out one-by-one, wondering who would make breakfast, making breakfast entailing setting out from the pantry and refrigerator the milk and the cereal and the bowls and the spoons and nothing else. Cobb took over the heavy work, trying to make as much noise as possible, hoping to arouse the kid or signal him that he could emerge.

The other three joined in banging, and Katie started singing.

And there he was, finally, looking as resolutely self-contained as always. He walked out of his room, sat on the couch, and then noticed Cobb fiddling, sprang up and started to help.

Then: "Good morning. Thank you for all that."

They all wished they knew what exactly "all that" was, but soon let it float away.

Cobb stopped his aimless fussing and moved back, just so that the kid would have something to do.

"You know how to cook anything good, Chef Louie?" he said, without looking at the kid.

"Roast dog," the kid said. "Boiled sparrow. Rat sandwiches."

Cobb then blundered in. "Ah, yes, the food of your people. Honest fare for poor but honest folk, sometimes honest."

"Just pretend honest," the kid said.

Cobb seemed to have learned when to stop, to shift gears.

"That where the spoons go? I always put them inside the bowl, but I don't have your restaurant experience." He said this easily enough, bumping against the kid in an extravagant charade of accidentally.

"You don't have any useful experience."

"That's true. You are the very one to know what kind of experience I need, where I most could use the help that only you can give. And you will give it, however reluctantly, thereby piling up points in heaven for your good works. Where will you begin?"

"Teaching you how to dress?"

"Well, yes, but how, outside of clothing, to attract women. I've never mastered that art."

Silence.

"Shit, I'm so sorry, buddy."

"Why? I was just thinking. You know, I don't want to be mean, but I have to think about that. You and girls. I mean, it's like...."

"It's like what?"

"It's like trying to make two things get along, you know, like trying to have a fly and a black widow go out on a date."

"Oh, well...."

"Or a coyote and a kitten, or a hawk and a birdie, or a shark and a minnow, or a wasp and a bare butt, or a...."

"You trying to make me feel bad, kid?"

"Yes. No."

Then a pause.

"Maybe."

"What a shit you are!"

The others wondered if they should stay put, see if this act would resume, this impossible duet. It didn't, so they went out and scattered themselves into the chairs circling round the tiny table.

The kid was still finding the cereal boxes, no help from Cobb or anyone else, so, when he did finally locate them, he was the last one to sit. Everyone half-stood, ready to make room anywhere and were probably surprised when he ended up between Katie and Joss.

They ate in silence, but not for long.

"Well," Katie said, "let's solidify our plans, even if they aren't plans so much as misleading directions, spinning pointers leading us just where we don't want to go. That okay? We were thinking of Donner Pass, so that's out, since it was planned. Right?"

For some reason she was looking at the boy.

When nobody else said anything, he did: "I don't know."

"I'll take that as an agree — from all," Katie said. "So, Donner Pass disappears into the future or into nowhere, for now, though it may be resurrected in the name of being idiotically inconsistent, and we are left with what?"

"Swimming and water-skiing!" Joss said.

"That'd be ever so fine, and unexpected, but maybe too obviously suicidal here with the icebergs floating," Katie said.

"Skiing?" the kid said, clearly not understanding.

"Okay, if you insist," said Cobb. "I'm a little rusty and never was what you would call an Olympic champeen on the slopes in my best day. But you can give me tips, right, alpine ace?"

The kid looked steadily at Cobb, didn't grin.

Brad took over. "So, since it's in the air, let's clutch at it, do it. There's some ski places around here, absolutely, and we have the ability, not to ski, maybe, but to drive to the very spot where skiing can be done."

"Snow-boarding, too," said Katie.

"I think we need to get clear information on where to go," Joss said. "Me and Buster here are very good at doing that, know just the filling station to hold up for the best inside dope. We're off."

And they were, at least to the door. Joss didn't notice the paper fluttering to the floor, but the boy did.

He picked it up and handed it to Joss, who gave it back to

him, hoping to joke. "Whassa matter, kid, you lazy? Help us out. I happen to know your reading skills are top-rank."

He didn't bother to look up, just read the paper: "Sorry to have missed you. Catch you next time."

"Shit!" Joss sputtered, truly angry. "I'm sorry, kid. That's not for you, so don't be scared. It's these creeps stalking us, I suppose, the Wilfreds. You know them?"

The kid looked at her, no confusion on his face. But he said nothing.

Joss at least knew when not to stop: "You one of them?"

The kid's expression changed, but it wasn't clear how.

Cobb cut into the mess: "Joss, for Christ's sake!"

Joss looked at him as if she were about to say something wounding, didn't. She reached to grab the kid's arm, so as to usher him out, but drew back when the kid flinched a little.

So they drove down the road a mile or two. Joss went round the aisles inside the gas station picking up things they didn't need just so their salesclerk friend wouldn't think they were using him as nothing more than the local tourist bureau, of which there doubtless was one, Joss suddenly thought, were they able to locate it, which, with minimal effort, they could.... Oh, fuck it.

"Hi!" said the handsome boy behind the counter, who seemed not to resent his role in all this. "What tips today? Tattoo parlors, hunting supplies, movie theaters, water sports, massages — which you can get right here?"

"Nah, just a date," Joss said, almost smiling.

"I'll abandon the shop. We taking your brother here along?"

The boy didn't bother to look up.

"We'll just take these overpriced essentials, if you please," Joss said, "along with your best recommendation on skiing. Is there a ski place around?"

"There are twenty-seven ski places around, counting two that have been condemned but insist on operating anyhow. All will be delighted to rent you stuff, instruct you, cart you up the hill and charge you about $3 thousand dollars per person — that's midweek and half-day rates, of course."

The kid did look up at this, with a half-smile. Both Joss and the clerk noticed. The clerk was about to try his friendlies on the boy, thought better of it.

"Which is the best of all, the premier spot?"

"Actually, you're better off going to any of them pretty early in the morning, get a few runs in before the lift lines get real long. If you can, I'd put it off for a day."

"Oh. I don't know what we'd do today," Joss said before she thought.

"You know, you wouldn't have to ski. There are places with hot tubs and that sort of Yuppie fun."

He looked again at the boy, who was now smiling more fully.

"Or, even better, one place I know of with dog-sledding. They also offer ever so many other diversions: snow-tubing, snowmobiles, even old-fashioned sled-riding on hills especially designed."

Joss nodded, nudged the kid: "That okay by you?"

He elbowed Joss back. She wondered if he was starting a fun game, decided he wasn't. "Tell me straight, Elbow-Elmer, is that okay or not?"

"Yes, Joss. That is okay."

"You gotta shoot me straight. I can't read your damned mind."

She stopped and looked more closely at the boy.

"I wish you'd really tell me, kid. I don't remember what it was like to be your age, don't know if I ever was. Anyhow, I know nothing about you. I'm sure that's how you want it, but I do wish...."

The kid looked straight at her, didn't blink.

The clerk seemed as much a part of this as anyone, decided he'd insert his views: "I think you would like this place a lot, I really do. Kid, you would for sure. If you don't enjoy one thing, try another. And this operation I'm pointing you to, with my excellent directions I've been sketching out on the company napkin here, isn't all that expensive. It ain't free, but it's not as repellant as Squaw Valley or them there spots."

It was thus determined.

* * *

Back at the cabin, the four took counsel on the Wilfred situation. Cobb had done a run around the house, looking for tracks, just like Chingachgook. Trouble was it was snowing a bit, and Joss and the boy had made prints walking to the car and.... Nothing conclusive.

"I think what we can do is pose for them, accept our role as sitting ducks," said Joss.

Nobody seemed to have a better idea.

"Just keep our guns with us," Brad said. They probably know we have them, but there's still a chance we can spot them first or, at least, find a way to save ourselves from being staked and flayed alive."

"Jesus, Brad. How's you skin, by the way?"

"Much better, Katie. I assume you mean the skin that was. Anyhow, enough about me. I'm going to go talk to the boy."

Nobody bothered to ask Brad what he meant to discuss with the boy or why he wanted to do so. He appeared to know what he was doing.

Brad knocked, softly asked permission to enter.

"Yes."

The kid was, as directed, getting on warm clothes, layer after layer. Right now, he had on only his underpants and socks. Brad was not prepared for the display of bones and scars. So little there that seemed healthy or sound — so much torment.

"I'm sorry. I'll come back."

"That's okay, Brad. You can stay. Should I stop?"

"No, no. Keep going. I just wanted to talk with you about you and us and the Wilfreds. Do you mind?"

"No."

"Do you mind if I call you 'Huck,' after the novel? You seem a lot like him — on the run, trying not to be caught, sharpening your eye for traps set by everybody around you, people like the Wilfreds — and people like us."

"Huck? Thank you."

"You know what I mean by traps, don't you?"

"I don't know."

"C'mon. This right here is not a trap."

"Brad, I do know about traps. I try to."

"Right. I don't know if it helps that we try to know about them, too. That's why we're doing all this crazy shit, trying hard to break out. But our traps are different from the ones set for you, I know."

"Not all of them."

"Thanks, Huck. Anyhow, I'm not trying to get inside you, uncover your secrets or anything. Please believe me."

The boy nodded.

"And please go ahead getting stuff on. I didn't mean to spy on you."

The boy nodded again, resumed dressing, keeping his eyes steadily on Brad.

"I guess I'm not sure what else I wanted to say — just that we don't, down deep, mean to be hurting you and that we know we are doing just that. And — I think I know the answer to this — is there something you'd like us to do for you?"

"What do you mean, Brad?"

"I don't mean buy you stuff or give you money. I just mean, is there some way we can help by, say, loosening the reins, opening up, getting out of the way?"

The boy seemed to understand, said nothing, though, waited.

"I know we have surrounded you, tried to protect you, all along knowing that was the wrong thing to do."

The boy dropped the sweatshirt he was holding and stood.

"Worst of all," Brad said, standing too, "we have not kept ourselves from loving you, wanting things for you that are not ours to give."

The boy made no avowals, advanced no farther into the room. Something, however, had changed.

Brad knew he should switch grounds. "You know what I'm talking about when I mentioned the Wilfreds, right?"

"Yes."

"Okay, Huck. Get yourself dressed. Sorry to have yammered at you for so long."

He turned to go, felt a hand on his arm. "I do know what you are talking about, Brad."

"Oh."

"About the Wilfreds. About everything."

"I thought you did."

"Yes.

Chapter 21

They did the best they could to have a day of fun, found the place without any difficulty and dutifully engaged in all the activities, starting with dog-sledding, the best part of which, for sure, were the dogs. They all — the four big people, anyhow — imagined that the dogs would be well-trained forms of pit-bulls, anything but the wagging, slurping cuddlers they turned out to be, once unharnessed and able to connect. The kid, of course, responded most fully to that part, getting in with them and rolling around.

They hated to call him out of the pen and such a romp, so they didn't. The guys running the place seemed to sense something or maybe just didn't give a shit and let the frolicking go on for some time before hitching up the dogs for another set of customers. The dogs seemed sorry to go. For sure, the boy was.

None of the other three had taken to calling him "Huck." Maybe it was a private matter between the kid and Brad.

Private times did occur up here, as they found themselves splitting off, as they hadn't done in so long, into boy-boy/girl-girl pairs. The kid was shifting among the four, being hustled into the high-priced activities and sometimes left to fend for himself.

Brad and Cobb had run into one another at the bottom of the hill, spilling and rolling over in the snow. They clambered to their feet, brushing snow away here and there but enjoying the feel, the idea of being rumpled and thrown.

"I'd forgotten what a kick in the ass sled-riding is, Brad!"

"Yeah, me too."

"Like you ever did it before, LA boy! Tell the truth."

"Maybe not. I can't remember, Cobb. Damn. Did some day-trip things up to Big Bear, but I guess that was skiing and snowboarding. No, wait — yes, sled-riding, too. Ran into a tree."

"Without which no experience is complete. You think your kid is having a good time?"

"Here, you mean, today? I'd say no. He sees too much, Cobb, smarter than hell, but you know that."

"He sees right through *us*."

"That he does."

"Where does all this lead, Brad? I know we're not supposed to think that way, but, hell, we more or less have taken in this child, kidnapped him, one might say."

"That's what I'd say myself. Not technically, but maybe so. We could have reported him, gone to some agency or other, the police."

They were still standing at the bottom of the run, endangering other sledders who were forced into making a choice between sudden swerving and collisions. Finally noticing, Brad reached for Cobb's shoulder to pull him away, missed, started to slip in the snow, righted his body only by attaching himself firmly to Cobb's hand (luckily the uninjured one), school-children in a line, taking care of one another.

"Watch it there, Waldo," Cobb said, not releasing the hand. "Anyhow, taking this kid to the cops is going to land him right where he's trying to escape from, likely. Don't you think, Brad?"

"I do."

"So, what if we let him think this through, try ourselves to stay clear, not force it? He'll let us know."

"If he can."

"He can, Brad, no question about that."

"You're right, Cobb. There's no good answer. He knows we're a snare, no matter what. But...."

"But what?"

"He may be able to escape us, fly by the nets we're setting up."

"I can't help hoping he doesn't."

"Yeah. I know. We all feel that way. Wish we had more going for us than hope."

"Do the Wilfreds know about him, Brad?"

Brad wished he could brush off Cobb's concern, necessary as it was. He tried to call up a sneer, dismissing such an obvious question. Failing that, he fell back on silence.

* * *

Katie and Joss had been together less often than Brad and Cobb the last few days but still had to work to avoid the same raw subjects. They had escaped the hilarity of snowmobiling (the shorter track) and found the snack shop, treating themselves to hot drinks, relishing some fatty confection made with heavy chocolate and whole milk and, like thousands of others, imagining that the exercise and cold weather excused it.

"Do you know where the kid is, Joss?"

"With the boys, maybe."

"Don't you worry that he may get lost, or.... Okay, he's sure to know where we are."

"If he cares."

"Well, Joss, I think he cares, if only to avoid us."

They were sitting side-by-side on picnic-style benches in the hoked-up rustic dining room, arranged to discourage long-term sitters. Katie had loosened her ski jacket and taken off her hat, letting her blonde hair stream out, seductive and careless.

"Joss, what can we do that makes any sense?"

"Keep ourselves between him and the Wilfreds."

"You think they're after him?"

"I don't know. They can't be unaware that he's with us. Remember where we found him."

"Or he found us."

"Yeah. You know, Katie, I thought at first he might be part of them, a fiendish decoy."

"He was creepy as hell then."

"Not now?"

"No, not creepy, not at all But he knows something about the Wilfreds, clear as anything. Not that anything's very fucking clear." Katie laughed, put a gloved hand on Joss's arm. "I'd love to know. Wish he trusted us enough to tell us. That might help."

"If he thought it'd help, he'd tell us. Not like we're as big a threat as they."

"At least we're a threat with different snares."

"Want a refill?"

"Oh yes. And tell you what, you get 'em. You pay, too."

* * *

As Joss was looking about to orient herself, find the line to the counter, she happened to see him, over in the far corner, hidden for a minute behind a hot chocolate cup of his own, then, when she shifted, coming into view. There was a man opposite him, a big man, talking to the boy, who did not appear to be part of the conversation, seemed intent on examining his cup.

"Hssst. Katie. Over there!"

Katie stood, turned, saw the pair. "Let's get him."

"Wait, Katie. Maybe he knows the guy. We don't want to rush in, assume it's an abductor, make things worse."

"Oh, yeah."

So they did their best to act casual, approaching the area, then pretending they only just at that moment spotted the kid.

"There you are!"

Both were looking at the man, who looked back, none too

happy to see them, they thought. Maybe that's what they wanted, in some perverse way, to see: danger and intrigue, a charming mystery they could solve.

The boy looked up, his face, as usual, indicating nothing whatever.

Katie and Joss slid in on either side of him.

Silence.

Joss: "You two know one another?"

The man now smiled, seeming a good bit less imposing up close. He looked across the table at the kid, clearly giving him first dibs, should he choose. He didn't.

"I just got off a mobile, came in to get warm, saw the child here alone, took it upon myself to get him a hot chocolate, keep him company. Hope that's okay. He was filling me in on things."

"He was? You were?" Joss and Katie were dumbfounded.

"Well, I'm afraid I was dominating, running my mouth the way I always do. I'm sorry. My name's Walter Corrigan, Wally to my friends, both of them."

The thing was, Wally's joke about having no friends seemed to both Katie and Joss almost certainly no joke. All of a sudden, he seemed less like a practiced abductor than a lonely, lonely guy, hoping the kid would give him what he never got — a smile, laugh, answer back.

Both were struck by what a bad choice he'd made: one Bartleby chatting it up with another. Two bits of wreck in the mid-Atlantic.

Neither Joss nor Katie spoke, ensnared in so many emotions: wonder, puzzlement, pity. Finally, the kid did: "Mr. Corrigan bought me the hot chocolate. Thanks again, Mr. Corrigan. He's been telling me about what he did back when he was my age."

That he was speaking at all was remarkable, that he was, just maybe, connecting with forlorn Wally Corrigan was right up there with the Lazarus miracle.

"Thanks to you, son. Yeah, I was recreating my childhood, the good parts."

He stopped, not wanting, Joss and Katie felt, to add any bids for sympathy, certainly not to the boy.

"Where did you grow up?" Katie asked.

He looked at her with undisguised gratitude. "Not too far from here. Silver City, which is the grand name without the grand thing, I'm afraid, though it was sure good enough for me. I had some happy times there. Are you all from California?"

The conversation had nowhere to travel, sputtered a while, Joss and Katie feeding the big guy questions, which were then bounced right back to them. Finally, vacancy took them over and the man stood to leave, first shaking hands with the women and smiling at the boy. As he started out, though, the boy ran to him and shook his hand, gave him what might be mistaken for a mini-hug.

He returned, sat down, frowned up at Joss and Katie and said in a voice they hadn't heard from him, low-toned and gruff: "Well?"

Neither had any idea how to respond, were still searching when the kid broke into giggles, proving that the first time was not their imagination.

"You are going to lecture me on not talking to strangers."

"Hell's fire, we're strangers, us four," Joss said.

"And I don't talk to you."

Katie laughed.

The boy went on. "Would you like me to tell you about my youth in Silver City?"

Neither knew what to say.

"Well, too late. You missed some very terrific stories. Not true but terrific."

This was not the kid they were harboring and used to, not their kid.

"What the hell is going on, Meatball? You have us all twisted in knots trying to figure you out, wondering what we should do, what would be best."

The kid looked at Joss, who had spoken. She wanted him

to think she was kidding, but she really wasn't, and the kid knew it.

"Well, it was me found you."

They hoped, Joss and Katie, that wasn't the end of it, so they waited.

"I found you. That tell you something?"

"What does it tell us?" Katie said.

"You should worry less. I'm nothing to be worrying about."

The impulse both women had was one they immediately distrusted, then blocked. Was he mocking them? Playing to their sentimental notions? Testing them?

"I don't know what to do," the boy said, smiling. "I didn't know what to do when I found you, so you haven't messed me up. Not too much. Not yet. I know you think that. Brad told me. You think you are trapping me. Stop thinking that."

"Brad told you we were trapping you?"

"He thought that's what I thought."

"Do you?"

"See what I mean? You're as bad as he is. Let's talk about something else, like going back where the dogs are."

"You want another ride?"

"No, no. I just want to see the dogs. Is that okay?"

They saw that the conversation, promising so much and delivering nothing they could locate, was over. Katie and Joss did take him back to the dog-sled area, discovered that the dogs were not to be wrestled with by nonpaying customers, surreptitiously slipped the attendant the fare and ushered the kid in where the animals were clearly happy to see him.

They both watched and waited, realizing that the day had wound down, that nothing was left but to find the larger boys and retreat. No enlightenment had arrived, no new maps. Perhaps nothing had happened. But neither girl believed that.

* * *

They had thought about locating a fancy restaurant for dinner, then realized how bad an idea that was. Most importantly, the boy would hate it, find it just one more torment. So, they veered sharply to the other extreme, picked up canned chili, soda crackers, and ice cream. They found it to be just the thing — delicious, food of the gods. Made them wonder why they ever served up anything else.

The boy had appeared in the kitchen, seemed anxious to help, so they let him open the cans, heat the grub, set the table, dish up the ice-cream, which he himself ate as a prelude and accompaniment to the chili.

They talked very little during the meal, mostly just grunted.

Afterwards, everyone just about sleeping in their chairs, Katie said, "Should we give in to our natural instincts and collapse, setting alarms for early-early so we can beat the crowds to them lift lines at the fancy resort we're going to bless?"

Nobody seemed to register anything she said except for the part about sleeping, nobody except the boy, who nodded slightly. Brad noticed. "Yeah, Huck?"

"Thank you. I think you all are needing more rest. Brad and Cobb need rest, that is certain."

Nobody seemed to react, perhaps not registering what he said.

"I need rest."

The boy got the personal plea out with visible difficulty, the last card in the deck.

Joss saw most quickly. "You think we're spending too much money."

The boy looked at her.

Joss saw what the others didn't, it seemed, at least kept at it. "You recognize that we're being led around by the nose, really, doing stuff that's in the vicinity because we happen to be here, not trying really to enjoy ourselves but letting these asshole outdoor-snow-fun corporations define for us what we should be doing and charging big bucks for our sheep-like compliance. You see it all, kid. Goddamn you. You're spooky."

She didn't smile but the kid did.

"So, you bossy shit, how we going to pass the time tomorrow, what plans you have for us?"

"No plans." He paused and repeated it, with some emphasis.

They all looked at the boy as if he'd whacked their hands with a ruler, reprimanded them sternly, reminded them of what they were doing, who they were hoping to be.

Chapter 22

Next morning dawned drearily enough, not that any of our four would have known it. The boy was awake but still in bed, studying the ceiling. He thought about getting up, getting the cereal out. He wondered if there were something else he could do: sweep, scrub, put a misplaced something back where it should be. But the noise he'd make doing that. As long as they were asleep....

It was some time before he heard anyone stirring about, a toilet flushing. He got dressed quickly, changing yet again into new clothes. Same hat, but clean and fresh-smelling socks, underwear, T-shirt, jeans. He'd never had jeans this soft, wondered how well they might hold up to rough weather, dirt. And these strange, rich-kid sneakers. He looked at the different sets of snow- and hiking boots settled beneath his bed, felt a momentary pang of guilt, or maybe fright, wondering if he might sell back the ski boots, give them to someone. But who that needed shoes could use ski-boots? He'd tried them on, knew they were too heavy for anything but skiing.

He'd also asked the boy working at the sled-dog place whether anyone could make good time on skis going through the woods, putting territory behind them. They'd told him it really wouldn't work, cross-country skiing, except on established trails. Established trails were no good to him.

He waited a bit more, waited for conversation, knowing it would be hushed, whispers to respect his sleeping. He found himself rubbing his right arm, an old wound. Trying not to recall the time or place that had given rise to it, he moved across the room, looked in the mirror. Some terrible thing looked back at him, hateful and challenging. How long since he had looked in a mirror? He studied the figure for a minute, did not change expression or try out different frowns and squints. So that's what he looked like. Ugly. He hadn't remembered that.

Then unmistakable voices, still low. Time to stop hiding.

* * *

"Hi, kid!"

"Hello. I can do that."

He pointed toward the kitchen. Cobb, who had begun piddling about aimlessly, smiled at him, considered a joke, couldn't think of one, and moved aside.

All four seemed a little shy, suddenly uncertain. The boy knew what that was all about, where to find a remedy.

"Today, I am in charge. You all must obey me. Anyone who does not — well, I do not need to tell you."

"Not the water torture, the ants in the jock strap, the tickling torment, the hair-pull, the nose squeeze!" said Brad.

"Much worse. Worse than you can invent. Worse than what's in the worst comic book or video game."

"We'll obey," said Katie. "What should we do first?"

"First, sit down right here in the kitchen while I get stuff out to eat. Anyone who doesn't sit gets no ice cream."

Cereal, ice cream, and, this time, *salsa* and chips. They all ate some of each.

"Anyone have any complaining to do? No? Good."

"So, what now, master? Do you want your feet washed, your back rubbed, your nails trimmed?" This also from Katie.

The boy looked a little sad.

"I think we can today rest a little this morning, stay indoors until it gets up to where we won't freeze right away, then start our outdoors things. What would you like to do? Or we can go outside right now if you want."

Cobb stood up fast. "I'll clean up here while you camp directors determine the daily schedule. It's not in my line. You leave it to me, I'm likely to insist on charades or RISK or hide-and-seek, even though the last one might not present too many challenges in this house without hiding places."

"I vote for charades and for making Cobb deputy director, rather vice-director, in case Whammo Boy gets tired of the position," said Joss.

So, charades it was, giving them all a chance to be uncomfortable, pass a little time, and wonder what the hell they were doing.

Cobb wanted to stay in the kitchen, pretending that he needed to do so to equalize the sides, two-each, but the others pointed out an oft-overlooked feature of the game: charades does not require equality, larger numbers on any side being, very likely, a liability.

Making up clues, though, was a tough one for both sides, all except the boy, who filled three blank cards at once: "The Mississippi River," "Shop Till You Drop," and "Make America Great Again." None connected in any way with the boy, but the phrases that did connect he rejected quickly.

"Okay. Brad gets to act out for Joss, that being the total population of the Shiny Team. They go first, Dull Team, so be silent and don't give it away."

Brad drew "Mississippi River," took the full sixty seconds allotted for considering, then started to act out what he realized he couldn't use — "first name, four syllables, first syllable, sounds like—" then a pantomime of missing, as in a bad basketball shot. Nobody knew what he was doing. Thinking fast, he came up with nothing, then thought of "kiss," sounds like, which was easy enough to get across, but led Joss to a lot of guesses so far off the mark as to be exasperating: *"Bismarck, Lusitania, Kiss the Girls and Made Them Cry, Mistletoe Madness."* Brad shoved the four-syllable sign (four fingers) in Joss's face, producing "Disanthropy,

Disestablishment, Fishmongering — give me another clue, asshole!"

With the help of some against-the-rules mouthing, Joss final got it, in a whizzing six and a half minutes.

The Dull Team pushed the boy out to the front. He drew from the hat and looked briefly at his clue. 4 words, first word: and he pointed to his eye and they got it, Katie did. Third word, sounds like: and he pantomimed getting burned, which brought forth: burned, stove, ouch, stop, and finally, hot, which sounded like shot, bought, tot, mot (?), and finally got. "I Blank Got Blank." Is it "I Wish I Got A — No, can't be that."

Second word. Sounds like — he went over to the wall and moved his hand up and down, producing " saw, plane, up-n-down, and wave." Then he waved his hands to cancel and suddenly rolled his eyes back and collapsed on the floor. That did it: "faint." Sounds like — and finally to "ain't." I ain't got blank.

"I ain't got shit? I ain't got time? I ain't got a date?"

It seemed to hit them both simultaneously, but neither wanted to say it. The kid stared at them and then, maybe for a clue, looked all around the room slowly and then up toward the ceiling, holding his hands out to catch something and then dropping them.

"Nobody. Oh shit, kid!"

The kid smiled, sat down, and not one of them wanted to play anymore. The four big people wondered how they could cancel all this, go back before that phrase entered the room, let the boy know that he wasn't attached to nothing, that he had them, always would. But each knew better than to produce what would look so much like a noose.

They sat in blunt silence for a full minute. Cobb, who was sitting with his feet resting, propped up on the edge of the coffee table was the first to become so edgy at the silence that he felt he had to break it. "When in doubt, stand and shout! I've got some clout, so just hear me out!"

Katie stood up from her hunkered position, walked over to Cobb, hauled him to his feet, and kissed him, full on the mouth. Then: "You made that up on the spot, right, Ace? You had no idea what might follow or why you said it?"

"I thought anything was better than silence — even that. As it happens, though, I do have an idea, though I should clear it first with Boss Man here. What do you say to the oldest game ever, 'I See Something You Don't See?' Huh?"

"Okay."

That left them no choice but to regress to that time-filler and then, after something less than ten minutes, pretend that it had warmed up a little, enough so they could venture out to cold-weather hilarity.

"Brad, could I see you — back there?"

"Sure, Huck."

The kid let Brad go first into his room and then shut the door behind him. Not saying anything at first, he collected his warm wear and started to exchange his tennis shoes for boots.

Then: "You guys are doing stuff you don't want to do at all, just to try and be nice to me. What would you be doing otherwise?"

Brad didn't bother to contradict him: "We'd probably be doing separate stuff along about now. You know — one person this, another that. Me, I'd be reading, I expect."

"Yeah."

"But that's okay. We can go outside and have a great time."

"Or—"

"Or, I guess we could do separate stuff."

"You said reading. How about if we read out loud, taking turns?"

"Really, Huck? We've never done that."

"Julie and I did. You know, what we came out and read to all of you."

"Yeah. That was great. Well, sure, then. I know the other three will love the idea. What book? You know one? You got one, I mean?"

"I do. I have four. You know, the new ones and the old ones."

Brad didn't try to decipher that, just looked at him, finally smiled. "Here's a thought, Buddy. We'll get everyone to read a favorite passage from a book, just like you and Julie did. Then you can do one, too. What about that?"

"A passage? Just a small part, you mean?"

"Yeah, we'll make up the rules, you and me: no real long things and no explaining them. Just read 'em and shut up. Whatdya say?"

The kid grinned, then added, "No singing allowed and no worrying about why it is you picked the passage you did." Then he shed his sweater and replaced boots with tennis shoes, retaining his green hat.

* * *

Brad announced the plan and its origin. Everyone looked at the boy, then nodded, then retreated to their private pile of stuff to find their book and their passage. Brad had allotted fifteen minutes for the search and recovery, but they needed far less, soon were reassembled, those who could manage it sitting cross-legged, staring at their chosen words, reading to themselves, moving their lips.

"Wait just a minute!" Katie hopped up or tried to, buckling for a second and then righting herself. She made it to the kitchen and shortly reappeared with a tray of sodas.

Brad then announced that as it was Huck's idea, he had to go last, the climactic slot, and that he, as the most well trained in elocution, would lead off. He repeated the rules: just read, no setting the stage, no explaining. You can leave things out or change words as you wish. Just don't tell us about it or justify it.

Then Brad set right to it. It didn't hurt that he was the best reader of the lot.

> *The Lisbon girls made suicide familiar. Later, when other acquaintances chose to end their lives—*

sometimes even borrowing a book the day before — we always pictured them on different paths, each having deciphered the secret to cowardice or bravery, whatever it was. And the Lisbon girls were always there before them. They had killed themselves over our dying forests, over manatees maimed by propellers as they surfaced to drink from garden hoses; they had killed themselves at the sight of used tires stacked higher than the pyramids; they had killed themselves over a failure to find a love none of us could ever be. In the end, the tortures tearing the Lisbon girls pointed to a simple reasoned refusal to accept the world as it was handed down to them, so full of flaws.

What lingered after them was not life, which always overcomes natural death, but the most trivial of mundane facts: a clock ticking on a wall, a room dim at noon. Then the rope thrown over the beam, the sleeping pill dropped in the palm with the long, lying lifeline, the window thrown open, the oven turned on, whatever. We couldn't help but retrace their steps, rethink their thoughts, and see that none of them led to us. We couldn't imagine the emptiness of a creature who could put a razor to her wrist and open her veins, the emptiness and the calm. And we had to smear our muzzles in their last traces, of mud marks on the floor, trunks kicked out from under them; we had to breathe forever the air of the rooms in which they had killed themselves. It didn't matter in the end how old they had been, or that they were girls, but only that we had loved them, and that they hadn't heard us calling, still do not hear us, up here in the tree house, with our thinning hair and soft bellies, calling them out of those rooms where they went to be alone for all time, alone in suicide, which is deeper than death, and where we will never find the pieces to put them back together.

All were silent, not because they were obeying the

announced rules against commenting. Nobody was crying, though the boy seemed to be squinting. Probably it was just a trick of the light.

"I'll go now," said Katie. And she did.

The close questioning the three survivors received later at the Review revealed that their training in how to meet fire emergencies consisted of a small handful of instructions, four to be exact and only one of which had any bearing on their present emergency: "remember that, whatever you do, you must not allow the fire to pick the spot where it hits you." The chances are it will hit you where it is burning fiercest and fastest. According to Dodge's later testimony, the fire about to hit them had a solid front 250 to 300 feet deep — no one works through that deep a front and lives.

Dodge survived, and Rumsey and Sallee survived. Their means of survival differed. Rumsey and Sallee went for the top and relied on soul and a fixation from basic training. The soul in a situation like this is mostly being young, in tune with time, and having good legs, an inflexible destination, and no paralyzing questions about what lies up beyond. But no matter where you put your trust, then and now, you have to be lucky.

The accounts that come down to us of the flight of the crew up the hillside nearly all conclude at this point. Only a sentence or two is given to those who, when last seen by Dodge, were all going in one direction, and when last seen by Sallee were angling through openings in the smoke below him as he looked down from the top of the ridge. Although they are the missing persons in this story, they are also its tragic victims. There is a simple aspect of historiography, of course, to explain why, after last seen by the living, they pass silently out of the story and their own tragedy until their tragedy is over and they are found as bodies: no one who lived saw their sufferings. The historian, for a variety of reasons, can limit his account to firsthand witnesses, although a shortage of firsthand witnesses probably does not explain completely why contemporary accounts of the Mann Gulch fire avert their eyes from the tragedy.

If a storyteller thinks enough of storytelling to regard it as a calling, unlike a historian he cannot turn from the suffering of his characters. A storyteller, unlike a historian, must follow compassion wherever it leads him. He must be able to accompany his characters even into smoke and fire, and bear witness to what they thought and felt even when they themselves no longer knew. The story of the Mann Gulch fire will not end until it feels able to walk the final distance to the crosses with those who for the time being are blotted out by smoke. They were young and did not leave much behind them and need someone to remember them.

"Do we really have to keep quiet?" said Cobb, "no responses at all, not even short ones?"

"I just thought of a new rule," said the boy.

So strange was the comment, so strange he'd be commenting, that everyone froze, looked at him.

"After we're all done, we draw straws. You know what that means?" Everyone nodded.

"Okay. The short straw has to— You guys guess."

"Declare a winner?" Cobb ventured. Otherwise silence.

"Cobb! Who wants winners? That'd be none of us. Go again. The short straw has to," said the boy, looking solemnly around.

Nobody said anything.

The boy glared, maybe just mocking them, "Go a second time."

"How about you go?" said Katie.

"Nope. Against the rules to do that," he said, no glimmer of a smile. "Short straw, like it or not. That's the rule. So everybody prepare a second."

Joss went ahead and said what they were all suddenly thinking, "Kid, where in hell did you pick up all this here book-larnin? Back a few days ago you were speaking silly Spanish and pidgin English. Now you talk like a prep school hotshot. What the hell is going on?"

Now the boy did smile, smiled and then crossed his legs, an imitation, they all recognized, of Cobb's habitual flailings. Then he waved his hands in the air, flapped his shoulders back and forth, and bobbed his head, including everyone present in his parodies.

They recognized his authority in all this, his demand that no more questions be raised.

Cobb put up his hand, but nobody called on him, so he just launched into his reading. Seemed to start, but then broke the rules (again) by launching a preamble—"I should say that my choice, though I love it, is not, maybe, literary. It's...."

The kid, along with Joss and Brad, then waved their hands insistently before Cobb's face, reminding him.

"Oh," he said, and began.

> *Now, I must say a word more and then I will leave this with you where I should have left it long ago.*
>
> *I have stood here for three months as one might stand at the ocean trying to sweep back the tide. I hope the seas are subsiding and the wind is falling, and I believe they are, but I wish to make no false pretense to this court. The easy thing and the popular thing to do is to hang my clients. I know it. Men and women who do not think will applaud. It will be easy today; but in Chicago, and reaching out over the length and breadth of the land, more and more fathers and mothers, the humane, the kind, and the hopeful, who are gaining an understanding and asking questions not only about*

these poor boys but about their own, these will join in no acclaim at the death of my clients. But, Your Honor, what they shall ask may not count. I know what is the easy way.

I know the future is with me, and what I stand for here; not merely for the lives of these two unfortunate lads, but for all boys and all girls. I am pleading for life, understanding, charity, kindness, and the infinite mercy that considers all. I am pleading that we overcome cruelty with kindness and hatred with love. I know the future is on my side. Your Honor stands between the past and the future. You may hang these boys; you may hang them, by the neck until they are dead. But in doing it you will turn your face toward the past. In doing it you are making it harder for every other boy who in ignorance and darkness must grope his way through the mazes which only childhood knows.

I am pleading for the future; I am pleading for a time when hatred and cruelty will not control the hearts of men. When we can learn by understanding and faith that all life is worth saving, and that mercy is the highest attribute of man.

I feel that I should apologize for the length of time I have taken. This case may not be as important as I think it is, and I am sure I do not need to tell this court, or to tell my friends, that I would fight just as hard for the poor as for the rich. If I should succeed in saving these boys' lives and do nothing for the progress of the law, I should feel sad, indeed. If I can succeed, my greatest reward and my greatest hope will be that I have done something for the tens of thousands of other boys, or the countless unfortunates who must tread the same road in blind childhood that these poor boys have trod.

I was reading last night of the aspiration of the old

*Persian poet, Omar Khayyam. It appealed to me as the
highest that we can envision. I wish it was in my
heart, and I wish it was in the hearts of all:*
> *So I be written in the Book of Love,*
> *I do not care about that Book above.*
> *Erase my name or write it as you will,*
> *So I be written in the Book of Love.*

"May I ask one question?" Katie ventured, after a long, long silence.

"Well," said the boy, clearly thinking 'No' and hoping she would read his thoughts.

She did. "Okay."

Joss stood where the other reciters had placed themselves, students in an old 19th Century schoolroom, reciting, caught in a set of official orders they had internalized, now so much a part of them that choice had nothing to do with it.

> *When they began the second round of that last dinner, it was past five o'clock, and nearing twilight. It was the time of afternoon when in the old days, sitting with the red cards at the table, they would sometimes begin to criticize the Creator. They would judge the work of God and mention the ways how they would improve the world. And Holy Lord God John Henry's voice would rise up happy and high and strange, and his world was a mixture of delicious and freak, and he did not think in global terms: the sudden long arm that could stretch from here to California, chocolate dirt and rains of lemonade, the extra eye seeing a thousand miles, a hinged tail that could be let down as a kind of prop to sit on when you wished to rest, the candy flowers.*
>
> *But the word of the Holy Lord God Berenice Sadie Brown was a different world, and it was round and just and reasonable. First, there would be no separate*

colored people in the world, but all human beings would be light brown color with blue eyes and black hair. There would be no colored people and no white people to make the colored people feel cheap and sorry all through their lives. No colored people but all human men and ladies and children as one loving family on the earth. And when Berenice spoke of this first principle her voice was a strong deep song that soared and sang in beautiful dark tones leaving an echo in the corners of the room that trembled for a long time until silence.

No war, said Berenice. No stiff corpses hanging from the Europe trees and no Jews murdered anywhere. No war, and the young boys leaving home in army suits, and no wild cruel Germans and Japanese. No war in the whole world, but peace in all countries everywhere. Also, no starving. To begin with, the real Lord God had made free air and free rain and free dirt for the benefit of all. There would be free food for every human mouth, free meals and two pounds of fatback a week, and after that each able-bodied person would work for whatever else he wished to own or eat. No killed Jews and no hurt colored people. No war and no hunger in the world. And, finally, Ludie Freeman would be alive.

The world of Berenice was a round world, and the old Frankie would listen to the strong deep singing voice, and she would agree with Berenice. But the old Frankie's world was the best of the three worlds. She agreed with Berenice about the main laws of her creation, but she added many things: an aeroplane and a motorcycle to each person, a world club with certificates and badges, and a better law of gravity. She did not completely agree with Berenice about the war, and sometimes she said she would have one War Island where those who wanted could go, and fight or donate blood, and she might go for a while as a WAC in the

*Air Corps. She also changed the seasons, leaving out
summer altogether, and adding much snow. She
planned it so that people could instantly change back
and forth from boys to girls, which ever way they felt
like and wanted. But Berenice would argue with her
about this, insisting that the law of human sex was
exactly right just as it was and could in no way be
improved. And then John Henry would very likely add
his two cents' worth about this time, and think that
people ought to be half boy and half girl, and when the
old Frankie threatened to take him to the Fair and sell
him to the Freak Pavilion, he would only close his eyes
and smile.*

   *So the three of them would sit there at the kitchen
table and criticize the creator and the work of god.
Sometimes their voices crossed and the three worlds
twisted. The Holy Lord God John Henry West. The
Holy Lord God Berenice Sadie Brown. The Holy Lord
God Frankie Addams. The Worlds at the end of the
long stale afternoons.*

They all looked at the boy, hoping he'd not be embarrassed, ready to let him off if he showed the slightest reluctance. He did not.

"Yes, I am ready. And remember, no questions or anything. You all agreed to those rules."

"Well, Boss Man, we didn't have a hell of a lot of choice," Cobb said, sprawling out so far he was nearly horizontal. "This a democracy or not?"

"Not," the boy said, not smiling. "So, we all set?"

   *Old Phoebe said something then, but I couldn't hear
her. She had the side of her mouth right smack on the
pillow, and I couldn't hear her.*

   *"What?" I said. "Take your mouth away. I can't
hear you with your mouth that way You don't like
anything that's happening."*

It made me even more depressed when she said that.

"Yes I do. Yes I do. **Sure** *I do. Don't say that. Why the hell do you say that?"*

"Because you don't. Name one thing."

Trouble was I couldn't concentrate too well. All that came to mind were those two nuns and this boy James Castle, a skinny little weak-looking guy with wrists about as big as pencils who wouldn't take something back he'd said about this very conceited boy Phil Stabile who then locked James Castle in his room and had about six other dirty bastards go at him, until James Castle jumped out of the window rather than taking it back, and when I got down the stairs, in my bathrobe and all, there he was **dead**, *and his teeth and blood were all over the place. He had on this turtleneck sweater I'd lent him and almost hadn't, since I didn't know him too well.*

"What?" I said to Phoebe. She'd said something I didn't hear.

"You can't even think of one thing."

"Yes I can. I like Allie."

"Allie's **dead**.*"*

"Don't you think I **know** *that?"*

She didn't say anything. Then, "Name something you'd like to be."

I couldn't for a minute, but I had to say something. Then it came to me: "You know what I'd like to be? I mean if I had my goddam choice?"

"What? Stop swearing."

"You know that song, 'If a body **catch** *a body comin' through the rye,' I'd like —"*

"It's 'If a body meet a body coming through the rye,' old Phoebe said. "It's a poem by Robert Burns."

"I **know** *it's a poem by Robert Burns."*

She was right, though. It is 'If a body **meet** *a body*

coming through the rye.' I didn't know it then, though.

"I thought it was 'If a body catch a body,'" I said.

"Anyways, I keep picturing all these little kids playing some game in this big field of rye and all. Thousands of little kids, and nobody's around — nobody big, I mean — except me. And I'm standing on the edge of some crazy cliff. What I have to do, I have to catch *everybody if they start to go over the cliff — I mean if they're running and they don't look where they're going I have to come out from somewhere and catch them. That's all I'd do all day. I'd just be the catcher in the rye and all. I* know *it's* crazy, *but that's the only thing I'd like to be. I know it's* crazy."

D.B. asked me what I thought of all this stuff I just finished telling you about. I don't know what the hell to say. If you want to know the truth, I don't know *what I think about it. I'm sorry I told so many people. About all I know is, I sort of* miss *everybody I told about. Even old Stradlater and Ackley, for instance. I think I even miss that goddam Maurice. It's funny. Don't ever tell anybody anything.*

Everyone was poised, waiting for the next sentence, which didn't come.

They tried not to add it themselves, figuring the kid had a reason. He had moved back to the sofa immediately upon finishing, waiting for something, maybe for someone else to take control. Nobody did, so he finally asked if anybody had straws, five straws, one of them short.

Chapter 23

The boy, nobody cheating, drew it. He seemed so distressed, Katie asked if they couldn't change the rules.

He looked even more distressed. Finally, "Okay. Here's what we do. I only know one other, and it's pretty short. And it's not really mine. Julie showed it to me."

He paused and added: "It's very hard. You won't understand it, but I do."

They all settled back, but he was still rooting around in his bag, for a book, they guessed. He found it but didn't start, kept rummaging and looking around, as if trying to locate something else. He must have done so.

"One other rule, the last rule. There is a bonus round, and it is won by Brad, as I am not going to go last, which is very bad luck and Brad won't mind, since he's already had all his bad luck. But Brad's passage cannot be too long, either, as we all must eat what I cook and then go outside, since we are not moles or bears hibernating."

Then he looked round, frowned, and seemed to consult with something inside. His face lightened, and he dropped the book back into his bag.

"I just changed my mind and that's okay. I have very good reasons, hidden from you. Hidden from me as well. Brad will go next after all and I will bring up the rear, where I am used to being. It will work much better this way. Trust me. Even if you don't trust me, obey."

The others all seemed stunned. Who was this?

Cobb broke the silence by asking directly, "Who are you?"

The boy seemed to be expecting it. "Nobody you don't know very well. I'm the same. Don't think too hard about it."

Cobb couldn't let it go. "I'm good at not thinking hard, or at all, but you're getting spooky, Mr. Shape-Shifter."

The boy looked at him, didn't answer.

Then, "Brad, your turn."

Brad seemed somehow to be ready, but that was a mirage. He excused himself, went to the room he and Cobb were sharing, banged around and emerged shortly. Brad realized his was the leadoff in this bonus round, a surprise, and he felt no need to apologize for the choice he was going to make, obvious and hardly fitting to this group, at least to the boy he was so anxious to contact. But what would connect with this kid, and was it right even to try?

Brad felt as if he should not stand, but he did, and, very shortly, started to read.

> *I cannot express it, but surely you and everybody have a notion that there is or should be an existence of yours beyond you. What were the use of creation, if I were entirely contained here? My great miseries in the world have been Heathcliff's miseries, and I watched and felt each from the beginning; my great thought in living is himself. If all else perished and he remained, I should still continue to be; and if all else remained and he were annihilated, the universe would turn to a mighty stranger; I should not seem a part of it. My love for Linton is like the foliage in the woods: time will change it, I'm well aware, as winter changes the trees. My love for Heathcliff is like the eternal rocks beneath — a source of little visible delight, but necessary. Nelly, I am Heathcliff.*

Brad was, as always, so moved by the passage, wanted to read it again, go back and live once more inside Catherine's anguish, her tragic declaration. He wanted to explain that

Heathcliff had been overhearing but had slipped out earlier, just a flicker before she declares her love for him—"he shall never know how I love him." She is wrong about that — he finally does know — but not wrong about how everything is stacked against them, how the conditions of this life will never allow for what they want, what they demand. They could compromise and live within the possible. They refuse to do that, however, and in that refusal offer to all of us the one impossible chance we have. Brad wanted so badly to say all that. More. The boy seemed to waiting for him to continue, but he knew better.

He finally slouched over to the sofa, waiting, like the others, for the boy, who seemed to have his lines right there with him.

"I said no starting explanations. That was the second rule, but the first rule has been that the rule-maker can be rule-breaker. Yes. So, I will say again that Julie showed me this. You can thank her. And you cannot ask me why I wanted to do this or what it means or, Cobb, who I am — as if you didn't know."

He then smiled, and they realized this was, in truth, the first genuine smile they had seen from him. It didn't last long, and he began:

> *For days during the rain Maria did not speak out loud or read a newspaper. She could not read newspapers because certain stories leapt at her from the page: the 4-year-olds in the abandoned refrigerator, the tea party with Purex, the infant in the driveway, rattlesnake in the playpen, the peril, unspeakable peril, in the everyday. She grew faint as the procession swept before her, the children alive when last scolded, dead when next seen, the children in the locked car burning, the little faces, helpless screams.*
>
> *"One thing in my defense," she says at the very end. "Not that it matters: I know something Carter never*

knew, or Helene, or maybe you. I know what 'nothing' means, and keep on playing. 'Why?' BZ would say. 'Why not?' I say."

He stopped and looked at them each in turn, as if adding something or asking for something. Not one of them could read him, though, so the moment passed, and he slid back into his corner sofa seat, remote as ever.

The others knew they had failed, had been too occupied with the obvious and irrelevant questions: How on earth? Where had he picked it up? Where had he been? Where had he come from, this little dark thing.

Chapter 24

"Okay. Now we need to eat, get ready for an afternoon of being cold. Is that okay?"

He seemed to have regressed, slipped back into a form closer to their field of understanding, but not close enough. That being the case, they abandoned themselves to the shifting current.

"Do we have anything to eat?" Joss said. I guess we could have cereal, but the milk's low."

"I'll go out and get milk," the boy said, "if you want me to." He didn't seem to be asking permission.

"Sure," somebody answered.

Brad threw him the keys. "You want company?"

"That's okay," said the boy.

"Money?"

"That's okay."

Then he was out the door. It seemed wrong to raise questions. Here was this kid, aged somewhere between twelve and forty, off on his own, without a license or shackles.

"That was real bright," said Joss. "What in Christ's name are we doing?"

"My worry is he has no money to buy anything — or, if he does, he shouldn't be spending it on groceries," said Katie.

"Screw that. What if he just keeps going, drives off and we're here with the Wilfreds, ready to serve as the life of their party?"

"He'll be back," Brad said. "He might not stay with us long, but he wouldn't leave that way."

"How do you know?" Cobb asked.

"I don't," Brad said, standing up and heading to the window; "I surely don't."

In any case, there was nothing for it but to wait, so that's what they did, sitting there and staring straight ahead. Finally, Katie got up and went to the kitchen, rattled around getting plates out for a meal and then putting them back, worrying that she might be preempting one of the kid's plans.

For sure, he was now the one in control.

Thirty minutes passed and no boy. Then there he was, rapping politely at the door, having somehow pulled in with no car noises at all.

They all rose, as if required to do so. If he noticed, the boy gave no indication of it, just proceeded with his three extra-full bags to the kitchen, making it clear that he needed no help.

Obedient all, nobody asked any questions.

In an impossibly short time: "Hamburgers! Chips! Salsa! Sodas! Beans! Cookies! Buns! I forgot the mustard, but maybe we have some left."

They filed into the kitchen, ready for anything. The smells were terrific, so warm and nose-tingly they couldn't imagine they were created simply by the long gap between breakfast and now.

Taking their seats, nobody insulting the cook by offering to help, they found the food before them and no prohibitions against gorging.

"What's in these hamburgers, Huck? You can't be mysterious on that. No need to tell us who you are or what magical powers you have, but do tell us your secret recipe for these wonders.

They boy didn't change expressions. By now, they knew he wouldn't. But he didn't ignore Brad's attempt to make things loose.

"It's peppers and chiles and that red powder you had and

a whole lot of salt and some of the salsa, not much, and some onions."

"Wow!" said Cobb. "That it?"

"Of course not, Cobb," said the boy. "There's a secret ingredient, two, that I have to keep to myself. I signed a paper."

Joss couldn't keep it in. "Recipes aside, kid, just what is going on? I know we've asked before and I know you won't tell us, but what is this? You start out as some mute waif and now are the most commanding person in the land. How can that be?"

He didn't seem angered by this, just looked at Joss with a new kind of suffering, and finally: "Like I say, you know very well who I am, know me. You do. And I'm not the most—whatever you said, Joss, commanding and all. Not even in this house and a half-mile around it."

It was Katie who thought she understood. "A half-mile. That's where the Wilfreds are?"

"Oh!" The boy seemed shocked. "I didn't mean that."

"Are you with them?" Katie continued, then wished she had not.

"Do you think I am, Katie?"

She didn't have to think. "No."

Silence.

"I mean it, my friend, I mean it. I know you're not some kind of plant. I know that. Believe me."

The boy seemed satisfied.

They finished the meal easily enough, thanks to Cobb and his repertoire of truly awful jokes, all of them requiring a straight man. Sample:

> *"Mr. Blotto, is it true you are UCLA's greatest comedian?"*
> *"Yes, it is true."*
> *"What is the secret of your—*
> *"Timing!"*
> *"Get it? Get it?"*

The kid seemed to have no objection to the whole team pitching in to help wash, dry, refrigerate, so they were finished quickly, stood around waiting for instructions.

"We need now to get out and work off the fat. Outside is where all the fun is, and we are going to find it!"

So unlike the boy, even his recent manifestation, that they none of them could find a response other than obedience. What would he have for them next? They retreated to their rooms and emerged shortly, draped with layers, with scarves and mittens, heavy jackets and boots. Then they collected on the side of the cabin, the side opposite the heavier woods

Just then, the kid's commanding presence vanished; either that or he decided not to disclose his ideas on what they would do now that they were out in the wild, or as much of the wild as could be found there beside the house.

Cobb to the rescue: "This snow is so thick, so goddamned deep, we can make not one, but two, snow forts, matching pairs, which we will then use as cover in the great war to come."

It was so cold the snow didn't pack all that well, nor did a few buckets of water fetched from the kitchen help. At this temperature, the water acted not as a softening but as an icing agent, which wasn't exactly what they wanted.

They had energy enough and even the skill to get the forts built, one turning out a good deal bigger than the other. That inequality mattered little, though, as they had constructed them too far apart, resulting in even the best-launched snowballs landing harmlessly in the no-man's land between. Being resourceful, they moved to the exposed front of their forts, created a cache of snow-weapons and let fire, charging and retreating, taunting and screaming in pain, most of it fabricated.

There was no reason to stop the game, so they let it go on and on, Brad finally calling a halt without meaning to.

"You know, this is the kind of thing we were after from the beginning, a sloppy game, one without rules or endings.

It battles time, a game like this, absorbs us, folds about us and creates an entire world, no winners. Keep the snowballs flying and the game will never end."

Somehow, though, saying it brought them all to the surface and then out, back to the world of afternoon suns and shadows, sequence, the need to keep thinking of what's next.

"How about dodge ball. We got a ball?"

They did, in the trunk of the car. Only the kid knew that, somehow or other. He retrieved the ball, and they did their best with it for a bit, the best being none too good in the frozen snow, on a slope, wildly uneven ground. After a time, it became too apparent that some players were slowing their pace in order to get hit, just to keep the game from collapsing.

"Fox and geese!" said Cobb, confident that he had found just the remedy for their flagging spirits. "Only let's go up the hill a ways. I think there's a flat place, up a good bit, behind that next row of house things."

"House things, Cobb?" said Joss.

"Cabins? Huts? Abodes? Mansions? Who gives a shit? Up there." He pointed, smiling.

Everybody noticed Cobb's hurt feelings, simulated enthusiasm, and trudged through the snow to where there was, indeed, a flat area, more or less, created just for fox-and-geese.

Nobody needed the rules explained, began the game preps at once, laying out a perfect circular trail, with random crossovers, some of which were out-and-out dead ends, cagily twisted so as to trap the hasty and the careless.

It was Brad who first saw trouble. "Has anybody been over here? I'm pretty sure not, but has anybody? See?"

Everyone stopped track making and came over.

Sure enough, there they were, what seemed to be footprints.

"Did any of us make them?"

Nobody bothered to respond, so, "How fresh are they?

Can we tell anything from the marks?"

They all looked at the boy, as if he really were a practiced tracking scout. He shook his head.

"There are other people around," said Joss. "I mean, other cabins and other vacationers. Seems funny to think of us vacationing, doesn't it? Seems more as if we were hiders, hiding in plain sight."

"Oh, hell with it!" Katie said. "If they're gonna, they're gonna. At least we can ignore this kind of shit. I mean, what's the miserable part of horror movies, huh? The fakes and the buildup and the shadows. When the heroine is finally beheaded, it's no big deal, right? I mean, it's not death that scares us but looking over your shoulder, trying to spot it coming at you from the least likely place."

When nobody said anything, she turned to the kid: "You agree with me, right, Freddie Krueger?"

"Yes," he said, now standing, not looking at the tracks any more, attending only to Katie.

She walked over to him, wiped her nose on her glove, and pretended to trip and fall into him, wipe her glove in his hair. He was braced somehow, put his arms around her, rocked her a little, as if in a dance. The boy took it all in stride, both the hug and the rationale for not thinking.

The others seemed to feel that any more inspection was somehow in bad taste, so they shifted easily to focus on the game, deciding the track they had made was too confined to allow for their top speed (blazing), enlarged it, and went stumbling at it, sometimes adding crossings, shortcuts, loop-de-loops.

After at least an hour, nonstop, Cobb leaned over, hands-on-knees, panting: "Anybody want to go back, warm up, get some bourbon?"

"No, Cobb, nobody is as flabby and wheezy as you are," Joss sneered. "And we don't have any bourbon, do we, kid?"

"I think we do," the boy said.

"What the hell? Do you drink?"

"Yes."

Nobody knew if Joss and the kid were talking about the same thing, and nobody knew how to make it all clear. Anyhow, who the hell cared? If he could drive, he could get drunk. Right? Besides, how old was he?

Finally, Brad did ask. "How old are you, Huck? Thirty-five?"

"You are close, Brad."

He didn't give any signs of inviting more. His age seemed just one more impossibility.

In any event, he was doing a fine job keeping things moving. He somehow let everyone know that there would be no retreating to the cabin, no warming up or cocoaing. Bourbon seemed still to be an open option, maybe later.

For the time being, they needed a new game, something fitting for the late afternoon, declining sun, and plunging thermometer. Boy to the rescue.

"Okay. We got time. We're going to play this great game. I know you have all played it before, at some point, one way or another."

The kid paused. "Am I right?"

"Yes, of course you're right," said Cobb. "Why'd you even bother to ask, you silly jackass?"

"Jackasses are not silly, Cobb. They don't put their feet into boiling water, anyhow."

Cobb stared at him, then laughed. "What an asshole you are, kid, making fun of a pathetic injured friend."

"Pathetic, for sure," Joss said. "You still wearing a dozen pairs of socks, Cobb?"

"Not so many now. Anyhow, Brad is the one who's hurt."

"I'm fine. Healing fast."

This little sideswipe into damaged bodies didn't deter the boy from his goal, the new activity, snuck into the last little bit of daylight.

"We'll play 'Track the Beast.' Three of us go off, way off, up there — " he pointed toward the thickly-forested hills behind all the houses — "and the other two have to track them down. When they find the first one — if they ever do — that poor sucker becomes one of the trackers, joins them."

Everyone stared. None of the others wanted to object, but they, each one of them, thought this was reckless — even for them.

Before anyone could find a tactful way to protest, the boy added, "The beasts get a twenty minute head start."

That detail did call forth something more than caution. What they felt now was fear, deep fear.

"No, kid, we don't have much daylight, and if...."

The boy nodded. "Five minutes."

"So, who are beasts and who are trackers?"

"Joss, Brad, and me are beasts. Cobb and Katie have to stalk. We'll get going right now."

The boy took off at once, straight up the hill. Joss and Brad both moved more slowly, exchanged what looked like knowing glances with the stalkers. Then they loped away into the bush, up only a little and to opposite sides.

"Do you think he's trying to escape from us, Katie?"

"He wanted to do that, he'd have gone off when he had the car. Maybe. Who the fuck can tell anything about him? Yeah, maybe he'll disappear. If he wants not to be found, we'll never find him, that's sure."

"Yeah, he's only staying with us to.... Wish I knew."

"You're right, Cobb. We should admit it: we have no idea why he stays. At first, I thought he was helpless."

"Me, too."

Neither bothered to say how deeply wrong they had been, to consider what that error might mean, to wonder if the boy's call for help had not registered.

Chapter 25

They set off together, following Joss's tracks, which might as well have been markers on an old-folks' jogging route. She was hiding behind a tree not a hundred yards away, happy as hell to have been found.

"Why did we ever agree to this?" The first words out of her mouth, hissed as soon as they were within range.

"We didn't have a choice, did we?" said Katie.

The other two nodded, and the three went off to collect Brad, who was scarcely more well-disguised or farther along. He actually stepped out from behind his bush, waved to them.

"You should congratulate Katie and me, Brad. We got to you and Joss in record time."

"Congratulations. Now, what the hell?"

"If we split up, we have a better chance of finding him," said Cobb.

"But we'll mess up any tracks, sure as shit," Joss said.

"We'll do that anyhow," said Brad.

"I hate the idea of him being out there alone. We don't talk about the Wilfreds, but we're probably playing into their hands by ignoring them. And who knows who they're after. Maybe him. Jesus, if we sent him off to them?"

Nobody agreed, exactly, but everybody felt the force of Joss's image: the boy out there in the snow, unspotted by anyone who wished him well, cold and darkness dropping down fast.

"To tell the truth," Cobb said, "I also don't want to be alone, so let's split the difference."

Nobody seemed confused, so they set off, Brad and Katie, Joss and Cobb, going higher, imagining they were doing just what good scouts should. It was very cold.

An aerial view would have shown the pairs keeping close, far too close if what they wanted was to cover ground. They actually stayed within visual range, which was, they recognized, stupid. But something was holding them locked together, despite wanting so badly, so very badly, to find the boy, the boy who no longer seemed to be playing a game, no longer his own agent.

They all knew they would not find him, started in saying so, outdoing one another in producing formulae of shock.

"Did we want to lose him? That why we let this happen?"

"We rescue him and then throw him away?"

"He'd rather fall off into the nothingness than return to us."

"We started on a flight into unpredictability and managed to be as lethal as our parents. Murderous and conventional at the same time."

Somehow, the babbling made them feel lighter, strangely adventurous. So, without proposing it, they finally divided into four units, spreading some and advancing directly into the fading light.

Whether they were, any of them, aware that they might be getting lost while seeking isn't clear. Whether they would have changed anything if they had so suspected isn't clear. Each of the four had a single focus now: to cover as much ground as possible, hoping not so much to find the boy as to place themselves where he would finally find one of them.

Cobb, though he never would have said so, was feeling shooting pain in his foot, so much pain that he finally started limping badly and then stopped going uphill, went laterally a few yards, and then quit.

He bent over, clutching his head and thinking only of the boy, who right then seemed to be thinking of him, came up from behind and caught Cobb in an embrace, reaching only a little above his waist.

"You found me, Cobb. You are the champion tracker."

"Oh Jesus, kid. Oh Jesus." Cobb was trying not to weep.

"We need to find the others. You stay here, Cobb, and I will return with them. If we both set off, we'll just add to the number of those lost."

He was back in ten minutes, somehow relocating Cobb in the dark and guiding them all back, hobbling and stunned, to the house.

They turned the left corner and bounced up the porch and into the front room, only Brad noticing: "Did we leave the door unlocked? Open?"

They all knew they had not, didn't need the predictable note on the floor to tell them who had come in, might still be there. That should have been the first concern, searching every area, all attics and basements and under the rugs. But instead they gathered round the note, all but the kid, who stepped back.

"We keep missing one another, playing friend-tag. Next time, we'll try harder."

Everyone looked at the boy, as if he could explain all this, if only he would.

He didn't spare even a nod, turned and headed straight into his room, not slamming the door, not quite.

"I think he's just going in to put on different clothes. You guys notice he changes daily, sometimes twice a day. That's, I don't know, touching."

"You find it touching, Cobb? Maybe if you didn't have six wardrobes full of shit you'd find it more than touching."

Joss fired that outburst, feeling some odd relief at having done so, then looked at Cobb, realized.... "Damn, Cobb. I forget you wear the same thing every goddamned day. You probably have but that one pair of jeans. More than one T-shirt, I hope."

"Fascinating as this is," Brad said, "there is this note. Let's check the house. Like they do in those horror movies, one of which we seem to be inside: I'll go to the basement, while you check the garage. Wait till the camera's on you before you open the door to the shed you thought was abandoned."

They split apart, investigated everything, including all the cupboards, and reassembled pretty quickly. Brad and Joss then went outside and circled the house, after turning on the couple of the energy-saving lawn and porch lights, offering only a faint hint of illumination. They expected to locate nothing, which they did.

"We all knew we'd not find them or their traces. Maybe their goal is to show us how vulnerable we are, utterly defenseless. Maybe that's what they want. Will always want. You think?"

"Maybe, Katie," Brad said, "but I imagine that'd get too familiar, even routine. Seems to me they're playing our game, in a parallel nightmare."

"And what's that kid doing?" Cobb said, laughing, realizing as he was permitting the laugh what it was he was ignoring.

Joss was closest to the kid's room.

She didn't knock, sprawled into the room, looking around frantically, at first not even seeing the kid, who stood there naked. She saw him after a minute but didn't register what she saw.

"Are you alone? Are you okay? Are there...?"

"What are you looking for, Joss? You think I snuck a girl in here?"

He did cover himself with his arms and hands, crouched slightly, but he stood his ground, challenging Joss to explain herself.

"Oh shit, kid. I do apologize. I was so scared, so scared. I thought you might be in danger. I didn't think about you changing or I would never have come in. I mean, I would have knocked. Only I was so scared, so that's why I didn't knock."

The kid stared at her, still crouched. Joss tried hard not to look at the welted, wounded body. Mostly she was worried that he wouldn't believe her story, the accident of her entry. She tried again.

"You understand, I'm sure. Only you don't. That note was.... Oh, hell. I am so sorry I embarrassed you. After what you said about undressing—us undressing you. I know you're shy."

"I am not shy."

"Yes, you are."

"Oh. I'm sorry. I am shy. It's just...."

"Oh, you dear lovely boy. It's my fault. That's okay. I'm leaving and going to get dinner ready, best you ever had."

"Thank you, Joss. I am sure it will be the best I ever had."

* * *

It couldn't possibly have been that, as Joss was a bad cook, the worst among them, working with lousy ingredients. But none of them gave any thought to food, anyhow, though they didn't let loose what was running through all their minds, talk it out. What, after all, was there to say?

Then, after the quick meal, the boy mumbled something and started cleaning up his area. Then he turned to the others. Katie hissed and started beating him on the head with a dish towel, initiating a mock battle and a giggling match.

"This is women's work, boy."

He looked at her, no longer giggling. "It's my work."

"Bull—fucking—shit!" she said, surprising all the others and herself, too, with the pitch of her joking.

The boy smiled, stood there awkwardly for a minute, murmured something, and then beat a retreat to his room.

Finally, Brad suggested they talk about the future, a solid future they could locate, their oft-discussed hike up to the Donner Pass. That destination would be fitting, Brad argued, not with great confidence, since they had previously adopted it and then, for very good reason, rejected it. Now, retrieving if from the wastebasket could count as primal deviance. Nobody seemed very happy with the idea, but it was Brad talking, so they sat on their discomfort.

True to their pledge to secure nothing, to maximize the unplanned, and to be as stupid as possible, they agreed not to consult maps or guides until the morrow, to content themselves for the evening with tales, true or not, of the Donner Party and their unrepeatable tragedy, see where that would land them.

Repeating would be alien to their ideals. Tragedy, not so much.

So, they made things tidy, armed themselves with beers, all five of them, and laid out a neat almost-circle — three would be planted on the couch with two chairs facing them — in their cozy room, first locking the doors, turning out inside lights for a minute, and checking the front and side yards.

They were not without some vague idea that this session would be valuable schooling for their boy. Whether he would be well served by this special bit of history, dished up with few designs on accuracy, was doubtful. Whether he would play the part of passive pupil was probable. If they turned their minds to it, they would have realized they knew nothing about him, about their menacers, about what they were about. If empty territory was what they were seeking, they could congratulate themselves on landing square at the center.

They all realized that they were being pulled toward the Donner Party disaster by the obvious: warmed-up horror to ignite their own, not shining brightly now, despite the unlocked door and the note. Cannibalism, disastrous wrong turns, criminal misdirection, freezing, killings — death everywhere.

They did all they could to make themselves cozy, lighting a fire, wood provided with the cabin rental, and gathering pillows from their two bedrooms to fluff up and snuggle into. It was only then they recognized that the boy was missing, still sorting out his small wardrobe, perhaps. They looked at one another, none of them willing to yell for the boy or seek him out.

"You could go back in there, Joss. You seem to have...."

"Shut your mouth, Cobb! He's had his privacy violated often enough. Anyone but you would know that."

Cobb didn't seem surprised by the attack, but wasn't able to turn it toward anything.

They sat silent again, thinking they were waiting for the boy to emerge.

Finally, Brad just hollered, "Hey, Huck!"

Chapter 26

And there he was, dropping down on the couch between Katie and Brad, as if nothing could be more natural.

"Who should start...?" Katie said, and then, "Okay, if you absolutely insist."

She looked around, saw no protests, and started right in.

"I did *not* do a report on this, I should say, nor was this material assigned in some class on "The American West in Story and Song," as if there were such a class, and if I would take it if there were."

This was Katie at her usual, so nobody bothered to respond, nobody but the boy, who looked at her and grinned, reached over and squeezed her knee, prompting her to initiate a hug and a kiss, completing the first and faking the second.

"I will tell you a little bit about Lansford Warren Hastings, the very model of the American entrepreneurial spirit in 1846, when the Donner party, all however many of them — one of you will tell us — set out. Hastings was a liar and a cheat, a murderer by proxy, and endlessly resourceful. A lot like Rockefeller, Carnegie, the Guggenheims, and Frick — except that Hastings wasn't very good at it. He wrote a book, though, that struck a chord with the Donner Party, whose footsteps we hope to follow and whose activities we hope to emulate. The book was called, *The Emigrants' Guide.* Hastings had indeed been to Oregon and California, and he thought others should come there, too, ignoring the fact that Oregon was jointly staked out by the U.S. and England, and that California had been claimed and was occupied by Mexico — never mind the Indians, of course, which they didn't and we don't today. Anyhow, these original miserable European shits were illegal immigrants, only, unlike today's exploited folk, bloody-minded and truly dangerous, thinking only of themselves and anxious to grab land and minerals therein, the filthy bastards, our forebears."

"Where was I?"

"Hasting's *Guide* and the Donner Party," said Joss.

"Oh, yeah. For reasons unclear to me but clear to Hastings, he hoped to lure people to California, maybe so he could be declared King or something. Anyhow, in his guide, he made a big to-do about a 'shortcut,' branching south at some point from the Oregon Trail and promising to save ever so many miles and maybe a month of travel."

"Hastings himself had never taken this route, cobbled it together from inaccurate maps and rumors, and sent it out to all and sundry, including the Donners and the others who would collect around them, still safe in a small town there in Illinois — I think it was Illinois. Anyhow, the route went, first, right through the Wasatch Mountains and then above where we are now. All those believing him and his promised shortcut were to lose at least a month, which, for the people we are now discussing, was fatal. I forgot to say that he did tell the Midwestern pricks he was luring that they should, on no account, leave on their trip after May 1. I think that was the only truth he spoke, and it was one our friends ignored, not getting their collective asses going until close to the end of the month."

"Thanks, Katie," Brad started, when she interrupted him.

"Oh, I forgot. The only person objecting to taking the wrong fork, this shortcut toward Fort Something and death, was my favorite of all, Tamzene Donner, who argued that Hastings was nothing but 'a selfish adventurer.' But she was outvoted or, more likely, just ignored, her being nothing more than a woman."

Everyone waited to see if she were through. She wasn't.

"In later life, Hastings ruined some business partners, was elected to public office, tried to make deals with Brigham Young's Mormons to ship goods to them from San Francisco down the Colorado River and through the Grand Canyon, impossible, of course. He was in the Civil War, on the wrong side, hoped to create a Confederate colony in California and then — get this! — in Brazil. He even wrote, yes he did, an *Emigrant's Guide to Brazil*, which I admit I have not read but which I am sure is even more worthwhile than his other, since, with Brazil, he can promise not just Indians to murder but slaves a-plenty, to whop and screw."

Katie had started out joking, but that's not where she ended up.

"Thank you, Katie," said the kid, after a considerable, itch-inducing pause.

The others looked at him, wondering how much of this he could possibly have understood.

"Bet you've run into assholes like this Hastings plenty of times," said Cobb, leaning over to touch the boy.

"Yes," said the boy, without expressing anything.

That seemed to put a stop to things, so Cobb, ever ready with the wrong thing at the wrong time, said it: "You want to go next?"

As he was looking at no one in particular, it was up to someone to answer, so the kid stepped in. "I'd like to go last again, if that is okay."

"It is," said Brad. "And just to head off Cobb, I'll go next — if that's okay."

Cobb pretended to be angry, upset, hurt — and then laughed, "I'll take the horror turn — one of them."

"Well, then," Brad started, fishing in his pocket and pulling out a battered sheet of paper, "I found this in my stuff and brought it along, in case we ventured near this scenic spot. It's about one Wakeman Bryarly, a young doctor originally from Baltimore, in what was probably the second wave of the gold rush, some few years after the Donners. He was with a bunch of others — probably a lot like our group — camping not too far from what was then called Truckee Lake...."

"And what's it called now?" asked Joss. "We might just want to go up there for some ice fishing."

"Before you answer, Brad, anybody want more beer? Kid?"

"Yes," said the kid.

"Shut the fuck up, Cobb!" said Joss.

"It is now called Donner Lake, Donner, you see, being the name stuck to most everything up in that area, whether connected to their expedition or not. Anyhow, here he was walking along on a warm afternoon, much like we will have tomorrow, despite its not quite being August for us, as it was for old Wakeman. Soon, amidst the weeds, flies, and grasshoppers, he stumbled across a cabin which had about it a number of sawed-off stumps. He went inside and didn't really find anything other than a partition separating two living areas and, I think, a fire pit or two. Maybe they were burial pits, but Wakeman didn't suspect that at the time."

"He went outside and looked about him and found just what you are imagining and what I wouldn't be telling this story had he not found — bones. What kind of bones? Cattle bones."

Everyone registered disappointment, then laughed.

"Nah. He found a nice complete human skeleton with grass growing up most picturesquely through the ribs. Then — are you ready for this? He checked around and found some boxes and clothes, too, including a child's sock that rattled when he lifted it for examination. Turns out it still had in it the foot bone of a small child, very good condition."

"Feeling exultant about his find and the status it would give him as a storyteller, able now to exaggerate things a little and make them almost interesting, Bryarly continued on to the Lake, whose cool waters felt so good on his naked skin as he sloshed around in the shallow water, being careful not to go out too far, both because of the many snakes swimming close by and because he had never learned to swim back there in Baltimore."

"Is that true?" Joss asked.

"Not so far as I know," said Brad.

"What isn't true, the snakes or not being able to swim? I mean, which did you make up?"

"Maybe one, maybe both, maybe neither."

The boy laughed. The others looked impatient. Brad responded only to the boy: "Thanks, Huck. You're the only one here with a sense of humor — or any other kind of sense."

"Anyhow," he continued, "here was Wakeman, naked as a naked person, careless of all the onlookers, swimming or maybe wading cross the lake and back several times, having trouble finding his clothes, wondering if it mattered, deciding it did, and then finding them after all, putting them on, and heading back. He got lost, he did, or I think he did, and was wandering through a pine forest, when he came upon the remains of yet another cabin. Here's where I need to consult my notes."

"This cabin had been burned to the ground, but Wakeman went sifting through the ashes and logs, unearthing many more human bones. According to my sources, femurs and tibias had been split open with an ax, skulls cut with a meat saw."

"After he returned he composed a note, which I copied out, finding it an odd and wonderful combination of stilted Victorian prose and a kind of poetry.

> *To look upon these sad monuments harrows up every sympathy of the heart and soul, and you almost hold your breath to listen for some mournful sound from*

these blackened, dismal, funereal piles, telling you of their many sufferings and calling on you for bread, bread.

"Was that repetition of 'bread' in his note or did you add it?" Joss asked.

"I didn't add it."

"I find that so moving," Katie said. "Do you think the idea of bread came to him because he knew of the cannibalism and...."

"Better than saying, 'kidneys, kidneys,'" said Cobb, immediately sorry that he had and looking to Joss for her certain rebuttal.

Finally, she roused herself: "How about you go next, Cobb, then me, and then our lead speaker."

Cobb was ready enough.

"I don't have notes, like some of you, but I remember this pretty well. Anyhow, I can make up what I don't remember. It's a long story, but you won't mind. Well, you will mind, but I'll not notice — and I will be respectful of your capacities, limited, sorely limited."

He paused for no good reason, until the boy, of all people, said, "Cobb?"

"Oh, yeah, rude twerp. So, anyhow in November and much of December, the Donner Party and associates were all — I don't know how many exactly — up at or near Truckee Lake, where that jackass went swimming a few years later. Some were there at this lake and others were at a place called Alder Creek nearby. They were snowed in pretty completely and faced impossible conditions getting out, having to find a way around the lake, through huge heaps of snow and then somehow over high mountains ahead, swamped with even more snow. Getting out seemed impossible, but they were running out of food by December, in some cases had already run out of food, so it was a kind of suicide, it seemed, either way."

The Graves family, my favorite bunch, got the idea of making snowshoes as a way of traversing the impossible drifts — twenty, thirty feet, I think — and then somehow allowing them to climb up the sides of canyons and claw their way westward to arrange for help to be sent back. I never had snowshoes on myself, so I can't really imagine. Any of you guys know?"

"We don't, Cobb. Keep going," said Katie, reaching over and grabbing his thigh, wondrously high up, and squeezing, leaving her hand right there.

"Well, if you put it that way. On December 14 — how's that for being exact — they set out, not all of them, clodding their snowshoes carefully around the corpses, which is probably an exaggeration, though for sure some people had already died and many more were dying. They made their way over to the eastern edge of Truckee Lake, like I said, just as the sun came up, reflecting off the lake as they snowshoed across it and bouncing off the granite mountains above them. Of course they didn't have sunglasses — duh! — so several of them were becoming snowblind, though they didn't yet know it. This would be real bad, though, as, without protection, your eyes blister just as sunburned skin does. And then you're blind, which in fact happened to at least three of these poor people."

"How many were there?" Brad asked.

"I was about to tell you, though don't hold me to absolute accuracy. Two turned back a little ways into the lake crossing, the two without snowshoes, which left, I believe, fifteen."

"All men?"

"Nope, Katie. I think about half and half, plus a boy. I don't know how old the boy was, pretty young," he added, looking at their own boy.

"That first day they barely made it across the lake and up a medium-sized hill before they stopped for the night and built a fire. I forgot to say this whole expedition is called 'The Forlorn Hope,' though that wasn't their name for it, of course. Some later historian with a taste for melodrama."

"The next day they rousted themselves very early and started up the canyon toward the pass, which they could see, as it was only three-quarters of a mile away. But it was also a thousand feet high, damned near straight up. Of course, as they tried to climb, it got progressively worse, not only steeper and more frozen but offering less and less oxygen, so they had to stop real often to rest. They were up about 7000 feet, I think, maybe higher, as they got to floundering within the deep, deep snow, even deeper toward the summit. I also forgot to say that, along with the snow-blindness, they faced the terrors of hypothermia. Anyhow, sweating fiercely and wallowing in deep drifts, with weakened bodies and not enough time or information and no help anywhere to be had, they were in a hell of a spot."

"By the time the sun was ready to go down, they were, somehow or other, at the top of the pass, in modern times called Donner Pass, looking down into the valley to the west and around at various peaks. Mary Ann Graves, my favorite, as I mentioned, wrote about what a beautiful view it was, how she paused to take in the grand vistas. If only she had known."

"They didn't go much farther that day, set up camp just past the summit, I think, and bedded down. Meanwhile, one of their number, an older guy, was having great troubles of various kinds, snow-blindness among them, but also general exhaustion. I forget his name. Anyhow, he was hours late getting into camp and then, after that, didn't move again ever, just settled onto a stump, sat there and relaxed, willed himself to die. I'm not making this up. He just did."

"Anyhow, here were the others, running out of food fast and still with fifty miles or so to go. They trudged along, though, only to be hit by a monstrous snowstorm. They were six days out from where they started now and things began to worsen. They were getting desperate and were about to make the worst decision of the trip — other than the one to embark on their westward adventure and trust Hastings."

"At the end of what's called The Six Mile Valley, they ran into a small hill, facing them on, I think, the left. If they had climbed it — it really wasn't high, but it blocked the view — they'd have got right to what is now Emigrant's Gap. From there, it was all downhill into Bear Valley and safety — food and warmth and even some kind of medical treatment. But they couldn't see, poor desperate people, and they didn't know, they just didn't know."

Cobb paused a minute. Nobody objected.

"Straight ahead of them was a nice easy slope, or that's what it looked like. I mean, they had this choice: go straight ahead and nicely downhill or start climbing again. What would you have done? I know about me — starving and freezing and hardly able to see."

He paused again.

"So they did what we would do. They went straight ahead, only to find that the gentle downhill became steep and then almost vertical, leading into a canyon containing some fork of the roaring American River, which they also couldn't see, since the canyon was about 3000 or 4000 feet deep, with narrow walls, sometimes impassable water, and vertical ascents. It was the route into death, and, like us, they took it."

He stopped very suddenly, looking for some reason at the boy, who nodded.

It seemed the natural thing for somebody to ask for more details: how did it go from there? how many made it? what the hell happened? But nobody spoke. Instead, they just sat there, immobilized, looking at nothing in particular.

Then Brad got up and went to the door, turned on the outside lights and disappeared. Everyone knew what he was checking, and in a minute joined him, all but the boy, who stayed where he was, waiting.

As soon as they returned, Joss started right in.

"I won't take long. I also have notes, knowing we'd be doing this."

Nobody seemed surprised, felt moved to ask how she knew that.

"Mine are copied, probably not too accurately, from written messages we have from members of the party. All but the first are letters from survivors sent back home to those plopped in tediously safe places such as Illinois or Indiana. Here's the first, from Reason Tucker, who formed part of what was called the Fourth Relief, on reaching the Truckee Lake cabins:

> *Death and Destruction. Horrible sights. Human bones. Women's skulls sawed to get the brains. Better dwell in the midst of alarm than to stay in this horrible place.*

Joss looked around. Then, "I'll try not to comment on these, but do notice that 'in the midst of alarm.' Ain't that chilling? Sorry. Of course it is, and I just screw it up by mentioning it. I won't do that again. So, here, from those now out of the mountains and settled into relative safety, next spring, 1847, on the west side of the divide. First, one Virginia Reed, writing to a cousin:

> *Oh Mary, I have not wrote you half the trouble we have had but I have wrote you enough to let you know what trouble is. Don't let this letter dishearten anybody. Never take no cutoffs, and hurry along as fast as you can.*

"I know I said I wouldn't gloss these, but you're going to ask about 'dishearten' and if she's being coldly sarcastic. I cannot even guess, and if you're going to guess, keep it to yourself. Cobb, you hear me?"

She looked at Cobb, who kept staring at the floor, so she continued:

"This is from Sarah Graves, to her aunt and uncle, longer than most, but...."

> *It is with a heavy heart that I inform you of our mournful situation. I cannot enter into the details of our sufferings; I can only give a brief account. We got on well to Fort Bridger. There we took Hastings Cut Off and became belated and caught in the California Mountains without any provisions except our worked down cattle and but few of them. They made snowshoes, and on the 16th of December, father, Mary Ann, my husband, myself, and eleven others set out. We got lost but resolved to push on, for it was but death any way. It snowed for three days and all this time we were without fire or anything to eat. Father perished at the beginning of this storm, of cold; four of our company died at that place. As soon as the storm ceased we took the flesh of their bodies, what we could make do us four days and started. We traveled on six days without finding any relief. On the night of the 6th my husband gave out and could not reach camp. I stayed with him, without fire. I had a blanket and wrapped him in it, sat down beside him and he died about midnight, as near as I could tell.*

And here's from Mary Ann Graves, her sister, whose letter is also a little obscure but that's just what it is:

> *I have told the bad news, and, bad as it is, I have told the best. No tongue can exceed in description the reality. I will now give you some good and friendly advice. Stay at home — you are in a good place, where, if sick, you are not in danger of starving to death. It is a healthy country here, and when that is said, all is said. You can live without work if you are a complete rascal; for a rascal you must be if you are to stand any chance at all. In the number of rogues, this country exceeds, I believe, any other.*

And, finally, from Mary Murphy, fifteen years old:

> *"I hope I shall not live long, for I am tired of this troublesome world and I want to go to my mother."*

Joss tried to sustain herself but did not, began shaking and then sobbing. If they were embarrassed by her response, anxious to move on, nobody gave that indication. Nobody did a thing.

There is no telling how long they might have stayed that way, had not the boy finally stood up. He said nothing until everyone was looking at him.

Chapter 27

"Thank you," he said. "I am glad to have been here and to know all this. I had heard before of this group, The Donner Party, and had always wondered what was wrong with them."

He paused. "You mean why they ate one another?" said Joss.

The boy looked at her, for a moment almost with scorn, it seemed. "No," he finally said, "why they would come out here at all, why they didn't leave people alone? They couldn't stand the idea that other people were happier than they were, couldn't stand it."

Nobody said anything.

"I mean," the boy said, "they weren't starving back where they were or being hurt all the time. They just couldn't take it that somewhere people might be making more money. But it's not even money. They'd run out of people to hurt in wherever they were, and they heard that out here in California there were lots of Indians and Mexicans they could hurt all they wanted. I know that was it, but I can't understand it."

He was on a roll of sorts, looking both pained and excited, his eyes squinted up and his hands working at the bottom of his new T-shirt: "Awesome Dude!"

"I know they were eating one another after they were dead, and, Katie told me, two of their Indian guides, murdering them first so they'd be easier to cook. But why did they start eating people? Huh?"

Nobody responded, not because they had no opinions but because they had never seen the boy like this, agitated and, it sure seemed, enraged.

"Huh?" he repeated.

"Because they were starving?" Katie offered, timidly, her voice shaking a little. This was dangerous territory, and she was the only one willing to stick a foot into it.

The boy looked at Katie, his anger suddenly gone. "I know it seems like it, Katie. They didn't have anywhere else to look for food, and they had to have food. That what you think?"

"I don't know, dearie. I just wanted you to keep going."

She hoped he'd smile. He didn't.

"I don't think they had to. I don't think that was it. You all say they'd not had anything to eat for six days, or not much, that right?"

He didn't wait for a response, steamrolled right ahead.

"Six days! You think that is a lot? Do you? You can go a lot longer without food, a lot longer. Yes, you can! Six days!"

Everyone seemed stunned. Perhaps the boy noticed it, lowered his tone.

"First off, they had plenty of water. And I'll bet there were bark and acorns and even grasses for food. But, even if there weren't...."

He paused and took a new direction.

"They had an excuse to do it and that's what they wanted to do. They liked it. They said afterwards they didn't, but they probably liked thinking about it, wishing they could do it some more. I know you don't want to hear this — especially Brad."

He stopped a second, not looking at Brad. Then —

"They got to peel off the clothes and the skin and everything. They could do what they wanted to the other person, whether he was dead or not. Some they ate, you said, were kids, some girls. They got to do anything they wanted to them, opening them up and looking and eating. And there was nothing the bodies could do about it. Nothing at all. The bodies, those people, were helpless and the others could do whatever they thought about, peeling everything off, everything, and then putting it in their mouth and chewing. I bet they chewed real slow, loving it, looking at what was left and anxious to move on to the next person."

"Next body?" Cobb offered.

"Next person!" the boy said, now with tears in his eyes. "They were people they were eating, hurting as much as they could. They gave them no chance. They just keep peeling away and hurting. And they did it because that's what they wanted to do. They didn't have to. They might never get another chance, so they just did it, over and over, peeled and ate as many as they could. Ate them."

He paused. "And hurt them."

Another pause. "People don't hurt you because they need to. They do it because they want to."

"Oh. Huck!" said Brad, standing up and moving toward him, probably with a mind to embrace the kid. But he was either too slow or too willing to give the boy an escape. The kid, anyhow, backed toward his room, stopped, and then gave some signal — they could not have told you what it was for sure, but it seemed like defeat.

* * *

No one could think of a good way to transition to another mood or activity, so Cobb blurted out, "You know it's still early and we might try another round-robin, don't you think?"

Lame, but even Joss didn't want to say so. However, nobody said anything, which threatened to leave them where they were, nowhere at all, so Cobb extended his weak idea: "We'll go around the circle and everyone gets to tell their most embarrassing experience ever, embellishments encouraged."

After a short beat, Katie entered. "That's terrific, Cobb,

but how about we do something more uplifting? Even we suicidal break-necks need some uplift after all that Donner stuff, huh?"

She was looking over at the boy, still poised outside his door but now seeming to lean a little back into the room.

Joss hit it, or at least hit what nobody could improve upon: "We all tell the story of the happiest experience of our lives — up to this point, of course." She immediately seemed embarrassed by the sappy suggestion, ready to withdraw it, but all the others drowned any hesitation in a wave of agreement so strong even the boy would have had little chance to protest.

He did, however, blurt out, "I'm hungry," immediately retreating into a kind of apologetic alarm.

"I know we just ate," he started, when Joss cut him off. "We're all hungry, kid, which is something we must not ignore, even if it means postponing briefly this next go-round and diving into unhealthy snacks, of which we are low on — notice the elegant phrasing — and which you and I will now procure from the nearby emporium, to which we will travel by auto, while the other lazy fatasses stretch a little and relieve their bladders."

The boy seemed to recognize the rescue and be grateful for it, even blinked a kind of response to Joss and started toward the door, watching her closely.

"Get your coat, doofus. It's about twelve degrees out there. Get your warm stuff and then we'll go."

He did and they did.

Returning into the driveway, the Prius now packed with junk food, the boy suddenly braked the car and switched off the lights.

"Did you see that?"

It wasn't a question, but Joss answered anyhow.

"I don't know."

"That light, back of the house on this side, sort of like a mirror reflecting."

"Yeah?"

"You take the bags in. I'll check it out."

His voice was so commanding, Joss, who was the last person to submit to be commanded, did as she was told.

Once she was inside, though, the others let her know how careless she had been.

"He's out there by himself?"

Joss stood, still holding the bags, while Brad and Cobb went for their coats. Katie didn't bother, was out the door, so quickly that by the time the others made it down the six steep steps and into the snow she was out of sight.

"Shit! You take that side, Cobb. Joss and I will do over here. Wait — stay where you are, and I'll go in and get flashlights."

Trouble was Brad could find only one flashlight, his, and wasted a minute or two looking to see if more might be in plain sight, which they were not. He didn't want to rustle through others' stuff and he didn't want to spend any more time, so he turned on the inadequate outside lights on the front (the open side and the back had none) and burst out the door, nearly whipping himself off the end of the porch and into the snow without benefit of the steps. In righting himself, then, he somehow activated the long-latent pain from his lancings. He had tried to forget about all that with a little success, but now he couldn't shove it down at all and was somehow face to face with the maniacs again, then seemed to see them, vividly, out there with Huck and with Katie, on them.

He threw the flashlight to Cobb and grabbed Joss's arm, whipping her with him around the opposite side and quickly up the hill into the sparse trees, and then the woods behind the house. Cobb, he figured, was flanking them.

"There's that flash," Joss said, not a minute up the hill.

"What flash?"

"The one the boy saw as we were pulling in. I didn't see it

then but just did, like a strobe light or something, not quite that, just a single sharp light, maybe a reflection."

"Damn!"

Cobb had circled around the house and now was in sight; then he was right there with them. Brad noticed that they were now one bunch, covering no ground, but said nothing.

"You see a flash, Cobb?" Joss asked.

"I might have. Can't be sure."

"That's real useful," she sneered, angry even now.

Before Cobb could retort, sulk, or shrink into himself, he spotted Katie up ahead, standing there, doing nothing at all, or so it appeared. She saw them at about the same time and allowed them to join her, form a unit.

"You see the kid?" Cobb asked.

Katie didn't bother answering, just indicated with sharp hand gestures that they should divide in two and proceed, the flashlight-less pair using the moonlight as best they could.

They didn't need directions more specific, set off at once to mimic an efficient search party, trying not to rush, trying not to panic. But they were wrestling with paralyzing dread, every one of them, feeling sure that there was something ahead of them, or behind — who knew? What they felt was an obscure sense of sly motion, of concealment, the sense we get in wild places from small hiding things — rabbits, deer, and mice. But whatever was causing these flashes was neither small nor set on hiding, not for long. For our rescuers, the flashes were both there and not, phantom and solid. Right then, however, not one of them thought of her own skin, only of the boy's, wondering if he were still out there on his own, out there at all.

And then he was. Suddenly. Tugging on Katie's jacket.

"Oh fucking hell, kid. Oh fucking hell!" It was Joss yelling the loudest. But they all wanted to say just that, turn their fear into a welcome.

The boy could not have known that, but somehow he was able to direct his energies to apology, to helping these four older ones, who as yet understood nothing about how to live.

"I am sorry. I should have stayed closer and checked back. I am sorry."

They all knew. After all, he was just trying to help them, put himself between them, the flashing lights, and whatever misery they were coding.

For some reason, nobody had tried to bridge the dozen or so feet separating them from the kid, maybe regarding the distance as important to his integrity, maybe marking their fear. Anyhow, once they became aware of the odd separation, it disappeared.

Back inside, the boy went to the kitchen to gather together the junk food, along with five beers, and, somehow from somewhere, cloth napkins.

He came back in and spread things around, much like an experienced waiter, even the silverware ending up in the right places, glasses for the beer, coasters.

The others were by this point past wondering.

The ate pretty much in silence, nobody wanting to bring up the latest scare. Finally, the boy spoke.

"There were tracks."

"Well, kid, people live around here. Maybe...."

The kid stared at Joss.

"Okay. You think the tracks are from our menacers."

"Who?" the kid asked.

"The ones after us."

"Yes."

"What should we do, kid?"

Joss's question might have seemed stupid at another time, addressed to a different child.

"I wondered why you were not doing anything."

Cobb looked at him closely, shifting around at the table

so he could see better. He had no impulse to make this into a joke, this comment coming from a kid who seemed older, in possession of something that might allow them to turn a corner.

"You think we should be doing something, don't you?" It wasn't a question.

"If they are wanting to hurt you, they will," said the kid.

"Unless?" Cobb prompted.

"I don't know. Unless you hide. I guess you could hurt them first, kill them."

"And how could we do that? Attack them, I mean. The hiding part doesn't seem like a workable scheme, since they keep showing up. Or I think they do. I'd be happy to kill them, if we had a way. I don't know how others feel."

If they thought he was joking, they didn't show it. The boy understood. He looked at Cobb and nodded.

"That's why you got the guns, right, so you could kill them? You got us all guns and then left yourselves open to them, hoping they would come."

Brad was first. "Jesus, Huck, is that what we've been doing?"

"Yes."

"Probably you're right. I didn't even know that. Holy shit."

Silence for a minute and then Katie. "Is this a smart thing, what we're doing?"

She wasn't looking at the boy but they all knew he was the one addressed.

"No. I don't mean you're not smart, Katie — any of you — but it's like a deer wants to win against a hunter by finding an open field and standing there."

"But our guns?" asked Cobb, feebly enough.

"You'd never have a chance to use them. You even know that. Is that what you want?"

They took the question seriously, but they had no answer.

"If you were going to attack them, kid, or save yourself at least, what would you do? Would you call the cops?" The kid whirled around on Katie, looked almost angry, then let it fall away.

"No. That'd be worse. You won't do that, will you? Please."

They seemed to know what he meant. As if he were apologizing, the kid looked around the table sheepishly, tried to smile, then tried to reassure them.

"I think what you are doing is best. That's what I think. You are having a good time, not letting them run your lives. If they want to do what they want to do, they will. At least, you have this time and they are not running it. At least you have that. That is what I would do."

Everyone had finished eating, but nobody stirred. Finally, Brad announced that they should adjourn, not to bed, early as it was and primed as they were by the recent storytelling, but back to the living room and more beer and more tales, not of the most embarrassing thing they'd ever fallen into but the happiest, the best.

Chapter 28

Nobody objected, but nobody was waving flags either, so Brad added:

"You might think Joss's earlier plan about happiness stories is a little silly, but I'm a little silly and, down deep, so are you. All but Huck here, who is a tough son of a bitch you don't want to run into in a dark alley. But he'll go along with the plan — either he does that or I'll force him to go to Sunday school tomorrow and praise Jesus."

It wasn't like Brad to babble so, but it got them out of the kitchen and back into the room with the sofa and chairs, beers-in-hand. It seemed the most natural thing in the world for Joss to get all their guns and hand them round. The kid had his with him to start with.

So, they sat there rummaging about in their brains, trying hard to remember times they had been happy, not just feeling happy but somehow encased in the feeling, unable to imagine anything beyond.

All this mental scrambling seemed to produce nothing but embarrassment for some time, as they stared helplessly at floors, ceilings, walls, and then, finally, at one another, bursting simultaneously into kiddie giggles, all but the one kid among them.

Cobb finally released them.

"I'll start, as I am the most tragic among us and have the least to be happy about. In fact, I regard happiness as the final inauthenticity. Even more than that...."

"Shut the fuck up, Cobb, you drooling moron." Joss didn't seem to be kidding him, but Cobb decided to regard her contempt as comradely joking.

"Right. You cannot contain your eagerness for me to happy us all up by telling of my supreme bliss."

Suddenly he turned grave.

"I was happiest my freshman year at USC when a drama class I was in did a production of 'Who's Afraid of Virginia Woolf.' It wasn't so much a production as just a reading, a classroom reading at that, and parts were not assigned but drawn by lot. Still, I was lucky enough to get these lines uttered by George, and they made me feel like I never had, not ever. That's true. The character George, in the play I mean, may be making all this up and may not be, like most of what he says. But for me, it wasn't make-believe. These lines, this story, allowed me into places I didn't know were there, inside me or anywhere else, spaces so frightening they went way beyond that into pure joy. But I'm getting ridiculous and will just say the lines. I remember them perfectly."

> *When I was sixteen, and going to prep school, during the Punic Wars, a bunch of us would go to town the first day of vacation, before we fanned out to our homes. And in the evening we would go to a gin mill owned by the gangster-father of one of us, and we would drink with the grown-ups, and listen to the jazz.*
>
> *And one time, in the bunch of us there was this boy who was fifteen...and he had killed his mother with a shotgun some years before. Completely accidentally, without even an unconscious motivation, I have no doubt at all. And this one time this boy went with us and we ordered our drinks, and when it came his turn he said, ''I'll have bergin. Give me some bergin please. Bergin and water.'' We all laughed.*

He was blond and he had the face of a cherub, and we all laughed. And his cheeks went red and the color rose in his neck. The waiter told the people at the next table what the boy said and they laughed, and then more people were told, and the laughter grew and grew.

No one was laughing more than us. And none of us more than the boy who had shot his mother.

And soon everyone in the gin mill knew what the laughter was about, and everyone started ordering bergin and laughing when they ordered it. And soon, of course, the laughter became less general, but it did not subside entirely for a very long time. For always at this table or that someone would order bergin, and a whole new area of laughter would rise. We drank free that night. We were bought champagne by the management, by the gangster-father of one of us. And, of course, we suffered the next day, each of us alone, on his train away from the city, and each of us with a grown-up's hangover.

But it was the grandest day ... of my ... youth.

* * *

Then somebody in the play asks, "What happened to the boy? The boy who had shot his mother."

And I say, "I won't tell you." And then:

The next summer on a country road, with his learner's permit, and his father sitting to his right, he swerved to avoid a porcupine and drove straight into a large tree. He was not killed, of course. In the hospital when he was conscious and out of danger, when they told him his father was dead, he began to laugh, I have been told. And his laughter grew and would not stop. And it was not until after they'd jammed a needle in his arm, not until his consciousness had slipped away from him that his laughter subsided. Stopped.

When he recovered from his injuries enough so he could be moved without damage should he struggle, he was put in an asylum. That was thirty years ago. And he is still there. I'm told that for these thirty years he has not uttered ... one sound.

* * *

Nobody bothered to mock Cobb, not even Joss. Brad did look carefully at the boy, trying to detect signs of confusion and failing to do so.

Katie didn't give them much time to react, just started right in.

"Like Cobb, my happiest time was indirect, I guess you could say. But it didn't seem that way to me. It was right there, right before and inside me, and I wasn't just reading a book but was, first, there on that boat, The *Pequod*, in the night, my hand on the tiller covering Ishmael's — and, then, my hand was his and his mine. But that's not important. What Ishmael allowed me to see was rapturous — and I'll turn the mike over to him now.

I don't have it memorized, like Cobb, but I brought the book along with me. Almost always do, and I sure wasn't going to be without it on this voyage. It'll do more for me than any gun. So here it is. It's not short, but I ain't apologizing:

> *Look not too long in the face of the fire, O man! Never dream with thy hand on the helm! Turn not thy back to the compass; accept the first hint of the hitching tiller; believe not the artificial fire, when its redness makes all things look ghastly. Tomorrow, in the natural sun, the skies will be bright; those who glared like devils in the forking flames, the morn will show in far other, at least gentler, relief; the glorious, golden, glad sun, the only true lamp- all others but liars!*
>
> *Nevertheless the sun hides not Virginia's Dismal*

Swamp, nor Rome's accursed Campagna, nor wide Sahara, nor all the millions of miles of deserts and of griefs beneath the moon. The sun hides not the ocean, which is the dark side of this earth, and which is two thirds of this earth. So, therefore, that mortal man who hath more of joy than sorrow in him, that mortal man cannot be true- not true, or undeveloped. With books the same. The truest of all men was the Man of Sorrows, and the truest of all books is Solomon's, and Ecclesiastes is the fine hammered steel of woe. "All is vanity." All. This willful world hath not got hold of unchristian Solomon's wisdom yet.

  But even Solomon, he says, "the man that wandereth out of the way of understanding shall remain" (i.e. even while living) "in the congregation of the dead." Give not thyself up, then, to fire, lest it invert thee, deaden thee; as for the time it did me. There is a wisdom that is woe; but there is a woe that is madness. And there is a Catskill eagle in some souls that can alike dive down into the blackest gorges, and soar out of them again and become invisible in the sunny spaces.

Katie stopped and looked at the blankest of the walls, trying to collect herself. "I expect it seems strange," she finally said, "but I find this so — I don't exactly know. It's not that I myself have hold of unchristian Solomon's wisdom, but I have never been happier than in times I have tried."

Joss was first to react. "Well, aren't we the absolute stereotypes — plays and novels. Any of us had any life at all?"

Katie tried not to look hurt, then exploded. "I don't think life and books are two different things, Joss. Maybe you do. All I was trying to do was tell the truth, tell about the happiest time ever. Ever!"

"I'm so sorry, Katie." And she was.

"Just for that, I'll go next," said Brad.

"Mine has to do with football and my older brother —

and, no, it doesn't feature me scoring the winning touchdown for old Central High and bringing home the state championship that my brother had been responsible for losing four years earlier. It has to do with shame and fear and, I suppose, trying so hard to feel neither."

Brad looked so sad as he launched into his story that the others squirmed with him, wondering how such obvious embarrassment could connect to happiness. Only the boy spoke: "Happy, Brad. A happy time. This wasn't, was it?"

Brad looked apologetic. "It turns out just fine, Huck. Really, it does. The happy part is at the end of the story, the way it should be. I wrote all this out once — I won't tell you why. I'll just read it."

> *I grew up way back in a little factory town in Ohio, where all the factories were beginning to shut down. Not that any of that relates to my story, which is about coming of age as a boy by way of football. I suppose the first part of my story is banal enough: I felt I should play football, which is what real boys did, no two ways about that. Was I a real boy? No, but there were no other roles being handed out, so I stepped right into this really bad fit.*
>
> *Everything was fine until the seventh grade. Up until then it was just little kids horsing around, small enough not to cause any real hurt and kind enough, too. But then everything changed. Parents became interested. Coaches came along and expectations and uniforms with pads. With the pads came pain and lots of it, not just smashing and banging but clawing and gouging and mashing. Fingers and eyes and pinches of skin and private parts.*
>
> *For me, football was no more than pain leading to a desire to avoid the pain, in any way possible, not disregarding ways leading to humiliation, leading to secret tears, leading to deeper shame, and finally*

back again to pain. I could not bring myself to do what you would call "play the game." That's not possible when you are so single-heartedly devoted to protecting yourself, inventing ever new ways for letting time go by without being injured in it. No artist ever made such calls on imaginative ingenuity. For me, it was not art, of course, simply shame and degradation, a feeling that I had descended into a kind of sewer. I vividly recall even the smells: old pads, old sores, old urine, old Absorbine Jr., old fungussy socks, old men hanging about, old lamentations.

We must have had a team of the lowest rank, since, lousy as I certainly was, I still found myself in games, on the line, wondering what to do. I found myself developing elaborate thespian abilities, trying hard to avoid the cleats that chewed you up, the hard turf, the humiliating open field. Sometimes I'd try to make deals with opposing linemen — fake it, don't get hurt, roll around in the dirt together. A few times that worked, but it made me feel even worse, naturally.

But avoidance meant shame and plenty of it. Here I was a boy, but not a real boy, so what in the name of cowardly yellow chicken-shittedness was I?

I was certainly no worthy inheritor of my older brother's mantle. Bob had been a star all through high school, a lineman and a linebacker as well, playing all four years and, as I say, covering himself with glory and making our dad proud. This last was everything. I could have stood up under the open ridicule of the rest of the town, strode past billboards proclaiming my chicken-shittedness, had it not been for my dad. My brother, too, who was the one who had made our dad feel worthy of fatherhood.

I did not. He never said anything, Dad, but I knew, of course. His primary feeling toward me was, had to be, repulsion.

Regret, too, naturally, but something more fierce. Imagine fathering a fake boy, a sissy, a yellow-belly.

Counting grade school, my brother had played a full six years. I crawled and cringed and evaded through only three, finally, after the last game of my freshman year, exploding into tears in the back seat of the car, issuing no words, only sobs, exposing myself to my dad. He didn't stop the car and eject me, said very little. But what he said planted the seeds for later bliss. "Brad doesn't like it. Just like Bob."

For some reason the second sentence didn't register at the time, took a few years, in fact, before it did. By then, my brother was in college a few hundred miles away, was engaged to be married, proving himself even more certainly a real boy, while I stuttered through some dating I wished I didn't have to do, crawling through high school.

Bob had invited me up to stay with him for a weekend, a testimony to his great kindness. He could not have found the presence of a young gangling hobbledehoy anything but an ass-pain. But he stayed with me the whole time, making me feel loved and whole.

One night, he took me to an actual college party, let me drink beer, and then to a restaurant whose name I forget. But its come-on was "Fried in Butter." For me, it was Delmonico's in the 20s, though, and I was floating, not on the beer, really — Bob had monitored me — but on the exhilaration of being in a new world altogether and finding it more like home than home had ever been.

And it was only to get finer. As we sat talking, it suddenly leaked out of me, all my shame and remorse, all the football failure. Before I could get well into it, though, Bob reached across and put his hand on my arm.

"Whoa, Brad! Remember that broken nose I had senior year, kept me out of seven games?"

"Yeah."

"A fake.'"

"Huh? A fake?"

"I hated every second of it, all of it. Every second. So, I know just what you mean. We share the same skin."

I was so flummoxed I couldn't say a word. "You know what else? Dad feels the same way, just figured he should be supportive if his boys insisted on being idiots. I didn't know that until last month or I could have saved you all that misery, jerked you right out of that nightmare."

Bob paused, and then, "I'm sorry, Brad — dear Brad."

Sorry! I felt as if I were ascending in a rocket, weightless and triumphant, everything forgiven. That was my happiest time ever. Nothing even close.

Brad didn't seem to want comments, even to lock eyes with anyone, so Joss stood up and started right in.

"When I was in Tenth Grade my grandmother died."

"Happy, Joss!" Cobb said.

"Did I interrupt you, Cobb?"

"You did. Oh yes, you did."

Joss almost smiled. "Well, that's very different, as you should know. I have a license."

Anyhow, my grandmother died in March and, as she was conventional as all hell, had a traditional funeral. The ceremony was held at the cemetery, right there at the grave site, the dirt piles discreetly concealed by quasi-velvet blankets. It was so cold, and everybody was trying to keep her teeth from chattering, out of respect, I guess, like my grandmother would have cared. The terrible part was that it was so fierce and blustery you couldn't hear the preacher. I don't mean you lost a word here and there. You could see his mouth moving but that was it. I looked over at my younger sister, Marie, and she had her head way bent over and her glove up to her mouth, and then I saw her shoulders quaking. That made me start laughing, too. My mother reached over to me. I thought she was going to hit me or something, but she hugged me and whispered, pretty loud so I could hear, "That's okay, sweetheart. Grandma is laughing, too.'" And that made me cry.

Anyhow, right there at the funeral, a couple of my friends came over and drew me aside. I was a little embarrassed — a lot embarrassed — as these were popular girls and I was always so anxious around them, even here at the grave, worried they'd discover how fucking uncool I was. And now they were going to offer condolences and I was going to be even more than usual uncool.

But I was wrong. What they did was look at me. So nice, and then invite me to a party. 'Just the thing to take your mind off your sadness, Jocelyn,' they said. 'Don't wear anything fancy, except your underwear, make that your best — unless you don't want to wear any at all.'

Not exactly condolences, but somehow it made the sun come out — you know what I mean?

I got through the rest of the day, the first part being back at our house, where there was tea that I didn't like and cookies that I did, and a lot of relatives and friends and especially friends of my grandma's. It would have been dismal and should have been, maybe, but I was really thinking of nothing but the upcoming evening and the party and what I should wear, underneath especially.

So, I got there, and there were four other girls, all very popular, and nobody else, I mean no parents or baby-sitters or anything. They even had punch, which they said was spiked — 'Be careful!' — but wasn't all that potent. It was perfect, really, made you relax and giggle, but not pass out.

After about an hour, we started playing games. I don't remember what the initial games were but then Celine, who seemed to be hosting, rang some kind of gong — I swear — and announced in this funny deep voice, 'And now the real fun!'

I won't keep you in suspense. The first games were old fashioned kissing games: post-office, flashlight, that sort of thing. I thought they were kidding about the kissing but they sure were not. At first, for me anyhow, it was just a peck, but then tongues came out and then, in a darkness that lasted longer and longer, hands began to stray and fingers grope. They apparently had been serious about not bothering with underwear. In any case, mine didn't stay in place long, nor did anyone else's. I saw all that when the lights came back up some time later, some time between ten minutes and ten hours, I have no idea. Bras and panties were all ooched up and down and backwards, and nobody seemed embarrassed, bothered to fix them.

I was thinking that was it and then I saw that wasn't it, wondered what in hell could come next, but not for long. I don't know who it was suggested we play doctor, but somebody did and before long we were without any clothes at all, not really examining one another but engaging in what I have since learned are pretty advanced lesbian techniques. At first, I think we were self-conscious, each of us eager to show just how unembarrassed we were. Somehow, though, and I think this was true for everybody, we were making love, usually in pairs but sometimes not, mostly kissing and cuddling but not only that. Not only that.

I have probably said too much, but I hope you believe me. What we achieved there was some coalition of excitement and friendship and ease that I thought would never end. I thought right then it was what adulthood would be, kind and together and naked. Touching and laughing.

Of course, after that night, it was as if it had not happened. Nobody ever referred to it, I don't think, not to me, and before long people were back on their own distant islands, not even bothering to wave to one another across the water. But there while it was, while it lasted, there wasn't anything else. It was all. It still is.

Cobb felt as if he should speak first. He could not have told you why, but he was not wrong: "I'm glad you had that time, Joss."

"Thank you, Cobb."

Chapter 29

Nobody knew what time it was — the clock was in the kitchen — but they all had voices in their heads telling them they should be resting up for tomorrow's big push. Nobody listened.

Suddenly it struck Joss what she had done.

"Kid, I didn't mean to embarrass you. Jesus, what was I thinking."

The boy said nothing, was sitting by himself in a wooden kitchen chair, removed from the others slightly.

"Did I make you uncomfortable?"

He looked up, no expression on his face. "I don't know. I cannot imagine anything like that." He stopped and stared all around, as if trying to locate something. "I can hear that you were so happy." He paused. "And then it went away."

Joss smiled. "But while it was there...."

"Yes," the boy said, "I do imagine that, while it was there."

Joss considered making light of the whole thing, assuring the boy she wouldn't try anything like that with the present ensemble, but she said nothing, hoping someone else would pick up the slack.

Wonder of wonders, it was the boy.

"What do you do about being afraid? It doesn't seem like you are."

"Are you afraid, Huck?"

"Yes."

"So are we," Brad continued. "I know it sounds awful,

but that's what we want to be, a part of what we want to be — you know, unsecured and open."

"Yes, I do know that."

"Does it seem to you stupid?"

The kid didn't answer Katie's question, whether out of politeness or some other consideration wasn't clear.

Cobb struck in. "It's different for you, honey, we know that. We're trying to throw ourselves into danger to avoid being dead while we live. We're serious about that and hope it isn't just a privileged-kids' game. All the same, the stakes are bound to be different for you. We can see that."

"Thank you, Cobb. I think it's the game that's different."

"Oh," somebody said.

The kid probably wanted to stop it there but was driven by kindness to continue: "I think you pull fear into the game. I think it's no game for you if there's no fear. That's not the game I understand. I see what you mean about games, though. My game doesn't ask me for the same things."

Joss looked hard at him. "You've been playing it so very long."

Changing subjects fast, the kid asked whether Cobb and Brad were okay. Something about the question made evasions seem cowardly.

While they were gathering their answers, the boy continued: "If we are doing a major thing — hike — tomorrow, I just hope your feet and your back and things are okay."

He recognized what he had said and almost laughed.

Brad went first. "They hurt sometimes, where they cut me. I've been good about dressing them, though. Truth is, they don't seem any better, but they're not infected or anything. So, I'm good."

Cobb: "I'm not so good, not right now. My hand is doing pretty well. It's my feet. I've been checking, though, and getting Brad to check where I can't see on the bottoms. The skin is still raw, to tell the truth, but it's not coming off now and the pain is worse when I'm not walking, if you can believe it, so I'm looking forward to our Himalayan trek! Yes, I am, and if anybody tries to block me from the summit, I'll kick his ass — or her ass."

There didn't seem to be anywhere to go from here, so they all shuffled to their feet and made as if to head off to bed. Before they left, though, the boy touched Cobb's arm: "Cobb, could I talk to you in my room?"

Once inside, he lost no time: "Cobb, you feel very bad when Joss is mean to you."

It wasn't a question and Cobb knew it. He just nodded.

"She is mean to you because she likes you. You ought to see that. She thinks you do not like her and she cannot stand that. And she's mean to you."

Cobb's jaw dropped. That's a corny expression, but here it described a reality that might have been funny had the boy been prone to laughing.

Cobb's instinct to talk when he was confused did not lock in. Finally: "Jesus, kid. Jesus Christ. How'd you ...? Never mind, you did. Okay. Well, Jesus Christ. Have you...? No, I know you didn't. Son of a bitch."

The kid let him take his time.

Finally. "Saying 'thank you' won't cut it, kid. I don't know how you do it. I don't know who you are or where you come from. I don't know you, but...."

"Yes, you do. Yes. You know."

"Do I?"

"You know you do."

"Jesus Christ. You won't say anything to Joss, will you?"

The kid stared at him.

"Sorry. See you tomorrow."

Cobb knew not to hug the kid, not to thank him. He backed up, didn't smile, gave the kid time to say, "See you tomorrow," and slithered through the door.

The kid looked out through his window, knowing he would see it, the mirrored light, a single flash.

James R. Kincaid

* * *

Nobody had set an alarm, but there they were, before even a false dawn had given them a signal. They hadn't discussed getting an early start nor why that would seem like a good idea. In fact, it most certainly did not seem like a good idea, as things developed around the breakfast table.

"It's snowing, not too hard, but look there in the light," Katie said, as if she were announcing something unexpected.

"It's been snowing a lot, which is amazing, it being February and all — just our bad luck," Cobb said, heading for the coffee pot. "Coffee, kid?"

"No, thank you. I'll have a beer, please."

Cobb stopped dead in his tracks, for a minute unable to believe that the boy, who never kidded, was kidding.

"You little shit. You'll get yours." He meant it to be only a feint toward the boy, but some signal or other pushed him to circle round and grab the pretend-resisting boy and lift him high up, then above his own head, making as if to throw him out the window, then spinning him round, and then whipping him upside down, his shirt falling over his too-skinny belly.

When he was upright, the kid almost laughed: "When you least expect it, Cobb, when you think you're all safe, that's when I'll get you."

"Ha! Just try it, asshole!"

Instead of continuing with the game — it had nowhere to go — the kid, holding center stage anyhow, announced that they needed snowshoes for any kind of hike and that they should wait until "the nice store down there" opened and get some.

They all stared at him.

"If we go very high up, the snow will be maybe twenty feet deep, maybe more, and we would never be able to get around the drifts. It'd be all drifts. But snowshoes will work. They open at eight, they said."

How would he know that? How would he know about snowshoes?

Nobody asked, just grumbled and accepted their lot.

"I can show you how to use them," he said, looking around. "They're not too bad once you get used to them. Not for most people. Of course Cobb there...."

Cobb made an obligatory snatch after him but knew that part of the morning, the game, had passed.

The others settled back in, ready to wait for 8:00. They could pass some time glomming down cereal, though, and set themselves to doing so.

Brad brought it up first: "Do we really want to do Donner Pass, that general area? I'm not opposed, but we all are pretty familiar with it, at least what it's like, even details. Is it a little obvious?"

They seemed ready to agree but waited for Katie to spell it out: "Well, there's the I-80, you know, which makes available to those daring souls with automobiles, about 600,000 adventurers per day, such remote spots as Donner Memorial State Park, Donner Lake and the Donner Lake Fishing Area, Donner Lake Village, Donner Lake Vista, easy trails for the whole family to Donner Ridge, a picnic area at Donner Summit, not to mention Donner Ski Ranch, a very nice road over Donner Pass, called Donner Pass Road, and several very nice monuments and markers, conveniently placed."

"I had no idea," Joss said. "That makes it as much of an adventure as that Anaheim Disney place, less. You could always fall off a ride at a park, but here there'd be too many people in the way, even of determined cliff-jumpers. Shit."

"So," Cobb asked, "what do we do?"

Nobody seemed to know. If the Donner Pass were eliminated, that left — a stroll around the lake, a ride on a ski lift, a trip over to Reno to spin the wheel?

By now, they were not surprised when the boy got them where they wanted to be. "We'll ask Gene down at the gun place, when we go there in a bit, you know, to buy our snowshoes."

That seemed to solve it, release them from a stupid uncertainty into one that might well become fruitful. They were all visibly uplifted and tackled the dry granola with simulated pleasure. The kitchen clock now available, they knew they had plenty of time to eat, clean, and get very warm, far too warm for being indoors.

"It's light now, just about, so why don't we go outside and get our temperatures adjusted to the freeze?" Katie's suggestion was as good as any of the others — there were no others — so they did just that, standing around, soon getting very cold, until it was close enough to 8 o'clock to justify a snowshoe shopping spree.

"Don't forget your guns," the boy said, raising many layers on his body to display his own gun, stuck into his pants, where a belt might be if he needed one. "That way we maybe won't have to come back here."

Brad locked the door, checked it twice, and then saw the others were watching him with what looked like alarm. He wanted to make a joke to divert their thoughts from the one area they should have been locked in on. But no joke came to him, probably none existed, so they crammed into the Prius and headed to their shop and information center.

Somehow, Gene seemed to understand just what they wanted. Gene wasn't at all the scruffy mountain guy you might hope to find in a last-resort gun and ski shop. He looked more like Harry Potter trying hard to grow facial hair.

"Yep. Just like you say, those wild hikes on the maps are about as wild as amusement park rides, the tame ones. You have in mind something more — more what?"

Everybody was ready to answer, but Katie did. "Well, we have in mind something certain to get us lost, even better, injured, and best, killed."

The boy looked at her and smiled. Gene, looking at the boy,

didn't smile, just reached into the cabinet to his left, rummaged around a good while, and finally produced a map.

Seeing how disappointed they all looked, he quickly said, "It ain't a map that'll get you anywhere, like to trails that will guide you along easily. There's trails, but they don't go anywhere, even when they are accurate, which hardly any are. I tried a few last summer, gave up. You'd be crazy to go up there in winter, but crazy's what you want, what you are, so that'll be $12.50."

Gene seemed to want them out of there, but they weren't half finished, forced him not only to dig into his snowshoe stock but to fit each of them.

"I'd give myself at least a day or two of practice on these down here on the level, but I know you won't, so don't."

"Some salesman you are, Gene. The owner know how devoted you are to insulting customers?"

"Your name is Joss, am I right? I am the owner, crazy girl." He did smile, now.

"Okay, owner, as if I believed that, where would you say we could most likely get ourselves in greatest peril."

Gene didn't even blink, took out the map and spread it on the counter-top toward them. "See up here, where it says 'Desolation Wilderness?' Maybe you been there; it's big. Anyhow, it's not too hard to get up to some parts of it, and it's not quite as desolate as they advertise. But, once you're there, just head over in the direction of Duck Lake or Lost Lake, pretty much either will do, though I know you'll go for Lost Lake, because of the sound of it. That's as far as I've ever been, and I only saw Lost Lake from a distance. Once you're around there, try to cut across General Creek, which they say is there and may be for all I know. Maybe you can cross it and maybe not. If you can and do, somehow, though I doubt that you'll even know you have, you could turn left, you see, toward Lost Corner Mountain. All around there are steep canyons, not too deep, and cliffs and thick woods and shit. I'm guessing that, but I'm probably right or there would be marked trails, trails and taco stands along the way. It don't matter what the names are, and I'm not too sure anybody's been where I'm telling you to go or if these places are there. I guess they are, since they're mapped. Probably from a helicopter's my guess. But you can get killed up there, especially with all the snow, especially not knowing a goddamned thing, like you do."

He stopped abruptly.

"Thank you, Gene," said Cobb, forcing him to shake hands, which you could tell he had no taste for.

As they were almost out the door, Gene said, in a whole new tone, "Don't go."

The boy turned. "Thank you. We have to."

* * *

They did spend maybe thirty minutes in a nearby field, thrashing around and trying to convince themselves their snowshoeing skills were on the upswing.

Then they took the damned things off, drove out of town in the general direction of what might have been a route to Desolation Wilderness (probably so) and to Lost Lake, General Creek, and Lost Corner Mountain (maybe).

It was a brilliantly sunny morning, no longer early-morning, and they were all equipped with the best in sunglasses (bought a pair for the boy, too), taking to heart the dangers of the snow-blindness that had struck the Donner Party. Even with the glasses, it was hard to see very far or very clearly, as they made their way up what was, even in the snow, unmistakably a trail. Well, the day and the expedition were still young. Plenty of time to lose their way.

As they trudged along on a moderate uphill, more bored than tingled, Joss suddenly dropped back next to the boy.

"There room for both of us on this here trail, fatty?"

"Yes, Joss."

"What's that up ahead?"

"The top of the hill."

"You're a regular woodsman guide, kid. There ain't nuthin you don't know."

He just looked at her, but she kept going: "Do you know why we're doing this and what it is we're doing? I guess that's two ways of asking the same question."

"Yes."

"Tell me, cause I sure as shit don't."

"You don't want to sit still and let those people just come and kill you."

"Holy shit, kid. That's what this hike is?"

"Yes."

"But aren't they still in control, keeping us on the move, running away?"

"You aren't running away."

"You are one spooky kid."

"Thank you, Joss."

By this time they were a few feet closer to the summit of this initial hill, and Joss was no longer bored. She had, however, run out of conversation, so she sank back another station and fell in with Cobb, wondering if she had chosen to be there.

Chapter 30

"Hi, Joss."

"Oh, it's you."

Cobb, mindful of so much new stuff squishing around in his brain, looked sideways at her and smiled, but said nothing. The silence was so alien to him, Joss was immediately upset, thought about being angry.

Before she could gear up, Cobb struck in.

"I'm glad you joined me, Joss. I know that wasn't your design, but I'm glad."

"Oh, well then I am fulfilled, as my mission on this trip, my mission in life, is to gladden your heart."

Cobb didn't lose his smile. "You don't have to do that, Joss. It's okay."

Joss had no idea what he was saying — rather, had an idea she could not quite let take up lodging. It couldn't be.

"Better than okay," Cobb added, thinking about taking her hand, rejecting the idea and then adopting it.

Joss didn't pull away, just looked at him, as if for the first time. "I have no idea what you are talking about."

"Yes, you do," Cobb said.

She didn't contradict him, hoped she would come to see what he meant. For now, though, their conversation was cut short by the topography. They'd reached the summit, expecting to find wide and level vistas, welcoming sights and paths. What they found was not even a top, exactly, but a confusing, multilayered jumble of snow-draped trees, declivities, hills, cliffs, mountains and now a clouding sky. Even that jumble was mostly painted in by guesswork, the actual vista being limited by trees and the wildly uneven terrain.

"Where do you suppose Lost Lake might be? I mean, which direction?" Brad was laughing, trying to do so.

"Did you see that flash, Brad?"

Brad had seen it, was resolved to ignore it, for now. "Fuck it. Which way?"

"That way," said the boy, pointing left, sort of.

"You want to lead, Huck?"

"No."

"Okay," Katie said, "then leave it to me. Off we go."

But it was tough to be off, even with the help of the snowshoes they now donned. They struggled through the dense cover for a good hour, getting somewhere, no doubt, but not to Lost Lake, or any lake. As they were now at what might pass for a level spot, they decided to stop and eat.

"This is more trouble than it's worth," said Joss, but almost as if she didn't really care, just thought she should say something.

One problem was that nobody had found a good way — any way — to sit down, what with all the clothes, the snowshoes, and the very deep snow.

Katie and Joss both noticed it at once, the patch on Brad's face — white, dead-looking. "Brad! Are you okay?"

"Huh?"

"Frostbite, I think."

"You think so, Huck?" Brad didn't seem concerned, more like interested in how the boy arrived at his diagnosis.

"Yes. You should get inside."

"Well, you know that's not going to happen. Pick on Cobb, whose feet are probably bloody shreds by now."

That ended it, and ended lunch. They made sure they'd left no trash — friends of the wilderness that they were — and saddled up, in a manner of speaking, heading off to what they hoped would be Lost Lake or some lake — or something.

They finally reached some cliffs that seemed impassable in themselves but that framed a depression that might very well, they figured, be General Creek, now frozen over and covered in snow. How they'd lit upon a creek which lay beyond the lake without first slopping into the lake was a real wonder, but then, they had not brought the map with them, for reasons all too obvious. Things being what they were, all of them were willing to suppose that they had found a shortcut. It occurred to them, naturally, that the Donners, too, had tried a shortcut, though they had literary sense enough to reject the parallel as far too corny and manipulative.

The creek, if that's what it was, rested farther below them than first appeared, but they walked — and then slid — down to it. There were no trees around, and the bottom was surrounded by hills or walls surprisingly high.

"This must be the very creek we been seeking!" said Cobb.

"I hope so," Joss said, trying not to sound too agreeable.

"Is it a creek at all?" said Katie. There seemed to be no indication of anything creek-like.

"Yes," said the boy. "It is there."

"Really?" said Katie, jumping into the declivity and then immediately through the snow and into what turned out to be water.

"Shit!" She lost her balance and found herself on her back somehow, still with only her feet in some kind of shallow stream.

"Be careful!" Joss said, pointlessly, rushing to haul Katie up and also trying to brush off her friend's feet, dry them or something.

"That's bad," Brad said. "Did your feet get wet?"

"I can't really tell," Katie said, now looking almost distressed. "Should I take off my shoes?"

They all looked at the boy.

"I won't say what I think, since you won't do it."

"We might."

"No, you won't."

"No, we won't."

And they wouldn't have — gone back, they figured he meant, if they could find their way back, even. But the real issue wasn't navigation, of course.

An hour later, getting on well past midday, they had made it out of the gorge, a grand term for a moderate-sized dip, and back up somewhere in between a pine forest and steep, sheer marble cliffs. The cliffs were not regular, of course, nor were they, in all their breadth, exactly sheer. Some seemed to be ice-covered, others not.

The flashings, which had come and then disappeared, were now back. They were again gone, though, before any of the party really could locate them, less a clear light in a field of vision than a memory, absent before it was present. But none of the four, or five, had any notion that these lights were natural or accidental. They knew they were lost, hopelessly and grandly lost, but they had counted on that. They had not counted on being tracked by these signaling mirrors, but were not surprised.

"What do you say we go after those flashes?" said Katie. "I'm fucking tired of feeling as if we're ignoring them, letting them seize the controls and keep them."

Nobody said anything. It was as if they were waiting for the boy to speak.

He was looking at the ground, maybe seeing something. If so, he didn't say what it was. When he noticed the silence, he looked up and saw four pairs of eyes grilling into him. He smiled: "Yes?"

Then he seemed to realize he was being cruel, forcing them to say it. They were cold, scared, and lost. They only recognized the first of these, but the last were the more dangerous.

"Now, we do something a little risky, but okay. The snow's not too bad." It was as if he were speaking to himself. Just as he said that about the snow, though, it started falling lightly and then seemed to pick up immediately, no longer floating through the tall pine trees but becoming forceful, each flake shoving the one in front of it.

"Our plan is to get up there, right, to Lost Corner Mountain, which we don't have a lot of daylight left for, even if we can get back fast."

They looked not so much terrified — which they should have been — as sad, so the boy changed his tune: "It'll be duck soup getting back: just keep going downwards. Even we can do that. For now, though, we need to split up, just for ten minutes, watch your own tracks and count to three thousand not too slow and then retrace your steps. See if you find a way up the cliff."

Katie started off even before he was finished, turning westward to hug the cliff wall and spot what she imagined she had glimpsed earlier, a kind of dip or maybe a crevice. As soon as her count reached one thousand she realized she could no longer see the top of the cliff — or much in front of her. The snow was blocking out everything.

Not quite everything. Through the smoke of the snow she could see Brad's back, oddly hunched over, as if trying to ask something of the snow. Just as she was about to call out, she either saw something or heard something — or just knew it could not be Brad. She kept her eyes on the veiled, stooped figure and backed away very slowly, keeping him in view as long as there was any view to hold onto.

She didn't have to tell herself what she had seen.

Katie was the last to arrive at the meeting point, breathless to share what she had experienced, hoping already that someone had a plan. She knew without giving it words where her own plan would end; she just didn't know how to get there.

The others were gathered, crouching in the snow, maybe hiding and maybe just trying to keep warm. They couldn't have been there long, but it seemed as if they formed the beginnings of some kind of igloo, so fast was the snow coming down. Katie found herself for a minute forgetting the figure behind her and thinking that they could not stay out in this weather very much longer.

And that's what she said when she joined the group: "Jesus Christ! We need to do something about this weather. Maybe send up a prayer?"

They all laughed, then: "You saw one?" She had, of course, and said so.

It now seemed the natural thing to turn to the boy for counsel, their leader, who could contain and direct their nervousness.

The boy understood that, looked at each of them carefully, crouched lower and said nothing. Then, "We will just get colder if we do not move. There's a little crevice not far to the east here, a dip in the cliff. Let's climb."

It was Cobb who asked, not in panic, "Will they...?"

"Yes, they will," said the boy. "That's okay."

Why it would be okay wasn't clear, but nothing else was clear, so they did as they were told, followed their leader through the snow, somehow more quickly now that they were a little more proficient with the snowshoes and were able to shlomp over to the crevice.

They had to take the summit on faith, as all that was above them was blotted out by the snow, now a grim curtain. None of them thought to ask why, as the afternoon wore on, they were moving farther and farther away from home, from heat and life.

They watched the boy and followed his lead, strapping the snowshoes to their back and forming a single line for the scrabbling and uncertain ascent, actually made a little easier by the snow pockets, outlining the hand-and-footholds and allowing them to dig into what otherwise would have seemed blank walls.

"Huck, do you know how high this is?" Brad was hissing, figuring they were going up in order to hide, maybe.

"Are you in pain, Brad?"

"Yes."

"You could go ahead of me and I could push on your butt."

"Yeah, like your eighty pounds of muscle could budge two-ton me."

"It's much closer, the top is, than it seems."

That was good enough for Brad, and they all made their unsteady way up, none of them slipping so badly as to bring on disaster — not yet. They spent much of their journey resting and looking down, though after a few feet there was nothing visible below them that didn't mirror what was falling on them from above. When they stopped to think about it, they realized that the snow disguising their view was also disguising their bodies, giving them a perfect cover. Only the boy was exempt from that delusion. But he said nothing.

They got to the top in a remarkably short time, given their worry — that they would soon be climbing in the dark. Actually, they still had an hour, maybe a little more, of good daylight, though they had no way of knowing how many daylight hours away from the house they might be.

That wasn't what they were thinking of now, though. They were trying not to think at all, the older four, transferring that burden to the boy, now their only hope.

"Is this Lost Corner Mountain?" Joss asked.

"No," the boy said, and then quickly, "But that's good. We don't want to be there. This is where we want to be. And what we need to do right now, right now, is split into two groups. I mean you four need to split up, Brad and Cobb going there and Joss and Katie over there, right over there."

Somehow his pointing seemed to make sense, though where exactly "there" might be no practiced mountaineer could have determined, much less these four beginners.

So they divided into equal parts, leaving the boy behind. They couldn't make out much more of the terrain than that it seemed to go neither up nor down very dramatically. It also was not forested any longer, seemed alarmingly blank.

There clearly was no place to hide, no way to find shelter from the snow and from threats more ominous than freezing.

Katie and Joss did as directed, moved several hundred yards away, stopping well short of a decline they could not have predicted was there, a decline that began, but did not remain, gentle, turning quickly into a sharp drop, a cliff.

Brad and Cobb pushed their way, moving away from the women, right to the precipice.

"Whoa, Cobb! You see that?"

He had. What neither had seen before was the trio just beyond the snow screen, moving up closer behind them, soon right there, only about twenty yards away.

"We meet again, dear buddies. Why you been avoiding us? We just wanted to renew old ties, form new ones, tighter ones."

They kept slithering forward slowly as they said this, mockingly, dividing the space in thirds so as to block any move away from the cliff or out of their line of sight. They were all wearing black, which made them easy to see — now that seeing them came too late to do any good.

"Let's move away from the cliff, Brad."

"Right into them?"

"Into them is better than over the edge."

"Okay. I love you, Cobb."

"Me, too."

These words would have to do as the dying declarations both knew they were making. Cobb considered amending his stupid sentence, but by then there was not time. The Wilfreds were only a few feet away, grinning as if happy to see them. Doubtless they were.

Figuring it was too late but knowing nothing else to do, Cobb reached behind him, inside his pants, for his gun, somehow failing to locate it, just as Brad threw himself toward the nearest Wilfred.

But the nearest Wilfred was somehow no longer before him and the gun Cobb was trying to reach no longer needed.

First, Brad's particular Wilfred slumped to the ground, clutching his leg, and then the other two started running, one holding his arm. Brad and Cobb had heard the shots but had somehow imagined, known for sure, they were the targets, though they could see by now that the Wilfreds were armed with knives, cruel and long knives now brandished, nothing that would create these loud reports, reports at first frightening and then welcome.

More shots, many more. Both Cobb and Brad were trying to count them, but both lost track. Cobb had by now actually located his gun back there by his ass and had it out and ready. Nothing in the way of a target presented itself, though, and he had sense enough not to open fire on empty space.

They saw them then, Katie and Joss, and were ready to run through deeper snow even than this to hug them. And then they saw something else.

The women were just standing there, looking away from where the rescued boys were approaching, backing up, still holding their guns, but above their heads.

It was soon clear enough. Cobb had his gun waving and Brad, very soon, his as well. Problem was, they could not see what or who had stopped the women from firing, had made them take up this submissive stance. Not wanting to make things worse, they decided without speaking it to creep toward the girls, trying hard not to recognize that they had no time to creep.

And then several things happened, happened simultaneously, it seemed, though that could not have been: first, an arm encircled Brad's neck, started to pull back violently and then suddenly was not there. What was there was in his ears, ringing and roaring. Then Katie and Joss were on the ground and there was more noise, repeated and terrible.

It took some time for Brad and Cobb to figure it out. At first, confusion only. Then there were Katie and Joss rising and coming toward them, then suddenly stopping. There was a figure behind them in the snow, not moving. Then there was the boy, still holding the gun.

They saw the bodies, many bodies. Nobody quite knew what had happened, but nobody was really in the dark.

They dug them quick graves, snow graves, and wondered.

Brad finally asked the boy. "Are there, you know...?"

"More?" the boy answered, letting them know the answer by the tone of his voice.

"Okay."

Nobody made any noise, turned their thoughts to finding an exit, any exit.

Naturally, they looked to the boy, now as always, their best hope, only hope.

"Follow me, please."

They did. Just as it was getting very dark, edging past that time when it would have been too late to leave, they found themselves coming within sight of their car, visible more easily now that the snow had let up.

They all seemed to know that it would be wrong to thank the boy, that no words would do, so they rode back toward the house, the boy driving. As soon as they got inside, though, he issued yet another order, more like a plea.

Chapter 31

"If you four will all go out to the store and get us the right things for a party, food and stuff, I'll get the place all fixed up."

They stared at him.

"All fixed up," he repeated.

So they did just that, finding no way to protest, no way to tell the most capable among them, their savior, to come along, not to be there or anywhere alone. They found the closest store shut for the night, drove on and located a general junk emporium that allowed them to get chips, sodas, and, most important of all, streamers and balloons.

They rushed back, almost hitting a cop car and luckily being ignored. Probably the police here were paid to look snappy and arrest no one who didn't fire directly at them. Better for the tourist trade.

A sign greeted them: "Big Party. All Are Welcome." By now, any sign seemed to them ominous, and this one seemed worse than any. Cobb was first up the steps, tried to shift all his bags to one arm so as to get the door opened fast, ended up dropping first one and then, in grabbing futilely for it, dropped the other two.

Joss rushed past him — jabbing him in the ribs, patting his ass, and looking round frantically.

But there he was, smiling and clear, standing in the middle of the neated-up living room in yet another new outfit, a T-shirt that said, "ZOMBIE FRIENDLY — DO NOT EAT ME."

They moved out to the kitchen, careful not to drop more of their bad food and good decorations. It was also tidy, table set.

Within a quarter of an hour, they had the balloons and streamers up, the pizza heating and the snacks in bowls. Not wanting to spoil the boy's work by ignoring the table, fit for a real banquet, they gathered there and took their time eating the pizza.

"I'm so fucking tired, I think I'll just sleep right here," Katie said, reaching over and giving Brad's cheek a pat and the boy's another. "What do you say we do something simple in the way of party fun, something that involves no movement whatever?"

"What do you think, Cobb?"

Joss's question was jarringly unexpected, but not so unexpected as her tone. She sounded interested — almost affectionate.

"Simple charades. Not like last time. Each of us writes his own, very simple, and that's that — I mean, then she acts it out — or he, I mean. Sorry. I'm loopy."

They beat it into the living room, pretending to be interested in the snacks. Tired as they were, they didn't have to pretend to be interested in the game.

"You remember this game, Huck?"

"Yes."

Cobb went first, naturally producing the most complicated phrase.

"Three words. First word. Four syllables. First syllable, sounds like—and he took off his shirt, went over to the light and draped it over it. After some time, they got "dim" and then "im," which wasn't much of a clue, producing "Immigrant," "Imaginary," and, more pointedly, "Imbecile." Cobb waved them off. Second syllable, sounds like: a throwing motion, repeated several dozen times until someone got "toss" and finally "poss," then "Impossible." Second word. Sounds like. And he made la-la-la mouth gestures, spreading his arms out and eliciting "sings" and finally "things." Not very long before they got it: "Impossible Things Happen." Probably everyone present hearing the phrase, applied it differently. Probably Joss landed closest to the truth. Joss and the boy.

Joss's was easier. Four words. 1st word. Sounds like. Blowing something — trumpet, bugle, and finally horn, which transformed to the right word, "Corn," which needed no more clues to become what she wanted: "Corn on the Cob."

There were no disguises left.

Brad got up, first going over and lifting the boy out of his seat so he could hug him. Then: one word, one syllable, sounds like. He hardly needed to make his hands into a straw and inhale. Suck — Huck.

Then Katie, who seemed near tears and was. "Three Words, Each One Syllable. First Syllable. Sounds like — Knee, which became We. Second word, hands on heart and then extended outward toward the kid. Third word, pointed directly at him. And then they all said it, standing but not advancing. "We Love You."

The kid, by common consent pushed to the climactic point, seemed unembarrassed. One word. Two syllables. First syllable. Sounds like — he struck his hands together — applaud, cheer, good — then went over and pretended to sit on Joss, pointed beneath him. Lap! Then sap, slap, crap, map — and at last Hap. Second syllable. Sounds like. He pointed to his knee. Happy.

"I know you're not supposed to explain. Is it okay if I do? Remember last night. The game we were playing. The happiest time of your life. Now, my life. The happiest."

He looked around slowly at everyone, held on to their eyes as if he never wanted to let go, never would leave or be without them — or they without him.

They all knew more had been said than they could absorb.

They went to bed quietly, nothing more said.

*　*　*

The next morning they slept in, seemed to wake together to an alarm no one had set, no one possessed. They strolled out into the kitchen, elaborately nonchalant, seeing nothing, not even one another.

"Hi, Brad."

"Hi, Joss."

"Hi, Cobb."

"Hi, Katie."

They sat around the table, saying no more than that, wondering who would be willing to look. It didn't seem fair to lay the burden on just one of them, so they scraped their chairs back, gathered their courage, and went in.

Sure enough, they found only an emptiness where once there had been everything. His clothes were still there — they checked — but in place of the boy was a note, written in his perfect hand:

I wasn't worth saving but you did. Now I am.

"Does anyone understand?"

But of course understanding was what they had, all they had now.

The End

ABOUT JAMES R. KINCAID

James R. Kincaid is an English Professor masquerading as an author (or the other way around). He's published five other novels (*You Must Remember This, Lost, A History of the African-American People by Strom Thurmond* and the Wendell & Tyler trilogy), thirty short stories and ever so many academic and nonfiction articles, reviews, and books, including long studies of Charles Dickens, Anthony Trollope, and Alfred Tennyson, along with two books on Victorian and modern eroticizing of children: *Child-Loving* and *Erotic Innocence*.

Kincaid has taught at Ohio State, University of Colorado, Berkeley, University of Southern California, and is now at The University of Pittsburgh.

Jim welcomes reader reviews in print or on line at Amazon.com, or GoodReads.com, or other social media sites. He invites your comments, be they words of praise or howls of execration.

You can friend Jim on Facebook or contact him at: kincaid@usc.edu

MORE BOOKS BY JAMES R. KINCAID

The Open Road Series

WENDELL & TYLER: WE'RE OFF! Open Road Series, Vol. 1, by James R. Kincaid.

WENDELL & TYLER: ON THE ROAD! Open Road Series, Vol. 2, by James R. Kincaid.

WENDELL & TYLER: END OF THE ROAD! Open Road Series, Vol. 3, by James R. Kincaid.

Single Titles

YOU MUST REMEMBER THIS, follows a common fantasy into uncommon territory, by James R. Kincaid.

LOST, traces the reckless expedition undertaken by two families, by James R. Kincaid.

A HISTORY OF THE AFRICAN-AMERICAN PEOPLE BY STROM THURMOND, by James R. Kincaid and Percival Everett.

Made in the USA
Middletown, DE
18 August 2017